HUNTLEY MOVED A FEW STEPS CLOSER TO THE DOOR, HIS GLOVED HAND REACHING FOR THE LATCH.

"By the by," he said, "your father issued an invitation to me to accompany him and Miss Heathergill to the theater tomorrow evening. It would please me greatly if you would consent also to join us."

Eliza smiled prettily. "I would be delighted to attend the theater with you, sir. Thank you for asking me."

He stood gazing down upon her for what seemed to Eliza like a very great length. Finally, he said, "The pleasure is all mine, Eliza."

The silent interval between them was broken a few seconds later by an insistent *me-ow!*

Huntley glanced down to find the gray-and-white cat nudging the toe of his boot with his head. "Do you wish also to attend the theater, Sailor-boy?"

Eliza laughed. "I believe he just wishes you'd pet him. He's quite spoiled, you know."

Huntley directed another penetrating look at Eliza. "And you, my dear, are spoiling me," he murmured.

Then he was gone.

MISS ELIZA'S GENTLEMAN CALLER

MARILYN CLAY

Zebra Books
Kensington Publishing Corp.

http://www.zebrabooks.com

ZEBRA BOOKS are published by

Kensington Publishing Corp.
850 Third Avenue
New York, NY 10022

Zebra and the Z logo Reg. U.S. Pat. & TM Off.

First Printing: December, 1998
10 9 8 7 6 5 4 3 2 1

Printed in the United States of America

*In loving memory of
my sweet kitty,
Sailor,
who gave me eighteen
years of companionship and laughter.*

I miss you, Sailor-boy.

CHAPTER 1

"A TROUBLESOME MATTER"

"But, you cannot marry Miss Heathergill, Papa! You cannot!"

Sir Richard Foxburn, a handsome man of some forty years, with laughing blue eyes and wavy black hair, turned a look of mild amusement on his only daughter, eighteen-year-old Eliza. Her wide blue eyes, a perfect match to his in both color and brilliance, were becoming a deeper shade of azure as she regarded her father with growing horror.

As was their habit since Lady Foxburn had passed on two years ago, Eliza and her father were enjoying a leisurely cup of tea following breakfast as they discussed the coming day's events with each other.

Sir Richard seemed in especially high spirits this morning. He continued to gaze steadily at his tight-lipped daughter as he sipped from the delicate bone china cup in his hand. "Tell me, Eliza," he began, a bemused expression on his face, "why you find the idea of my taking another wife so very monstrous?"

"It is not that I object to your marrying again, Papa; although it is quite soon after . . ." Eliza's tone faltered as she inhaled a sharp breath. Her long dark lashes fluttered against her silken cheek as she fought to maintain her composure.

She fully expected her father would marry again one day. He was far too handsome and affable to spend the remainder of his days alone. His appealing good looks—strong shoulders, trim waist and hips—were once more showing to advantage now that he'd ceased wearing black and begun to step out more frequently.

From beneath her lashes, Eliza cast a guarded glance at the costly maroon coat her father had donned this morning. A snowy white cravat cascaded down his tucked linen shirtfront and—her brow furrowed—was that another new pair of gray pantaloons he had on? Her lips thinned. Apparently Papa's interest in this Miss Heathergill was having the added effect of increasing his tailor's coffers.

Not that she begrudged the expenditure or thought it excessive. Although not terribly wealthy by *ton* standards, the Foxburns were comfortably well-put. They wanted for nothing and with both a lovely town house—albeit situated on the veriest fringe of fashionable Mayfair in London—and a pretty new cottage in the country that Papa had only just built for Mama before she passed on, they were considered plump in the pocket. More plump in the pocket than some. Apparently plump enough to tempt a certain Miss Heathergill, Eliza thought irritably.

"Well?" Sir Richard prompted, his blue eyes trained on Eliza. "I realize you've not yet met the young lady I've been squiring about, but I trust when you do, you will find her above reproach."

Eliza's nostrils flared afresh as she worked to keep her emotions in check. Although she could think of any number of reasons why she would not, *could* not, ever find Miss Heathergill above reproach, she chose to keep her opinions to herself.

But, try as she might, she found she could not remain completely silent on the subject. "You have only just met Miss Heathergill, Papa," she blurted out. "I think it entirely possible you are acting in haste. As you well know, Mama always said you were . . . reckless," she concluded haltingly.

It was true. All her life, Eliza had heard her mother scold her father when one or another of his ill-thought-out schemes had gone askew, some of which, when Eliza learned of them, had put her to the blush. Why, the very evening of her come-out ball, Papa had astonished everyone by quitting the party early to nip over to the infamous Cyprian's ball at the Argyle Rooms!

Eliza had had the devil of a time explaining her father's sudden exit to her friends! Mama had borne it well, not in silence, but well. The same as she had a vast number of Papa's outrageous pranks.

Eliza knew her father did not mean to embarrass them. He simply acted without thinking. When Lord Hamilton asked him to attend the Cyprian's ball, he'd gone on a whim, without taking thought to what his actions would mean to his wife and daughter.

The same as now. Papa had no idea how it would look if he were to actually wed Miss Heathergill! It was bad enough that he had already been seen about Town in the company of the objectionable young lady, but to marry her? Eliza could never countenance that, not ever.

"You know very well why Miss Heathergill would not suit," she told her father now, her tone quite even given the circumstances.

She watched as her father reached for the silver teapot between them and, with slow deliberation, topped off his cup. Without asking Eliza if she would like more tea, he nestled the silver server back into the cozy and dropped a fresh lump of sugar into his own cup.

As he lazily stirred the contents, she noted a slow grin

begin to curve his full lips upward. When crinkles appeared at the corners of his bright blue eyes, and they began to twinkle merrily, she could only wonder what was going through his head now.

"Miss Heathergill is every bit as pretty and accomplished as you are, Eliza," he remarked pleasantly.

She shifted in her chair. Papa's infectious grin and artful flattery had always had the power to disarm her. As a little girl, she had loved nothing better than to be the object of her handsome papa's attentions. The sound of his merry laughter echoing throughout the house was uppermost in her childhood memories. Papa was always eager to indulge in childish games with her, getting down on all fours and pretending to be a pony as three or four of her little friends, all giggling merrily, climbed atop his back. Though she was never quite sure what he might do next, Papa's lively antics kept her highly entertained, then.

At bedtime, with Mama quietly looking on, it was Papa who read her her favorite stories, his rich baritone rumbling in her ear as he'd attempt to alter his voice and act out the various parts. Eliza suspected he made up a good deal of the stories as he went along, for they often grew more and more amusing with each of the tellings. As her squeals of laughter increased, it was always Mama who'd call a halt to the proceedings, firmly telling her husband that his antics were becoming raucous and that their little child would never fall asleep.

But, in those days, those long-ago days, Eliza did sleep. Safe and secure in the knowledge that with her beautiful mother and handsome, fun-loving papa to love her, life was perfect.

A pang hit her now as she realized afresh that Mama was gone forever. In the last months, Eliza had begun to fear that Papa's joyful attitude and lighthearted laughter was gone, as well. In her darkest hours, she had missed both her parents. Papa's once-twinkling blue eyes seemed instead to stare unseeing at the world, as if the spirit that once animated them was also dead and gone.

It was Eliza who'd finally sent for Papa's sister, Aunt Louisa, to come and look after them. It had been Mama's habit to see to the Foxburn household, the accounts, and to Papa. When everything landed upon Eliza's inexperienced shoulders, she didn't know which way to turn, or how to cope.

Aunt Louisa had stayed with them a twelvemonth, her firm hand and quiet manner assuming all of the household management. She also took it upon herself to instruct Eliza in the fine art of running a home. Eliza'd been pleased to discover it was not the arduous task she'd once feared. Fortunately, the Foxburn staff was small—consisting of Briggs the butler, the housekeeper Mrs. Allen, Cook, a handful of upper and lower maids, the requisite number of footmen, and only a few groomsmen and stable hands.

A month ago, confident that Eliza could manage on her own, Aunt Louisa had taken herself back to the country, wishing to be on hand when her own married daughter gave birth and would require help with the newborn.

Because of the upheaval in the Foxburn household, this year's social season had passed unnoticed by both Eliza and her father. Things were only now beginning to return to normal. Eliza had resumed a light schedule of morning calls, sometimes taking tea with her girlhood friend Jane Anders, and Papa had begun to go out, dining with acquaintances or at his club on occasion.

And then, a few weeks ago, he met Ivy Heathergill.

"Well, speak up, Eliza." The baronet's good-natured tone shattered his daughter's reverie. "It is plain to see you've something else to say on the subject of my marriage. Despite what you think, sweetheart, I shouldn't wish to marry a woman you do not approve of."

"Well, I cannot approve of Miss Heathergill!" Eliza sputtered, then bit her lip. Her temper often got the better of her. Mama'd always said her quick tongue would one day be her ruination. It did not surprise her when Papa did not respond to her impertinent outburst.

Trying to calm herself, she became aware of the fresh morning breeze wafting through the open window beside them. She drew in several deep breaths of the fragrant air and a moment later, in a considerably more even tone, said, "What I meant to say, Papa, was that you have only just met Miss Heathergill. Perhaps she is not . . . all that she seems."

"I suppose that is possible." Sir Richard nodded solemnly. "But, as reckless as you appear to think me, Eliza, the moment I met your dear mother, God rest her soul, I knew I wished to marry her. I confess the lovely Miss Heathergill has inspired the same sentiment within me."

"How can you say such a thing, Papa?" Eliza cried, her unruly tongue once again overcoming prudence. "Miss Heathergill can never be on a par with Mama!"

"I do not mean I could ever love Miss Heathergill as I loved your mother, Eliza. No one will ever replace Margaritte in my heart."

"Then, why, Papa? You and I are . . . we are getting on quite famously now. Why must you marry at all?" she pouted.

Sir Richard's blue gaze softened as he beheld his only child. "Because I am a man, Eliza. And I must," he concluded firmly.

Still studying her, Sir Richard took another long, slow sip of tea. "It is time you gave a thought to marrying as well, my girl. You cannot spend the remainder of your days looking after me. You are a delightful young lady, and you will make a fine wife to some lucky chap." He leaned over to bestow a fatherly pat on his daughter's white-knuckled hands, clasped before her on the table. "The time has come for you to settle on a young man and marry."

Eliza tilted her chin up stubbornly. "I have no interest in marrying, Papa. And, I am not likely to meet an eligible

gentleman anytime soon. As you well know, this year's
season has already drawn to a close." Being deep in mourning, neither she nor her father had attended any society
functions in well over a year.

"But with the war just over," her father countered,
"London is a-swarm with young men returning home from
the Continent. Hundreds of dashing young officers are
filling drawing rooms all over Town. We are not the only
family who did not retire to the country this year. Certainly
one or another of your young lady friends has a brother
or cousin returning home. I rather expect you will soon
be receiving scores of invitations to this ball or that, given
in honor of the hero's safe return."

Eliza regarded her father obstinately. Perhaps she would
and perhaps she would not. Her own season had ended
abruptly with Mama's death, and if her lack of invitations
to society events this past year was any indication, she had
already been forgotten by nearly everyone in Town.

Besides, how could she possibly think of marrying now,
with Papa teetering on the very brink of disaster? Moreover,
what young man would have her if Papa *did* marry the
objectionable Miss Heathergill?

As usual, the consequences of doing something so caper-
witted as falling in love with someone of Miss Heathergill's
stamp had not entered Papa's head. It was bad enough
that the young lady's father was—even in her thoughts,
Eliza could barely utter the horrid truth—*in trade;* what
was far worse, the thing that Eliza objected to most strenuously, was that Miss Heathergill was less than half her
father's age! At nineteen, the young lady was barely a year
older than Eliza herself! It was perfectly obvious the girl
was simply after Papa's fortune and title. Why could he
not see that?

Eliza fixed a small smile on her lips as her father rose
to his feet and leaned down to drop a parting kiss on her
flaming-hot cheek.

"I am off to Tattersall's this morning, sweetheart. I am

determined to find another horse to match the handsome bay I purchased last week." He continued to grin down at Eliza as he twitched the points of his fashionably embroidered waistcoat into place. "Wouldn't do to have a mismatched pair pulling my handsome new phaeton, now would it?"

Eliza's stomach churned. A mismatched pair, indeed! Why could her papa not see that a mismatched pair was precisely what he and Miss Heathergill would be?

Moments after he had exited the room, Eliza heard the swooshing sound of the double French doors in the drawing room, situated adjacent to the breakfast nook, being opened—but *not* closed behind him—as Papa made his way to the mews at the rear of the house. With an exasperated breath, Eliza pulled herself to her feet and marched to the adjoining chamber to slam the doors shut herself. Situated this close to the mews, two doors standing wide-open were a positive invite to all manner of flies and vermin lurking 'round the stable.

Her thoughts still fixed on the troublesome direction her father's misguided affections were taking him, Eliza mechanically set about her daily chores that morning.

After writing out a lengthy list of items for Mrs. Allen to purchase at the market, she set two of the belowstairs maids to polishing the silver, which unfortunately hadn't been touched in quite a length. Another pair were sent to take up the carpet in the upstairs corridor and haul it outdoors, where the dust was to be beaten from it. Briggs was given the task, several times that morning, of running Eliza's cat, Sailor, to ground and carrying the fuzzy creature back outdoors. Sailor loved to curl up smack in the middle of Papa's bed, which never failed to set him sneezing at night when the covers were thrown back.

Despite his occasional lapses in decorum, Eliza loved her father dearly, which is why she spent the whole of that morning wracking her brain to think up a way to show him how foolish he looked with such an unsuitable and very *young*, young lady on his arm.

It quite unsettled her when by luncheon, she hadn't managed to think of a single plausible way in which to solve the nagging problem. Something had to be done, but *what*?

CHAPTER 2

"A DINNER PARTY . . . AND THE WAR"

It occurred to Eliza that perhaps the Foxburns' extended absence from *ton* functions might have contributed to the problem. Papa had simply not had occasion lately to meet the *right* sort of woman.

To reenter society, however, would mean that Eliza, too, would be obliged to leave off the safe cloak of mourning she'd hidden behind the past two years. It would further mean that without Mama's firm hand to guide her, she'd run the risk of landing in high thicket herself. After all, she couldn't very well seek Papa's counsel should she run into difficulty.

Still in a quandary about what she ought to do, Eliza decided to pay a call that afternoon on Jane Anders. Not that Jane would be of much help. She was still consumed by her own grief.

Though only nineteen years of age, the poor girl was already a widow. Her late husband, a gunnery captain in the Royal Navy, had been tragically killed on board ship when the gun he was tending recoiled after firing with such force it slammed him into the opposite wall. The young man fell instantly dead of a broken neck. Though the accident had happened over a twelvemonth ago, Jane had not yet recovered sufficiently from her beloved husband's death even to set foot beyond her parents' doorstep. Both Eliza and Jane's mother, Lady Villiers, were exceedingly worried about the girl.

"How lovely to see you looking so well and fit, Eliza!" Lady Villiers greeted her with a smile as the Villierses' butler primly showed Eliza into the cozy sitting room where she and her daughter were seated. "Jane and I were just speaking of you, were we not, Jane?"

Eliza turned a warm look upon the slip of a girl who was curled up on one end of an elegant green-silk sofa. Wearing a pale lavender wisp of a gown, Jane looked so frail and wan that were a gust of wind to come along Eliza imagined the force of it would scatter her about the room like a leaf.

"How are you feeling today, Jane?" Eliza asked gently. She made her way to the sofa and bent to place a soft kiss upon her friend's ashen cheek.

Jane managed a sad smile. "It is good of you to come, Eliza."

Eliza slid onto a straight-backed chair near her friend.

"I was just telling Jane that I think it high time the pair of you were once again in circulation," Lady Villiers admonished them. Wearing a lovely gown of champagne-colored serge, her gray-streaked hair done up in the latest style, the older woman looked the picture of aristocratic perfection. "I fear you girls are not taking sufficient thought for your futures," she added earnestly. "I cannot think that you are both destined to spend your lives on the shelf!" A long sigh of frustration followed Lady Villiers's grim pronouncement.

During the silent interval, Eliza cast about for something plausible to say. An anxious gaze flitted from Jane and back again to her mother. "I . . . confess I have given very little thought to marrying, Lady Villiers," she finally ventured.

Beside her, Jane's features remained drawn and impassive.

"All the same," Lady Villiers started up again, her tone growing stronger as fresh enthusiasm fueled it, "I have decided to take matters into my own hands. I mean to host a little dinner party next week, and I insist that both you girls, and your father, Eliza, consent to attend."

"Oh, I couldn't," Eliza rushed to say, her dark curls shaking from side to side, her blue eyes widening with alarm.

"But, of course you can, dear! It will be a simple affair, with only a few of our intimate friends present. Only a few of our friends are presently in Town," she added on a laugh. "With so many young men returning home from the war now, Jane's father is obliged to be in Town for the numerous receptions and reviews that are being held at the palace to honor them. I think this the perfect opportunity to bring both you girls out again, as it were. I have it on good authority there are earls and viscounts aplenty amongst the officers," she added brightly.

When this elicited no response from either young lady, she continued, "London is quite thin of eligible young ladies now, you know. It is the perfect time for you and Jane. You are both *very* pretty, and, I daresay, you will garner quite a good deal of attention."

Again, neither young lady said a word.

"If your dear mother were still alive, Eliza, I am certain she would support me on this."

Eliza shifted uncomfortably. "I daresay you are right, Lady Villiers. Mama would, indeed, wish me to . . . to . . ."

"Of course, she would!" Lady Villiers exclaimed.

The smile on Eliza's face wavered nervously. "T-Thank you for thinking of me."

"Of course, I think of you, dear. You and Jane have

been bosom bows since you were children. I care for you every bit as much as if you were my own child.''

Suddenly, it was on the tip of Eliza's tongue to blurt out her troubles to the older woman, but just as suddenly, she heard the firm voice of her mother in her thoughts, admonishing her to remain silent.

It is not wise to speak openly of one's personal concerns to others.

Clamping her lips tightly shut again, Eliza offered up a silent prayer of gratitude that even from the grave, her mother's guiding words were as vivid in her mind as if she were speaking them today. There were times, Eliza feared, that if left to her own devices, she'd be every bit as impetuous and impulsive as her father. As a child, her natural inclination had been to follow his lead, her own merry laughter ringing as gaily throughout the house as his. As she grew older, however, Mama had exerted quite a strong influence upon her, with the result that the bulk of Eliza's high spirits had been squelched in the interests of feminine seemliness and propriety.

Although Eliza wasn't at all sure which way to turn now in regard to Papa, one thing was certain. He definitely needed a firm hand to guide him, and since Mama was not around to do the job, that meant Eliza must. She simply must prevent her father from marrying the objectionable Miss Heathergill!

On impulse, she decided that Lady Villiers's suggestion that she and Jane reenter society was not amiss. The proposed dinner party would also present the perfect opportunity for Papa. Undoubtedly, one or two attractive young widows who would interest him would be there.

She squared her shoulders with resolve. "Your mother is quite right, Jane. We are both of us wasting away whilst we grieve. And to no purpose. I loved my mother with all my heart, just as you loved your dear Roy, but life goes on, as they say. And so must we." Her chin at a determined tilt, she turned to Lady Villiers. "I will be delighted to attend your dinner party next week, ma'am. And both my father, and Jane, will be there."

Once the dinner party at Lady Villiers had got under way Eliza was doubly certain she had made the right decision in coming. She'd even had a new gown made for the occasion, a pretty melon-colored sarsenet decorated with tiny satin rosebuds and a soft flounce at the neck. Her only regret this evening was that, at the last minute, her father had decided not to join her.

"If I recall correctly, Lady Villiers's dinner parties can be quite dull and tedious," he'd said, his blue eyes beginning to twinkle. "I confess I am in the mood for something more lively tonight."

"Oh, Papa," Eliza fretted. Heaven knew where he would get off to tonight, and Eliza didn't dare ask. However, she did admonish him to take thought for his actions. "Do promise me you will be home before dawn. And if you must play at whist, that you will not bet more than you carry in your pocket."

Sir Richard grinned mischievously. "You needn't worry that I shall be reckless tonight, sweetheart." He planted his black-beaver hat atop his dark head and jauntily twirled the ivory-tipped walking sick he carried. "May I remind you that the tiresome task of looking after me will soon fall to Ivy," he said gaily.

A flood of alarm engulfed Eliza. Parking both hands on her hips, she could not help retorting, "Well, I hope you have told her how daunting that task can be at times!"

Sir Richard merely threw his dark head back and laughed heartily. The sound of his merry whistle as he left the house further disquieted Eliza.

But, to the party gathered that night at the Villierses', Sir Richard's absence was barely noticed. Seated about the long mahogany dining table were at least two gentlemen for every lady present. Eliza was acquainted with some of the guests, friends her parents and the Villierses' shared in common. But she was acquainted with none of the handsome young officers, splendidly turned out this evening in their dashing scarlet-and-gold military uniforms.

Jane was seated between two young officers, and Eliza was flanked by a handsome pair of them herself. This being the first time Eliza had ever attended a dinner party without one or both of her parents also present, she felt a bit shy and reticent, which made it doubly difficult for the young men to draw her out. For the most part during the lengthy meal, Eliza contented herself by merely listening as the dashing young soldiers exchanged interesting tales of the war.

Nearly all of the officers present had seen action at Waterloo, the final battle of the war, and consequently the bulk of the conversation round the elegantly appointed dinner table and afterward, in the filled-to-capacity drawing room, centered around narrow escapes and daring deeds of valor performed on the battlefield.

Growing increasingly intrigued by the adventurous deeds she heard about, Eliza's ears were soon standing at attention. Were she a man, she, too, would have willingly fought for her country. What thrilling experiences these young men had had!

Jane, too, seemed to be enjoying the evening's diversion. At the moment, she was seated between two young officers on a sofa in the drawing room. The men were talking and laughing across her as they recounted yet another fascinating episode of the war they'd endured. Jane's soft brown eyes were quite large as she listened raptly to them. Eliza noted with pleasure that there was even an upward tilt to Jane's lips. She'd feared that surrounded by so many soldiers, some of whom were Navy men, Jane would sink even lower into her depression, but it now appeared quite the opposite was true.

"Jane does appear to be enjoying herself," Lady Villiers spoke softly into Eliza's ear.

She turned a smile upon the older woman. "Indeed, she does, Lady Villiers. This was quite a good idea of yours. Jane looks very happy this evening, and very pretty, too."

"As do you, my dear." The older woman reached to adjust the flounce adorning the low-cut neckline of Eliza's gown. "What a lovely shade of melon you are wearing. It sets off your blue eyes and shiny black hair to perfection. I am certain that all the young men think you look very charming tonight."

"Thank you, Lady Villiers."

"Come, I shall present you to Captain Worthington and his commanding officer, General Huntley. Both gentlemen are unmarried," she added with high satisfaction.

Eliza was well aware that the eminent General Huntley, known as Wellington's Master Strategist, was the highest-ranking officer present. She had easily recognized the gentleman earlier, for his likeness was displayed in almost every London printseller's shop window. General Huntley was quite famous. Throughout the war, Eliza'd read many glowing accounts of his genius and bravery in the *London Times*. She turned an appreciative gaze in the famous man's direction.

General Huntley stood a good head and shoulders taller than the other young officers. Despite the fact that his crimson coat with the wide bands of gold lace fit his well-proportioned form to perfection, it was obvious from his rugged, well-lined face that he was a good deal older and far more experienced than most of the others. His thick dark hair was sprinkled with gray, and there were distinguished wings of white feathering outward from either temple. Taken all together, General Huntley cut quite an impressive figure, she thought. As she and Lady Villiers approached the small cluster of men, Eliza decided General Huntley was, indeed, a very attractive man, in a fatherly sort of way.

When the introductions had been made and Eliza had smiled all around, the handful of gentlemen, which also included Lord Villiers, Lord Hamilton, and another elderly gentleman, a Sir somebody or other, fell again to talking.

"On my honor, that is precisely what Blücher said!" exclaimed young Captain Worthington with a wide grin. " 'The stuff is no use taken on the outside,' and then he drank it down!"

Captain Worthington's proclamation was followed by a burst of hearty laughter from the gentlemen.

Another of the young officers, whose name and rank Eliza had already forgotten, turned to address her. "Captain Worthington was just telling us about the battle at Ligny when Napoéon's army successfully routed the Prussians and Field Marshal Blücher's horse was shot from beneath him."

"Oh, my!" Eliza breathed, a shocked look that soon turned to sympathy when she thought of the poor felled horse crossed her face.

"When the company's surgeon arrived to rub Blücher's injured leg with spirits," the young man continued, "the field marshal snatched the whiskey from the doctor's hand and instead gulped the contents of the bottle right down!"

"Oh, I see." Eliza smiled.

"That the same battle that felled the Duke of Brunswick?" Lord Villiers asked with high interest.

"I believe it was," one of the men replied. A few of the others nodded.

Standing quietly beside Eliza, she noted that the highly decorated General Huntley, who thus far had said nothing, wore a rather fixed look of bored disinterest on his handsome face. The look plainly said that he would rather be anywhere but here, doing the pretty, in yet one more London drawing room.

"The Duke of Brunswick was killed at Quatre-Bras," the famed man said at length.

Hearing his voice for the first time, Eliza glanced again at the tall man, whose very presence dwarfed every other gentleman in the room. She was struck not only by his

superior air of quiet strength but by the authoritative tone
of his voice. It clearly told her that regardless what he said,
his word was law and not to be disputed. Eliza certainly
felt the utmost respect for him.

"The Duke of Brunswick was the first to leave the Duchess of Richmond's ball that night in Brussels," General
Huntley added, "and unfortunately, he was also among
the first to lose his life."

This remark elicited a hum of collective murmurings
amongst those present on how quickly and unexpectedly
one's life could end.

"The entire city of Brussels was shocked by the immense
toll exacted at Waterloo," remarked Captain Worthington.

"The battle was exceptionally brutal," mused another.

As others were still mulling the grim matter over, General Huntley further added, "I recall I was dancing with
the Duchess of Richmond's daughter Georgiana that night
when the—"

"You were actually present at the Duchess of Richmond's ball!"
exclaimed Eliza, her eyes round with wonder. Upon feeling
a hot flush of embarrassment flood her cheeks, a hand
flew to her mouth as she realized she'd actually spoken
her thoughts aloud and interrupted the great man. "Oh,
I do beg your pardon, sir!"

The general, his gloved hands clasped sedately behind
his back, turned to regard her from long narrow eyes.
"Indeed, I was present at the ball, Miss . . . ?"

"Foxburn," Eliza murmured.

"Ah, yes. You will please forgive me, Miss Foxburn. I
have recently met so many young ladies, I confess the
names all too quickly become a jumble in my mind." The
general eyed her for a moment longer, then said, "I am
acquainted with a Sir Richard Foxburn. Perhaps you are
relat—"

"He is my father!" Eliza replied brightly, then she felt
another warm flush color her cheeks. "Oh, dear, I seem

unable to refrain from interrupting you, sir. Pray, do forgive me again."

The tall man, the cool look of boredom still fixed upon his face, inclined his dark head the veriest notch. "Think nothing of it, Miss Foxburn."

"Do tell us more about Lady Richmond's ball, General Huntley!" exclaimed a plumpish matron, a bright pink feather atop her turban bobbing as she elbowed her way closer to him. "Was it terribly grand? Oh, it must have been quite grand!" she enthused. "I have never been to Brussels, but I understand the city is excessively beautiful!"

"Indeed, Brussels is quite beautiful," the general replied quietly, his tone aloof, his strong torso erect. "The buildings in the Grande Place are quite ornate, a good many of them rimmed in gold."

"Oh!" Eliza sucked in her breath again, which prompted the great General Huntley to cast yet another glance her way.

"I take it you have also not been to Brussels, Miss Foxburn."

"No," Eliza said simply. Her blue eyes were quite large as she gazed up with awe at the impressive man. He must have been everywhere! Beyond a few months of each year spent with her parents in the country and three years of schooling in Bath, she'd been nowhere at all in her eighteen years of life.

"The ball, General Huntley!" The matron snapped her fan shut and impertinently tapped the general's highly decorated chest with it. "I am dying to hear about the ball!"

One of the general's dark brows lifted as he cooly regarded the rude woman accosting him. "It was not so very grand, madam. Not nearly so grand as those given in Vienna whilst the Congress was in session."

"You were also at the Congress in Vienna?" Eliza cried, her enthusiasm once again overcoming good manners. "I do beg your pardon, sir." Of course, she knew he was in

Vienna. She had read detailed accounts of the goings-on at the Congress in all the newspapers. She bit her lower lip as the impressive gentleman's gaze flicked her way once again. But, her acute embarrassment over her outburst was lessened the veriest bit when she spotted the veriest twitch of amusement begin to play about the general's stern mouth.

"Indeed, Miss Foxburn, I was one of several of the Duke of Wellington's commanding officers who accompanied him to Vienna."

"Oh-h-h," Eliza breathed, her blue eyes still round with awe. Why could she not remember to take thought *before* she blurted out whatever was on the tip of her tongue?

"General Huntley was also in Paris," said Captain Worthington, who had moved closer to Eliza's other side. "I expect the ladies would also like to hear about the Duke of Wellington's banquet after the surrender, sir. In Paris."

The bored look again settled upon the general's face. He drew in a breath before he spoke. "Wellington's banquet was, indeed, a grand affair. With the fighting at last over, the allied forces had a great deal about which to celebrate."

"I daresay the only one amongst the troops who was loath to lay down his sword was Field Marshal Blücher," interjected Captain Worthington.

Eliza noted General Huntley's features visibly harden before he nodded in silent agreement. Longing to ask a question that would lead to the remainder of the story, she refrained, but was exceedingly glad when one of the others present asked the very question burning in her mind.

"Why did Field Marshal Blücher not wish to cease fighting, sir?"

Huntley drew in another breath, as if reluctant to repeat what in truth, amounted to gossip. At length, he began. "Blücher, it appeared, was quite incensed over the disappearance and destruction of a number of Prussian artifacts—Frederick the Great's sword and watch amongst them, and an important monument at Rossback. To vindicate the loss"—Huntley was speaking in quite measured tones—"Blücher issued immediate orders upon entering Paris to destroy several French monuments. As expected, the French resisted. As Blücher was preparing to blow up the Bridge of Jena, a skirmish took place involving Talleyrand, who had serendipitously happened along. To Talleyrand's face"—Huntley's stern voice became little more than a whisper—"Blücher declared he'd like that gentleman sitting atop the bridge when he blew it up." The narrowed slits of the general's eyes reflected his disdain at the field marshal's effrontery. The hushed comments elicited from the gentlemen clustered about him were in a like vein.

Watching the general, Eliza found herself fascinated by this giant of a man who, with a look alone, could command such respect. Why, she wondered, had her father never once mentioned knowing him?

A moment later, Huntley added, "The field marshal was still out of sorts a few days later at Wellington's banquet, given in honor of the official surrender of Paris. I clearly recall the disagreeable man's words as he lifted his glass in a toast: 'May the pens of the diplomats not undo what we have won with the sword!' "

This time all the gentlemen in the party gave way to laughter. A few of the ladies, although it is doubtful that they caught the full meaning of the general's remark, also tittered.

When the laughter had subsided, Captain Worthington cleared his throat. "With all due respect, sir, surely you were aware that behind your back, Field Marshal Blücher referred to you and some of the other officers as, 'Gentlemen of the Quill.' "

General Huntley's only response was another cool nod.

Eliza's eyes were still trained on the great man. "What did . . . that mean, sir?" she asked softly.

When those cool gray eyes once again turned to regard her, Eliza could not halt the thrill of pleasure that shot up her spine. The sensation was very like the special feeling she experienced when, as a little girl, her father fixed his full attention upon her, and her alone.

"It means," General Huntley began quietly, "that Blücher considered those of us who served in the diplomatic corps to be of lesser consequence than 'real' soldiers."

A pregnant pause followed, then in a booming voice, Lord Villiers said, "Well, that is scarcely true in your case, eh, Huntley?" He raised his glass of port in salute. "To Wellington's Master Strategist, a brave soldier *and* distinguished diplomat! Hear, hear!"

"Hear, hear!" chorused the ring of other men.

If Eliza'd had a glass in her hand, she, too, would have drunk a toast to the powerful man. What a courageous soldier he was! He had fought in all the major battles of the war, and in Vienna, had been instrumental in negotiating peace treaties between England and the coalition. She felt immensely honored to have met the great General Huntley. What a very good idea it had been to attend Lady Villiers's party!

Two days later, Eliza was pleased to receive an engraved invitation to a theatrical evening given by Lady Hamilton, with whom she'd become reacquainted at Lady Villiers's dinner party.

Still hoping to lure her father away from the unsuitable Miss Heathergill and back into appropriate *ton* circles, she tried quite strenuously again to persuade him to come along.

"Papa, you really should reconsider," she said to her father that morning at breakfast. "Your name was also on Lady Hamilton's invitation. Lady Villiers's dinner party wasn't the least bit tedious. You would quite enjoy hearing the fascinating stories the soldiers tell."

"I think not, sweetheart," Sir Richard replied absently. "I have invited Mr. Heathergill to sup with me at my club tonight."

"Papa, no!" Eliza cried. She was so very alarmed her fork fell from her fingers to her plate with a loud clatter. "What will people say?"

The outrage in her tone caused Sir Richard to glance up. "Let them say what they will. Heathergill is a fine man, and I am proud to call him a friend."

Eliza's nostrils flared with fresh anger when—her father's blue eyes twinkling merrily—he blithely added, "For all that, I expect I shall soon be calling him my father-in-law."

"Oh, Papa, how can you contemplate such a thing?" Eliza's fingers fairly trembled as she pushed her breakfast plate aside. She simply could not eat when she was so overset. She made no effort whatsoever to curb her tongue. "The man is in trade, Papa! What would Mama say?"

With a shrug, Sir Richard replied, "I rather expect your mother would have a good deal to say . . . and all of it disparaging to poor Mr. Heathergill." He turned again to the creamed eggs on his plate. After swallowing a forkful, he reached for his coffee cup to wash down the eggs. In a matter-of-fact tone, he added, "Heathergill owns quite a successful grocery establishment. He supplies a good many *ton* families with tea and coffee and other necessities. Heathergill's carries the finest selection of exotic spices to be found in London."

"Oh, Papa, you've haven't actually been to his shop, have you?"

Sir Richard snorted. " 'Course, I have." He reached for a steaming hot scone and began to slather it with rich yellow butter. "The day I met him, I walked with him back to his establishment. Was curious to see for myself, don't you know."

Eliza quite clearly recalled her father's account of how he'd become acquainted with the disagreeable Mr. Heath-

ergill. Quite by accident it was. Her father had been leisurely strolling along the Strand one afternoon and,
suddenly realizing he'd left his timepiece at home, simply
stopped a passerby to inquire the time. The well-dressed
man turned out to be Mr. Heathergill, the pretty young
lady on his arm, his daughter, Miss Ivy Heathergill.

The men struck up a conversation which culminated in
Mr. Heathergill's inviting Sir Richard and his wife—Mr.
Heathergill being unaware at the time that Sir Richard was
a widower—to partake of a meal at his home.

Eliza had listened calmly when her father told her of
the chance encounter that night but had thrown a royal
fit when she learned that her father meant to accept the
tradesman's invitation to dinner. Her fits had become
increasingly more royal with each encounter between the
men since.

"Your association with that man, and his daughter, is
just not seemly, Papa," she declared now.

"Not seemly? Need I remind you, daughter, that you
yourself have frequented a tradesman's place of business,
and I might add, quite enjoyed it."

Eliza's lips thinned with annoyance. Papa was, of course,
referring to Birch, Birch and Company, whose pastry shop
was quite famous with the *ton* for their delicious confections and enormous Twelfth Night cakes. Eliza and her
father had often dined in Birch's unpretentious, but quite
clean, dining room on extraordinary fare that included
turtle soup, venison, and oyster pies.

"Furthermore," Sir Richard added with high satisfaction, "as you well know, Samuel Birch—a mere pastry
chef—is now London's Lord Mayor."

"Which I think quite unseemly!" Eliza returned hotly.

"And what of Sir Edward Hungerford?" her father countered. "A bona fide gentleman-turned-grocer."

"That hardly signifies. Hungerford's Market has been
in the Strand for nearly a century now. No self-respecting

gentleman today would seek to restore his fortune by becoming a tradesman.''

Sir Richard eyed his tight-lipped daughter. ''To say truth, since knowing Heathergill, I have given the idea of engaging in commerce some thought myself.''

''Papa, you wouldn't!'' Eliza cried.

''And why not? Were I to operate a distinguished establishment such as Rudolf Ackermann has done, I'll wager the *ton* would flock to my door, as well.''

His features irritatingly impassive, Sir Richard brought the linen napkin in his lap to his mouth and dabbed perfunctorily at it.

But, when a quick grin suddenly spilt his face, Eliza realized her father had been baiting her. Some of her anger abated. ''Oh, Papa. What do you know of ladies' furnishings and bonnets?''

''Very little actually.'' Sir Richard winked rakishly as he rose to his feet. ''But I certainly know what pleases a gentleman's eye.''

''Oh, Papa. You are incorrigible.''

CHAPTER 3

"A NARROW ESCAPE"

The following evening, Sir Richard Foxburn handed Eliza up into his fancy new phaeton, then climbed up beside her and snatched up the ribbons. An expert flick of his wrist set the team in motion, the carriage behind it lurching forward with a jolt.

"She's a beauty, ain't she?" Sir Richard exclaimed proudly, as they headed for Lord and Lady Hamilton's town house in fashionable Grosvenor Square—Eliza to be delivered there while Sir Richard proceeded onward to collect Mr. Heathergill so the men might dine that night at his club. A look directed Eliza's gaze to the handsome new bay harnessed alongside the other prime go-er, both animals of a similar height and bearing.

"Daresay, I was damn lucky to get her!" Sir Richard added. "Had to outbid Fraser and Sefton, who both wanted her fiercely. Can't wait to show off my new team to Heathergill!"

Though Eliza bristled at the mere mention of Mr. Heathergill's name, she managed an appreciative smile over her father's good fortune at Tattersall's that day.

"Lord and Lady Villiers mean to see you home, do they?" Sir Richard asked with fatherly concern as the shiny green-and-black equipage skimmed over the cobblestone street.

"Yes, sir." Eliza nodded. "Jane will also be at the Hamiltons' tonight."

"Splendid. I expect that means she is at last coming 'round." Sir Richard held the ribbons taut in his hand as the perfectly matched team ahead of him trotted at a spanking pace. The baronet flicked an appraising glance at Eliza, who this evening was wearing a lovely blue-silk gown trimmed in silver braid, with a matching blue-satin pelisse.

Noting the direction of her father's gaze, Eliza inquired anxiously, "Do I look all right, Papa?" Again it seemed strange to be going out for the evening without the company of her parents. It had also seemed strange to have dressed for the occasion without her mother there to fuss over her. Her mother had had definite ideas about how to present her daughter to best advantage. Eliza sincerely hoped she had made the correct choice in her attire tonight.

"You look lovely, my dear," Sir Richard replied. He favored Eliza with an affectionate wink.

This past week she had spent hours pouring over the latest editions of the *Ladies Home Companion* and *La Belle Assemblee* in an effort to determine what young ladies of fashion were wearing these days. Her mother had generally had the last word on both the style and choice of fabric for Eliza's gowns. And during her many months of mourning, Aunt Louisa had seen to the procuring of proper attire for her, and in some cases, for Papa. Eliza had had very little experience in the actual choosing and ordering of her own clothes.

Today, for the first time since her mother's death, she and her abigail Betsy had set out alone to visit a fashionable shop in nearby Charlotte Street. Eliza had purchased a half dozen pairs of new gloves, two new bonnets, assorted ribbons, a new muff, and three pair of satin slippers for dancing.

"I discovered I have very little that is presentable to see me through the Little Season," Eliza told her father now. "I took the liberty of ordering Mr. Stultz to make up several new gowns for me, and two new pairs of half boots."

Sir Richard nodded agreeably. "Sounds as if that should serve." His tone was a bit absent as the demands of driving claimed his full attention again. At the moment, he was expertly heading the team 'round a high-sprung carriage that was lumbering along at a snail's pace. Once past it, he worked to execute a sharp left turn at the next corner.

Eliza watched, captivated, as her father, an excellent whip, feathered the corner within an inch. She had a secret desire to learn to drive. Many times in the country, her father had passed the ribbons to her as the small curricle they drove there wheeled briskly down a dusty lane. The powerful feeling it gave her to control such huge animals thrilled Eliza to the core. Of course, it would be far too dangerous in London to trust her inexperienced hand with the ribbons. But she hadn't given up the dream of doing so one day.

The fast pace the carriage was traveling sent a brisk breeze whipping past them. Eliza ran her gloved hands up and down her thinly clad arms in an effort to ward off the chill. Dusk was fast enveloping the city, which meant the air would soon grow quite crisp as it replaced the sweltering humidity that hung over London during the late-summer days.

"You have my permission to purchase anything you like, Eliza," Sir Richard said, as the high-stepping team before him settled onto a straight course again. "I trust your mother gave you sufficient guidance in that quarter. You may, of course, consult with Lady Villiers, or even Lady Hamilton, if you find yourself in a quandary over certain, ah . . . feminine matters."

"Of course," Eliza murmured. Then, suddenly, it struck her that this was the perfect moment to again bring up the *un*suitability of Miss Heathergill as a companion to her father. Since the other morning when they'd last discussed the matter, no opportunity had presented itself to broach that particular topic again. "And who will *you* consult with, Papa, when you find yourself in a quandary?"

Sir Richard flung a quizzical gaze at his daughter. "In a quandary? About what?"

Eliza tilted her chin up primly. "About what is and is not proper for *you*, Papa."

Not forgetting to keep a watchful eye on his driving, Sir Richard glanced down at the well-cut chocolate brown coat he wore, the exquisite jonquil yellow waistcoat, and form-fitting biscuit-colored pantaloons. "Is there something amiss in regard to my evening attire?"

"No, Papa," Eliza said irritably. "You look positively handsome. By proper, I was referring to your . . . your association with Miss Heathergill. You know very well Mama would advise you *against* furthering the acquaintance."

Sir Richard's mouth hardened visibly. "We have discussed this subject at length, Eliza, and you have made your views on the matter quite clear."

"Well, what would Mama say if she knew you meant to marry Miss Heathergill?" she blurted out.

One of Sir Richard's arched brows quirked. "Allow me to point out, Eliza, that if your mother were still alive, the question of my marrying another woman would likely not come up. Now, let this be an end to it," he concluded firmly.

Because her father's tone was so *very* firm, Eliza had no choice but to let the matter drop. For now.

In less than a quarter hour, she found herself being ushered into the plush drawing room of Lady Hamilton's elegant town house in Grosvenor Square. One of several large houses on the block, it sat a good distance back from the street, with its own parcel of well-manicured yard in front. Eliza had been here many times before, and generally she was quite entranced by the lovely furnishings and exquisite *objets d'art* that Lord and Lady Hamilton had collected from around the world. Being in such an ill frame that night, however, she took no notice of her surroundings.

She was far too agitated over her inability to make her father see reason. By all that was right and proper, *he* should be here with her, not nipping off to sup with some no-consequence tradesman whose primary aim in life was to leg-shackle his daughter to an unsuspecting gentleman of means. For the life of her, Eliza could not see why Papa was unable to see that he was being royally hoodwinked by this pair of scheming toad-eaters.

She worked to tamp down her frustration with her parent and present an amiable face to the crush of people crowded into Lady Hamilton's elegant drawing room. The same as last week at Lady Villiers's dinner party, there were only a few people with whom she was acquainted, and most of them were of an age with her parents. Upon spotting Jane Anders perched alone on a sofa in the corner, she headed that direction, on the way speaking with one or another of the elderly guests whom she knew.

"How lovely to see you, Miss Foxburn. Is your father well?" asked a Mrs. Pettibow. "You must both come to tea! I shall send my card 'round."

We shall be delighted to come, Mrs. Pettibow. Thank you, I'm sure."

She spoke also to Lord and Lady Villiers and noted with some interest the presence of a vast number of the same young military officers that she'd met last week in the Villiers's drawing room.

A funny little flutter of interest gripped her when she spotted the eminent General Huntley. At the moment, he was engaged in conversation with quite a pretty young lady, whom Eliza did not know. As she watched, two other young officers joined them, one of whom seemed especially enchanted by the pretty blonde. Though it appeared he was attempting to be secretive, he actually slipped an arm about the young lady's waist! My, Eliza thought, propriety had indeed dipped a notch or two since she'd been out and about.

Having reached Jane's side, Eliza eased onto the sofa beside her friend. They had begun to chat, when suddenly Lady Hamilton extricated herself from a nearby cluster of turbaned matrons and hurried over.

Eliza's parents had been friends with Lord and Lady Hamilton for years. The Hamiltons had two sons and a daughter, who were all married, and Lady Hamilton spent the bulk of her time entertaining the *ton*. She never tired of showing off her treasures and took especial pride in thinking up new and unusual ways to amuse her party guests.

"Eliza, my dear, where is your charming father this evening?" the older woman cried. A worried frown creased her well-lined face. "I was counting on his being here. I was counting on *both* of you being here. Dear me," the woman began frantically. "I shall have to alter my program now. I can't think whom I shall find to replace Richard at this late date. Do you come along, Eliza dear, and I shall explain it to you straightaway. You will excuse us, will you not, Jane?"

Flinging an apologetic look at poor Jane, who looked quite forlorn at being left alone again on the sofa, Eliza rose to follow the overset Lady Hamilton from the room. Once abovestairs, she led the way into a spacious bed-chamber at the end of the corridor.

As Lady Hamilton closed the door behind them, Eliza glanced about. Score upon score of elaborately decorated stage costumes were strewn about the large room. In one corner lay a pile of bonnets, some sporting huge plumes, others tall and pointed with flowing gauze trains. Eliza had seen pictures of such odd headgear in history books, but she'd never beheld such antiquated garments in real life. On the floor were at least a dozen pairs of buckled shoes and tall polished black boots such as a pirate or buccaneer might wear. Scattered across the canopied bed were brightly colored stockings, tights, petticoats, and multi-caped cloaks and robes. Obviously the chamber was to serve as the dressing room for the theatrical company that was set to entertain the guests later.

". . . was certain when I received your note that your acceptance for this evening included your father, as well," Lady Hamilton was saying.

Still eyeing the assortment of colorful costumes, Eliza murmured, "Father is . . . he had a previous engagement tonight."

"Oh, dear." Lady Hamilton chewed on her lower lip. "I had not meant to reveal my surprise just yet, but since you are here, I may as well tell you." Her face relaxed a trifle as a conspiratorial quality stole into her tone. "This evening's 'theatrical company' is to be chosen from amongst my guests." She paused, as if expecting Eliza to comment on the extraordinariness of her plan.

A bit stunned by the pronouncement, Eliza could only manage something that sounded like, "How interesting."

"I had meant for you and your father to play the parts of Helene and Reginald from the play *The Nocturnal Revenge.*"

Eliza's eyes widened. She'd never in her life entertained the notion of appearing on stage, not even as a lark. Perhaps her father's absence here tonight would prove a blessing in disguise for her.

"I am certain you will have no trouble at all in finding someone else to play our parts, Lady Hamilton," she said quickly.

"But I had counted on Sir Richard." Lady Hamilton reached to finger a brightly colored cavalier's costume draped across the bed. "Your father is so very dashing, with his dark hair and twinkling blue eyes. I shall simply have to make some adjustments, but you will not disappoint me, will you, Eliza, dear?''

From beneath the cavalier's cape, Lady Hamilton unearthed a voluminous white peasant blouse and a full-length gathered skirt, with a loud pattern of red and yellow flowers.

"This is to be your costume." She handed both garments to a stunned Eliza. "Now where did the mask and cape get to? Ah, yes, here they are. If you recall, the story is about a dashing highwayman and his pretty young daughter who accompanies him on his nightly escapades. The mask and hood is to shield Helene's identity," she told Eliza, who was holding the low-cut white peasant blouse up before her body. Lady Hamilton sighed. "I will simply have to find another gentleman to play the role of your father," she said with decision.

Eliza's brow puckered with dismay. How was she to learn the lines of the play in so short a time and be able to perform them adequately without a proper rehearsal?

Before she had time to voice her concerns, Lady Hamilton exclaimed gaily, "My dear, you should see your face! I declare, telling my actors and actresses of my plan tonight will be half the fun!" With a merry laugh, she gave Eliza's shoulders a quick squeeze. "Mustn't worry, my dear; you've no lines to learn. Come, I shall show you."

She snatched up the cloak and a pair of beribboned shoes that looked to be Eliza's size and ushered her guest across the hall into another bedchamber.

"Here we are."

Eliza looked about this room and indeed, saw a half dozen other lady's frocks and gowns, complete with shawls and baskets and even a shepherdess's hook, lying helter-skelter about.

Lady Hamilton indicated a vacant chaise near the hearth where Eliza might put her costume, then she snatched up a sheaf of papers which she proceeded to scan. "Yes, here we are. This is your scene."

She handed the pages to Eliza.

"Each scene is merely to be mimed," Lady Hamilton said gleefully. "The 'actors and actresses' will act out their part without speaking a single word! It's charades, with costumes and props, and instead of merely guessing the title of the book or play, the others must determine which scene is being presented and the exact names of each of the characters in the scene! What do you think?"

Despite her lingering trepidation, Eliza managed a weak smile. "I-I see."

As Lady Hamilton busied herself with sorting through the rest of the scripts and laying the pages alongside the appropriate costume, Eliza decided the woman was right about one thing, her papa would have been perfect in the role of the handsome highwayman.

"There," Lady Hamilton said. "Now then, we shall join the other guests, and after supper, when I ring the bell for the entertainment to begin, you will slip away and come straight up here to be dressed. There will be a maid on hand to assist you. Agreed?"

Beginning to feel somewhat excited about the plan, Eliza nodded. "It should be quite entertaining, Lady Hamilton. Please accept my apology for Papa's absence tonight. He will be most disappointed when I apprise him of all the fun he's missed."

Following her performance on stage, with young Captain Worthington gallantly stepping in to play the part of her father, Eliza hurried back upstairs to change again into her own gown. There were still a number of skits left on the program and judging from the hilarious antics she'd witnessed while awaiting her turn in the wings, Eliza did not wish to miss any of the remaining performances. This had been quite a good idea of Lady Hamilton's and indeed would not be an evening soon forgotten amongst the *ton*.

In the dressing room, Eliza joined three other ladies who were also hurrying out of their costumes, all the while talking and laughing as a pair of silent maids nimbly undid and did them up again. When the three other women exited the room, one of the maids turned to assist Eliza.

Suddenly, she heard the bedchamber door open and shut behind her and a feminine voice declare, "I should like to have the cloak and mask you are wearing, Miss Foxburn!"

Unaware who was addressing her, Eliza turned to find the pretty blonde she'd observed earlier conversing with General Huntley. She was wearing a lovely gown of pale pink silk trimmed with gold-lace rosettes.

"The cloak and mask, Miss Foxburn!" the pretty blonde insisted.

Eliza glanced at the plain gray woolen cloak in her hands, and back up again. Why would the young lady wish to cover her beautiful gown with such a repugnant garment, she wondered? Perhaps it was to be part of her costume, as well, she decided, with a shrug.

Suddenly the girl turned to address the maids, one of whom was busy gathering up an armload of disheveled costumes, the other just beginning to undo the tight laces of the stomacher cinching in Eliza's trim waist.

"You will leave us now!" the girl cried insistently, "and you will speak of this to no one!"

Eliza quickly undid her mask even as her eyes widened with alarm. When she had observed the young lady earlier, conversing with General Huntley and the other officers, she had seemed in quite good spirits. What could have happened to overset the girl between then and now?

Once the maids had scurried from the room, the agitated young lady turned to Eliza. "I mean you no harm, Miss Foxburn."

"Who are you?" Eliza asked. "And what do you want, apart from my cloak and mask, that is?"

"My name is Constance. I am Lady Constance Torbett. I need your help, Miss Foxburn. I observed you being kind to Jane Anders earlier. I am acquainted with Jane and I know of her great loss. She loved her husband dearly."

Lady Constance rushed to Eliza's side, a pleading look distorting her pretty features. "I, too, am desperately in love, Miss Foxburn. But my circumstances are a bit different from Jane's. I am not yet married to my young man. Charles is a lieutenant in the Life Guards. We met a twelve-month ago and have been corresponding with one another since. He has asked me to marry him, Miss Foxburn, and I must. I simply *must!*"

"But, why are you . . . ?"

"My parents have forbidden it. Charles is . . . he is not a *gentleman*. I am not even allowed to see him. My parents wish me to marry a title—my cousin, a pompous ass, whom I cannot abide! That is why Charles and I must run away to be married. Don't you see? It is the only way. But I must have your help!"

"But I fail to see what I can do to help you."

"I am in the final charade tonight, playacting opposite General Huntley. He is Charles's commanding officer, and he, too, opposes the match, though I cannot think why. Possibly because he is *old* and never been in love," she said with derision. "At any rate, if you take my place in the skit, Charles and I will have a few minutes in which to steal away. Oh, you must help me, Miss Foxburn, you must!"

Eliza was torn. "I don't know, Lady Constance. I . . . I really shouldn't. Your parents will not know what has become of you. They will worry and . . . ."

"Charles and I love one another!" Sinking to her knees, she reached to grasp Eliza's hand. "Please help us, Miss Foxburn, *please!* It is our only chance. My parents watch me every moment; even General Huntley watches me! Charles and I are desperate to be together!"

Eliza considered. She had never been in love herself. She'd often wondered what it would feel like. Several of her friends had professed to be in love and when it had happened to them, Eliza had marveled at the odd way love had of . . . of completely absorbing one's life! Why, it seemed to make even the most intelligent person act with total abandon, as if her senses had completely taken leave of her! Papa was behaving in such a fashion now. Did it mean he truly loved Miss Heathergill, or . . . what?

"Please, Miss Foxburn! I cannot live without Charles. I will surely die!"

Eliza doubted the young lady would *die,* but . . . "Oh, very well," she said, on a sigh. Cupid was certainly working overtime lately, first her father and Ivy, and now Lady Constance and Charles. The little fellow's aim left a lot to be desired, however. His indiscriminate arrows were doing far too good a job of leveling the classes.

She rather grudgingly handed the cloak and mask to Lady Constance. "But, I cannot like it that you asked me, Lady Constance. And I cannot promise that I will not tell your parents the truth if I am asked what I know of your whereabouts."

"They shan't ask," Lady Constance exclaimed as she hastily tied the mask about her eyes, then flung the cloak about her shoulders and drew the hood up to cover her golden curls. "Even now, my mother is preparing to keep an assignation with her own lover, and my father is too deep in his cups to notice where I've got to." She hurried to the door. Before opening it, she turned a grateful countenance upon Eliza. "Thank you; with all my heart, thank you!"

The girl was nearly out the door before Eliza realized she had no idea which costume to don next. "Wait!" she called. "What character am I to play next?"

Lady Constance smiled. "You are to be Isolde. The reconciliation scene from *Passion Rules Their Hearts.*"

Oh, my, thought Eliza. If she remembered correctly, Jason drew Isolde into his arms in that scene.

And kissed her.

Lady Constance had said the gentleman playing opposite her in this charade was General Huntley.

Oh, dear.

CHAPTER 4

"PASSION RULES HER HEART"

"I shan't be changing into my own gown, after all," Eliza told the wide-eyed little maid who scurried back into the bedchamber mere seconds after Lady Constance had vacated it.

The maid bobbed a quick curtsy. "What would 'ye be wanting to wear instead, miss?"

"That." Eliza pointed to a diaphanous gown that, she now realized, probably wouldn't fit. Lady Constance was several inches taller than she and a good deal more 'rounded' in places. "I expect we shall be needing some pins."

"Yes, miss."

Nearly half an hour later, Eliza, feeling quite rushed and anxious, clutched the long folds of the sheer gown about her and hurried again down the long winding staircase to the ground floor. From the sounds of shouting and laughter she heard, she ascertained that the previous charade had not yet drawn to a close. Quietly, she entered the darkened anteroom adjacent to that area of the drawing room that had been designated the "stage."

Her anxiety rose as she stood in the shadows, waiting as various ones of the guests tried to determine the correct name of the play and the characters in it.

On occasion, she glanced behind her, expecting any minute to see General Huntley appear. What would he have to say when he realized she was not Lady Constance, she wondered? Lady Constance had said the general vehemently opposed the lovers, but she hadn't said why. Eliza also wondered if the young lady and her beau had managed to escape successfully.

Suddenly a roar of applause rang out and the pair of actors who'd been on stage rushed into the wings, both talking and laughing at once as they breathlessly recounted their moments on stage.

"I thought you meant me to strike you when you moved to the side!" the young lady laughingly exclaimed.

"Indeed, that is what you should have done," the gentleman agreed, shaking his head sheepishly, "had I not become hopelessly confused and lost all sense of direction! I swear I shall never agree to such a thing again. I have made a complete cake of myself!"

"Nonsense, you did very well! It is I who was most unconvincing."

Amidst the bustle of the pair of them exiting the small chamber and the sound of Lady Hamilton's voice introducing the next performers—General Huntley and Lady Constance Torbett—Eliza was unaware when the general quietly stole up behind her. Not until she heard the gentleman speak, did she turn to look up at him.

His gaze was directed over the top of her head. "Do not concern yourself, my dear," he said in a hushed tone, "I shall not compromise you by kissin—"

At that moment, his long gray eyes met Eliza's clear blue ones. "Miss . . . Foxburn."

Eliza nodded. "Lady Constance has . . . taken ill, sir."

An arched brow lifted. "I see."

The sharp gaze that flicked toward the doorway of the anteroom did not escape Eliza's notice.

No further words were spoken, however, as it was time for their performance to begin.

The appropriate accoutrements for their scene were already in place onstage.

Eliza, or rather Isolde, was to recline upon a chaise longue with a tea table nearby, upon which rested a carafe of wine and two crystal goblets. When Isolde's lover, Jason, rapped at the door, she was to answer his knock and then pretend to be incensed by his effrontery at invading her private chamber. Once his considerable charm had melted her resistance, however, the united lovers were to fall into one another's arms in a passionate embrace that culminated with a searing kiss.

During the span when Eliza was to resist the general's advances, she merely thought about how angry she was with her father and stamped her foot and tilted her chin up quite convincingly.

When the time came for General Huntley, who Eliza thought looked quite splendid in a pair of white-satin knee breeches and a maroon-velvet coat to draw her into his arms, she, not yet ready to "give it up" as it were, slipped instead from his grasp and scampered back to the chaise, where she again flung herself in a tragic pose. Undaunted by the heroine's unexpected maneuver, General Huntley simply followed the young lady to the armless couch and perched upon the edge of it quite near her.

When he reached to touch Eliza's trembling shoulder, the quivering sensation she experienced had nothing whatever to do with the part she was playing. The plain truth was, she'd never been embraced by a gentleman before, unless one counted one's father, which Eliza didn't think one did.

Time seemed to stand still as she sat motionless, her frightened gaze locked with the general's reassuring one. She was sitting so very close to him, she could plainly observe the rise and fall of his powerful chest as he inhaled and exhaled each breath. The male scent of him—a pleasant mixture of musk, male and lime—seemed to envelop her.

To complete the scene, she knew she *must* let the handsome older man pull her into his arms. Finally, her own heart pounding wildly in her breast, she mustered the courage it would take to do so. Slowly, very slowly, she leaned into his strong chest. But, when his arms tightened around her, suddenly, a shudder of . . . of *something* quite alarming coursed through her!

What was happening to her?

There was no time to refine upon it, for at once a voice from the audience shouted, "Isolde and Jason in *Passion Rules Their Hearts!*"

"That is correct!" gaily called Lady Hamilton. She joined the burst of applause that shattered the tender moment unfolding onstage.

General Huntley at once released Eliza and put a hand out to draw her to her feet.

Her knees weak, Eliza rose and nodded a quick bow at the cheering audience, then, without waiting for the general to accompany her, darted through the anteroom and ran again toward the staircase.

She told herself she was running lest anyone question her regarding the whereabouts of Lady Constance, but deep inside she knew that was not the whole truth. The strange queasiness in her stomach had nothing whatever to do with the disappearance of Lady Constance. Though, to be honest, she wasn't entirely certain what it did have to do with.

Still, she knew she'd have to answer to Lady Constance's parents soon, quite possibly even to General Huntley. But she could not speak to anyone just now! Not until she'd regained her composure and stopped trembling like a scared housemaid who'd been caught with her arms wrapped about His Lordship's neck.

General Huntley was a shrewd man. He would know when a person was telling a falsehood. And, feeling as she did now, Eliza suspected any answer she gave at the moment would sound like a falsehood.

What had come over her the very second General Huntley's arms enveloped her? What did the strange fluttering in her stomach mean?

She hurried into the dressing chamber and began to tear off the robe she was wearing even before a maid rushed forward to help her.

"Ouch!" Eliza cried, as a pin she was attempting to remove herself instead penetrated her flesh.

Parking both hands on her hips, she forced herself to stand quite still while the little maid unfastened the remaining pins.

Then Eliza impatiently jerked apart the tapes and thrust aside the offensive garment. Suddenly, she wished only to be at home, where things were ordered and quiet, where life was predictable—that is, where life had been predictable before Papa'd met Ivy Heathergill and Eliza had decided to reenter society!

She tried to calm herself again as the maid did up the hooks on her own pretty blue gown. Eliza squirmed to peer into the glass and quickly pat her dark curls into place.

It had been close on an hour since Lady Constance had slipped from the dressing room, her identity shrouded by the cloak and mask. Would General Huntley be terribly angry with her, she wondered? Suddenly, the queer queasy sensation in her stomach beset her again. Oh, why was she so concerned over what General Huntley would think?

Hearing footsteps in the corridor, Eliza thrust the irritation from mind and advanced bravely toward the doorway of the dressing chamber. She only hoped Lady Constance's parents did not hold her entirely responsible for the unfortunate episode. Lady Constance had been quite insistent, after all.

"My dear child," cried Lady Hamilton, rushing into the room, "What have you done with dear Lady Constance?"

Eliza flung a worried look from Lady Hamilton to the attractive woman on her heels. Judging from her even features and pale blond hair, she looked to be a mature version of Lady Constance.

Before Eliza had a chance to utter a single word of explanation, two elderly gentlemen, one of them being General Huntley, came bearing down upon her.

"What have you done with my daughter?" demanded the more portly of the pair, his words slightly slurred as he spoke.

A sharp pang of guilt assailed Eliza. "I am so very sorry, sir. I should not have consented to help her, but—"

"Undoubtedly, it was not this young lady's fault," cut in General Huntley, his tone quite firm.

Though Eliza felt enormously grateful to him for coming to her aid, she knew she was not innocent of all blame. "I should have refused to give Lady Constance my cloak and mask, sir."

"It was not your cloak and mask to give her!" Lady Hamilton retorted angrily. "I gave my word to the theatrical company that all of the costumes would be returned intact!"

"I will gladly pay for the missing—" Eliza began.

"Rubbish," spoke up Lady Torbett, who thus far had said nothing. "My husband and I shall bear the expense. Constance obviously viewed this young lady's costume as too good a disguise to pass up. She is quite a headstrong girl, and she has been determined from the outset to marry Charles Langston."

"The question is, what's to be done about it now?" bellowed Lord Torbett. Despite his rather bosky condition, he appeared to be a powerful man who was also quite accustomed to having his own way.

"Appears they've got quite a good head start on us,"

General Huntley interjected matter-of-factly. "If we make haste, we should still be able to overtake them."

"I'll send f' my carriage at once," Lord Torbett said, "and a bottle." Apparently noting the purse of his wife's lips, he added, "Fortification, don't you know. 'Twill be a long night." Lord Torbett seemed to weave a bit as he headed for the stairwell. "Ye' coming, Huntley?"

"In a moment, sir. I mean to see Miss Foxburn to her carriage, first."

Eliza glanced up, a mixture of surprise and . . . . yes, pleasure, in her eyes.

"Mrs. Anders was quite overset when she learned of Lady Constance's plight," he said. "Lady Villiers asked me to see you down, Miss Foxburn."

"Thank you," Eliza murmured, a wave of relief washing over her. To return home now was uppermost in her mind. She turned to Lady Hamilton. "It was a lovely party, ma'am. I am so sorry for . . . whatever trouble my actions may have caused." Her gaze darted to Lady Torbett. "I am indeed sorry for your loss, Lady Torbett. I pray you can forgive my part in it."

The attractive woman shrugged. "I cannot hold you responsible for my daughter's willfulness. Constance is a great deal like me, I fear. A hopeless romantic." With another resigned shrug, she turned to General Huntley. "You are on a fool's errand, sir. I daresay wherever you overtake them, Constance will insist she has already been compromised. Your efforts to save her will come to naught."

The general nodded. "Perhaps you are right, madam."

The elegant woman's head shook. "I warned Constance to follow my lead. She could have married well *and* had her precious lieutenant."

Hearing such plain talk, Eliza ducked her head to avoid looking at the scandalous Lady Torbett, or at General Huntley.

"The girl is, indeed, behaving quite foolishly," Lady Hamilton agreed.

Feeling a light touch at her elbow, Eliza lifted her chin.

"If you will come with me, Miss Foxburn," General Huntley said, "I will show you to your carriage now."

A grateful smile on her lips, Eliza slid past Lady Hamilton and the outspoken Lady Torbett. For a few paces she and the general said nothing. Walking beside him down the stairs, Eliza ventured an explanation.

"I truly did not wish to help Lady Constance flee with her young man, sir."

"I am certain you did all you could to detain them, Miss Foxburn. Lady Constance is quite a willful young lady and I daresay, her mother had the right of it when she said her daughter would not have given up until she found a way."

"I take it you are acquainted with both Lady Constance and Charles," Eliza said. "I confess she told me that you vehemently opposed the match."

The general snorted with derision. "Indeed, I do oppose it. Lieutenant Langston had no business setting his cap for that young lady. She quite plainly . . . outranks him."

Eliza's eyes widened. She could scarcely believe her ears. "Are you saying, sir, that you disapprove of the match because Lady Constance's station is . . . superior to his?"

The general's head and shoulders were quite erect. "That is precisely what I am saying, Miss Foxburn. Charles is a miller's son, with nothing to recommend him but a fancy uniform and a medal for valor on his chest. He is an exemplary soldier, but he is not a gentleman. The two have nothing but heartache ahead of them. Lady Constance's family will ostracize him, and, I daresay, when Lady Constance tires of him, she, too, will toss him aside."

The force of his words were so very strong, Eliza was stunned into silence by them.

He cast a sidelong look at her. "None of which would have happened," he added firmly, "if the young man had

had the decency to choose a bride . . . closer to home."
He paused, then beneath his breath, added, "Langston is
being quite vulgar."

Eliza could scarcely believe her ears. General Huntley
was, indeed, the most brilliant man she'd ever met! If only
she could persuade him to speak to her father; surely he
could make Papa see reason.

Her breath coming in fits and starts, she said, "I recall
you saying you were acquainted with my father, General
Huntley?"

They had now reached the ground floor and were
advancing toward the foyer.

"That was quite a long time ago," the tall man replied
absently. "Your father and I were classmates long ago at
Eton."

Upon reaching the marble-tiled entryway, the general
turned to address the liveried footman posted near the
huge double doors. "Has Lord Villiers's carriage been
brought 'round?"

The footman's eyes remained properly downcast. "This
way, sir."

Eliza could barely contain the excitement bubbling
within her. She hurried to catch up. "I am quite certain
he would like to see you again, sir."

Ahead of her, General Huntley stepped through the
elegant mahogany door that a second footman had flung
open for them. Striding across the gleaming portico, he
advanced down the steps to the drive.

Close on his heels, Eliza repeated anxiously, "I am certain my father would like to see you again, General
Huntley."

The general was now standing alongside the Villierses'
shiny black equipage, the four handsome bays in front
pawing the pavement. He placed a gloved hand on Eliza's
elbow to assist her into the carriage.

"Shall I tell him you will come, sir?"

The tall man seemed only now to hear her. "I beg your pardon, Miss Foxburn, were you . . . addressing me?"

Eliza smiled sweetly. "I said my father would be delighted to see you again, General Huntley. I wonder if you'd be good enough to take tea with us tomorrow afternoon? Would four of the clock suit?"

General Huntley sketched a polite bow. "Thank you, indeed, for the kind invitation, Miss Foxburn. But, I haven't the least clue where I shall be at four of the clock tomorrow. I will, however, consent to call upon your father when I return from . . . from wherever it is I am going."

"Indeed," Eliza murmured. "I quite forgot, sir. Very well, then. I will tell my father to expect you . . . whenever." She smiled into the handsome general's cool gray eyes. "Thank you, sir. You have been most kind."

General Huntley nodded. "Good evening, Miss Foxburn."

Eliza climbed into the Villierses' carriage and settled herself beside a distraught-looking Jane.

"I simply could not abide remaining in that house a second longer," Jane gasped. In the darkness, she reached to clasp Eliza's gloved hand and held it tightly as the coach wheeled down the curved drive away from Lord and Lady Hamilton's town house and onto the cobbled streets of Mayfair.

"Constance has made a grave error in judgment," Jane went on. "After she marries Lieutenant Langston, he will return to his post and be killed. She should never have married him. Do tell me you tried to stop them, Eliza."

"Indeed, I did, Jane. But Lady Constance was most insistent. Perhaps her young man will not be killed," she added hopefully. "The war is over."

Jane dabbed at her nose with a moist scrap of linen. "Of course he will be killed! One should never marry a soldier. It only brings heartbreak."

"There, there, Jane," Lady Villiers said in a soothing tone. "I expect General Huntley will succeed in bringing

her back to London before she . . . that is before they"—
she flung a furtive glance at Eliza,—"before the deed is
done."

Eliza gave Jane's hand another squeeze. "I am certain
your mother is right, Jane, dear. It will all come out right
in the end."

At length, the women fell silent, which left Eliza free to
mull over the extraordinary events of this most unpredictable evening. Most unpredictable of all was discovering
that she and General Huntley were of the same mind on
the gravest of Eliza's concerns—that of the unsuitability
of her father and Miss Ivy Heathergill. How very fortunate
she was to have met the great man! And how fortuitous
that he, of all people, would be the one to come to her
aid.

An excited smile crept over her features.

Now, all she need worry about was how to keep Papa
home every afternoon for the next several days. It would
not do at all for him to be away when General Huntley
came to call.

CHAPTER 5

"PARIS BECKONS"

She was unsuccessful the following three afternoons.
Papa was taking Ivy for a drive in the park, or to Gunter's
for an ice, or sparring with Mr. Heathergill at Gentleman
Jack's. Eliza grew more agitated and anxious with each
passing day. If General Huntley did not set Papa straight
soon, they'd be related to a tradesman, and she'd have
a stepmama who was little more than a year older than
herself!

On the fourth afternoon, Eliza was seated before the
pianoforte in an upstairs sitting room, when Briggs, the
Foxburn butler, appeared in the doorway.

Briggs politely cleared his throat in order to gain her
attention, then he said, "You've a caller, Miss Eliza."

"Oh!" Eliza sprang to her feet, her blue eyes round.
"Do show him in, Briggs, do!"

Briggs cleared his throat again. "The caller is not a 'he,'
Miss."

Eliza gazed quizzically at the white-haired retainer.
Briggs had butled in the Foxburn household since her
father was in leading strings. They both knew it was long

past time to retire the elderly servant, but neither had the heart to turn the old fellow out. Instead they endeavored to be patient with his somewhat quirky ways.

"He is a she," Briggs clarified. "What I mean to say, Miss, is that it is not a him, it is a her."

Eliza's face fell. "A her?"

"Yes, miss."

The butler's voice was all but drowned out by an insistent swish of skirts and a female voice declaring, "Oh, do stop babbling, Briggs, and step aside."

Eliza wordlessly watched as Lady Villiers sailed past the stoop-shouldered butler and entered the room.

"I declare I was growing roots waiting to be announced!" she said. She flung a peevish look at Briggs, who apparently of his own accord had decided that that would be all and was now shuffling toward the corridor.

A half smile on her lips, Eliza turned to her guest who, also without waiting to be told, or in this case, asked, was already arranging herself comfortably on a small settee before the low-burning fire. When suitably settled, Lady Villiers turned an expectant look on Eliza. "A cup of tea would be nice, dear."

"Of course," Eliza murmured, realizing that in her disappointment over the fact that Lady Villiers was not General Huntley, and that Briggs had very nearly put her caller out of curl, she'd completely forgot her manners.

"Briggs!" she called, expecting that the slow-moving man had likely gotten no more than a few feet down the corridor. She waited a few seconds for him to reappear, and when he didn't, she crossed the room to the bell rope and gave it a smart tug.

"I expect Briggs didn't hear me," she said in the old man's defense. "He is a bit . . ." She tapped one ear significantly.

Lady Villiers sniffed. "Doddering old fool is far more than a *bit,* if you ask me. Can't think why Richard insists on keeping him about."

"Briggs does rather seem like one of the family," Eliza remarked, then, after the housekeeper, Mrs. Allen, had arrived and she'd given her instructions regarding the tea, she joined her guest near the hearth.

Lady Villiers waited 'til Eliza'd taken a seat, then in a bright tone, said, "I have come to tell you my latest plan, dear. As you know, Jane was quite distraught over the unfortunate episode between Lady Constance and her husban—"

"They are married, then?" Eliza blurted out. "Do forgive me for interrupting, ma'am. I confess I have been quite a-tremor to hear the outcome."

"Indeed, they are married," Lady Villiers replied crisply. "Apparently Lord Torbett and General Huntley did not reach the runaways in time. The ceremony . . . or *something*—" she said pointedly, "—had already taken place. In any event, I can assure you, the news quite upset my Jane. She simply refuses to believe that Lieutenant Langston will not be killed or that when the inevitable does occur, Constance will survive the loss."

She paused to draw breath, during which Eliza hastened to ask, "General Huntley has returned to London, then, has he?"

Lady Villiers seemed a bit thrown by the off-subject question. "Well, yes, I . . . expect he has . . . but the point I am trying to make, dear, is that Jane has declared she will attend no further functions in Town where there are soldiers present. I have been quite beside the bridge about it. She'd made such a good beginning, you know, and now . . . this. Which is why I was forced to cast about for a new plan. And managed to come up with quite a good one, I daresay." her lips pursed smugly.

"A new plan?"

"Indeed." Lady Villiers nodded. She rearranged the ribbons of her reticule in her lap in quite a deliberate fashion. "I have decided to take Jane to Paris. I am certain the diversion will be the very thing to bring her back around. In addition, Eliza dear, I insist that you accompany us."

"Oh!" Eliza sucked in her breath. *Paris!* She'd always wished to go to Paris!

"With all the celebration going on abroad," Lady Villiers went on, "I think it the perfect time and place to prod Jane from the dismals. Paris is swarming with nobility these days. It would be simply delicious if Jane, or you, were to meet a French marquess, or a Russian count. Jane's situation is quite similar to Lady Constance's, you know. Both girls should have married titles. The sooner my Jane is wed again, the better. And it's high time you gave a thought to your own future, as well, Eliza. So, what do you say? Are you up for a little sojourn?"

"Oh-h . . ." Eliza was having trouble drawing breath. "Of course, Lady Villiers, I would like nothing better than to . . . Oh! Oh, my! I don't know what to say!"

The older woman laughed. "There is only one thing to say, dear." She reached to pat Eliza's hand affectionately.

"And, that is, that you will come! I fear Jane will not be persuaded if you do not agree to accompany us. I have not yet presented the idea to her, you see. I wished to tell her at the outset that you were to be along."

"Well, I . . . I shall have to consult with Papa, of course."

"Of course. But I am certain he will agree. Why wouldn't he, for pity's sake? It is the perfect opportunity for you to—"

At that instant, Mrs. Allen appeared with the tea tray, and Lady Villiers took the liberty of not only giving the Foxburn housekeeper instructions as to where to put it, but of pouring a cup for herself and one for Eliza.

Whilst the above was taking place, Eliza's thoughts were in a whirl. Paris! What a perfectly splendid idea! What a perfectly splendid city! She'd always wished to go to Paris. She'd always wished to go somewhere . . . *anywhere!*

Oh, my! It all sounded so very thrilling . . . but . . . oh; oh, dear. What was she thinking? She couldn't go. Not now. Someone had to look after Papa. But . . . wait, Lady Villiers had said that General Huntley had returned to London. Surely that meant he would call upon them very soon and once Papa'd heard his views on the pitfalls of marrying outside one's class, her troubles would be over and she *could* go to Paris!

She was so a-tremor over the prospect, she absently brought the teacup in her hand to her lips and took an inordinately large sip of the steaming brew, then cried out in pain when the steaming hot liquid scalded her tongue and throat.

"*Oh!*" She flung the clattering cup and saucer to the nearby tray and snatched up a slice of lemon to suck on. "I-I have burned my tongue!"

Lady Villiers grinned. "Well, I only hope Jane will be as excited over my little plan as I can plainly see that you are." She set her own teacup aside. "I shall be off now. You will let me know what your papa says. I should like to leave for the Continent within the week."

She rose to her feet and continued talking on her way out. "There will be no need to purchase a thing for the trip, dear. We shall spend every spare minute in Paris . . . that we are not attending balls and receptions, that is . . . shopping! It will be glorious, indeed. Ta!"

At the door, she cocked a brow. "No need to ring for Briggs to show me out. I shall be halfway home before he makes it up the corridor."

Still contemplating the delightful prospect just presented her, the sound of Lady Villiers's gay laughter as she headed toward the foyer did not penetrate Eliza's consciousness. However, it did suddenly occur to her that if the general were to call upon them and ask for Papa, and he were not at home, Briggs would very likely turn the great man away. Stirring herself from her reverie, she went at once in search of Briggs.

She found him on his hands and knees in the butler's pantry, an uncorked bottle of McCutheon's Health-Giving

Tonic on the sideboard. She and her father both knew that, as the day progressed, it was very often McCutheon's Tonic that kept Briggs going.

"Ah, there you are, Briggs."

"Blasted cork done rolled away," Briggs muttered.

"Do get up, Briggs, I shall send one of the housemaids in to help you find it," Eliza said. It would never do for Briggs to sprain something while crawling around on the floor. "In the meantime, I have come to tell you that I am expecting a gentleman caller any day now, that is, *Papa* and I are expecting the gentleman, and I wished you to know, Briggs, that even if Papa is not at home when the gentleman calls, that *I* wish to see him myself. Do you understand what I am saying, Briggs?"

His head barely visible from beneath the sideboard, the old man nodded. At least, Eliza took the nervous twitching of what she could see of his head as a nod.

"Good. The gentleman I am speaking of is General Huntley, just home from the wars. He is a most impressive man, quite tall and broad-shouldered and . . . uh—" Suddenly, she realized that so detailed a physical description of the man was not necessary, as it was likely not to be noted, or remembered, by Briggs.

"The thing is," she hurried on, "I am uncertain as to the exact time or day when the general will call; I simply wished to alert you that he is expected and to please not turn him away. Are you certain you understand me, Briggs? Briggs?"

The old man, the elusive cork now in his hand, pulled himself to his feet, a resounding burp escaping from the folds of his double chin as he did so. Once upright, he recorked the bottle of tonic and busied himself putting it back on a shelf in the tidy pantry.

"Did you understand what I just said, Briggs?" Eliza asked.

The butler turned a somewhat florid face upon his

employer's daughter. "I am to turn away none of your gentlemen callers, Miss Eliza."

"Hmmm," Eliza murmured. He seemed to have gotten the gist of it, so, she supposed, that would have to do.

She decided it would be wise to go and change her dress and brush her hair, in case General Huntley arrived in time for tea this very afternoon. She did so wish to look as presentable as possible for him, though why that was an important consideration to her was unclear just now. The thought uppermost in her mind at present was how *desperately* she wished to go to Paris!

Her life, to this point, she realized, as she made her way abovestairs, had been prodigiously dull. In all her eighteen years, she had not done *one* thing even remotely exciting. Instead, she'd excelled at being the dutiful daughter, performing each and every task given her by her mama, her papa, her nanny, her governess, and every tutor and teacher she'd encountered at home and at school, in an exemplary fashion. Which meant that, her life had been quite ordered and predictable. And dull.

Except where Papa was concerned, of course. Papa was not predictable. Or dull. One never knew what Papa might do next. Of course, if she were to be entirely honest, Eliza would admit to rather admiring that trait in him. Papa was not afraid to be daring and outrageous. In some instances, Eliza allowed, daring and outrageous was not *un*desirable. All the young soldiers she'd met were daring . . . and they'd lived such exciting lives! Now, it appeared that, at long last, *she* was to have the opportunity for adventure. To go to Paris was, indeed, quite daring!

And whilst there . . . she might even do something outrageous.

Reaching her bedchamber, Eliza opened the clothespress and absently sorted through the somewhat sparse selection of pretty gowns hanging there.

Even Jane, poor sad soul that she was, had already had a more interesting life than she. Jane had been in love and more importantly . . . Jane had been with a man! A shudder of something *scandalous* rippled through Eliza. She knew next to nothing of such matters, only what she'd read in books. Not that the books she'd read could be considered reliable sources of instruction for that sort of thing, most of them being romantical novels. Like *Passion Rules Their Hearts*. Suddenly, the odd queasiness that had plagued Eliza on the stage in Lady Hamilton's drawing room gripped her again. What did it mean?

She shook her head as if to shake the strange sensation away as she drew forth her favorite lemon yellow sprigged muslin and spread it across the bed. Betsy would be along shortly to help her dress. Her thoughts still fixed on the upcoming Paris trip, Eliza crossed the room to her dressing table and absently reached for her hairbrush.

A long sigh escaped her as she drew the brush through her ebony locks.

How dearly she had yearned for adventure! Even during her many months of mourning for Mama, she'd often sat for hours just gazing from her bedchamber window, or alone in the garden, dreaming of faraway places, wishing she were anywhere but London. And, now, suddenly she was presented with the very opportunity to go somewhere smashing! To have an outrageous adventure at last! And, best of all, she did not have to defy convention, or disobey anyone to do so.

Unlike Lady Constance.

What courage it must have taken for that young lady to go against her parents' wishes—and those of the formidable General Huntley—to approach a stranger and demand she give over her cloak and mask so that she might flee incognito with the man she loved! What a daring, wickedly daring, terrifyingly daring, thing to do! But, Lady Constance had done it! And by all accounts, had been successful at it. Of course, Eliza did not approve the match, but she heartily admired the girl's courage! Lady Constance was indeed an adventuress.

Her hairbrush poised in midair, Eliza gazed at her own image in the glass.

"Eliza Foxburn, you are as dull as oatmeal," she said aloud.

"Beg pardon, miss?" came Betsy's voice from behind her.

Eliza whirled about and in a determined tone added, "I am as insipid as a . . . a leaf of boiled cabbage!"

Betsy's lips pursed. "Sounds to me as if you might be feeling a bit peckish, miss. It's nigh-on teatime," she added, heading for the bed and scooping up Eliza's pretty afternoon gown.

Eliza turned back to her image in the glass. She hoped General Huntley was on his way to their home. All her hopes for the future hinged on his making Papa see reason.

After changing her dress and freshening up, Eliza decided that whilst she awaited General Huntley, she'd brush up or her French. She used to be quite proficient in the language but it'd been some time since she'd spoken more than a few words of it. On her way to the library, her attention was arrested by a curious swooshing sound coming from the drawing room.

She glanced through the arched opening and was quite astonished to see the tall figure of General Huntley standing near the mantelpiece doing . . . what *was* the general doing?

In one hand he held what appeared to be a rolled-up newspaper and he was swatting at . . . what *was* he swatting at?

"Good afternoon, General Huntley," Eliza began, her blue eyes round with curiosity as she advanced into the room. "I was unaware that you were here, sir."

The dashing officer, still holding the rolled-up newspaper, glanced up. "Good afternoon, Miss Foxburn, I was just . . . ah . . ."

"Oh, dear," Eliza murmured, her gaze fastening on the half dozen or so dead flies strewn about the floor at the general's feet. She flung a glance at the double French doors that led to the mews. Sure enough, they were standing ajar. "If there are flies in the drawing room," she said matter-of-factly, "that must mean Papa is at home. Is he aware that you are here, sir?"

"I . . ." The general turned a puzzled look on her.

"Oh, dear. If you'll excuse me, sir, I'll just go and fetch him."

"Of, course."

In her excitement, Eliza, herself, forgot to shut the outside door and on her way back to the hallway, was startled when suddenly a fuzzy gray-and-white cat streaked past the general and came running after her. As the cat dashed past her legs, Eliza gave chase and sure enough, managed to catch him. She bent to scoop up the squirming creature. Turning back around, the cat tucked under one arm, she glanced at General Huntley. "You haven't by any chance seen a mouse, have you, sir?"

"A mouse? No, I . . . can't say as I have." He paused, the curious look on his face deepening. "Should I have seen a mouse?"

Affectionately scratching the cat's ears, Eliza grinned. "I hope not, sir. My Sailor often streaks into the house when he's after a mouse, you see."

"Your . . . sailor?"

"My kitty-cat. His name is Sailor. I named him Sailor because he's always sailing about." At that moment, Sailor wriggled from her arms and darted back out the still-opened doors that led to the the garden. "Oops! There he goes." Eliza walked to the double French doors and closed them firmly behind the cat. "There. I do hope he wasn't after a mouse."

The general's features relaxed a mite. "I promise to be on the lookout for it, Miss Foxburn."

Eliza smiled up at him. The older man looked quite dashing this afternoon in his scarlet military coat with the blue cuffs and gold braid. His crisp white breeches were tucked into gleaming black Hessians. Eliza's gaze was drawn to the distinguished white wings of hair that feathered outward from his temples. General Huntley was really a *very* handsome man.

Suddenly, she realized she'd been staring overlong at him. "Well, I . . . I shall just go and get Father."

"Perhaps he has seen the mouse," the general offered.

Eliza grinned sheepishly. "I rather doubt that. Papa rarely notices anything these days, which is why I wished you to speak with him, sir. Any advice you can give him will be greatly appreciated," she said, her tone gravely serious.

The puzzled look reappeared on the general's face. "Ah-h."

On the way to fetch her father, Eliza met up again with Briggs.

"I have put your gentleman caller in the drawing room, Miss Eliza," the butler informed her.

Eliza paused. Unlike most of Briggs's pronouncements, this one required not the least bit of deciphering. It made perfect sense just as he'd said it. She blinked. "Thank you, Briggs."

He turned to shuffle off.

"Oh, Briggs."

The elderly man glanced over one shoulder. "Yes, miss?"

Eliza's lips pursed. She did not wish Briggs to put General Huntley out of curl as he had managed to do earlier with Lady Villiers. "I have not yet said 'that will be all,' " she added peevishly.

The balding retainer cocked a brow. "Would you be needin' something else, miss?"

"Indeed, I do. Will you please ask Mrs. Allen to prepare a nice tea for us? With a good many sandwiches, please. There are two very large gentlemen present, and if General Huntley is anything like Papa, I expect he will want more than a thin slice of cake with his tea."

Briggs stood motionless for a second or two, then he

cupped one ear with a hand, his thinning white head at a tilt.

"What is it now, Briggs?" Eliza asked, irritation again creeping into her tone.

"I was wondering if that was all of the all, miss? I shouldn't wish to miss the rest of the all if it t'weren't."

A sharp gaze pinned him. "You may go now, Briggs. But please do not forget the sandwiches."

Eliza hurried to her father's suite, on the way stopping a housemaid and sending her to sweep up the dead flies in the drawing room. When she did not locate her father in his suite, she hurriedly returned belowstairs, where she was pleased to discover both men now in the drawing room and already having a pleasant chat.

As she stole noiselessly into the room, her father glanced up from the sideboard, where he was busy pouring his guest a brandy. "May I present my daughter, Eliza. Eliza, this is—"

"The general and I have already met, Papa. If you recall, I told you that General Huntley was present at Lady Villiers's dinner party and again at Lord and Lady Hamilton's." She cast a suddenly shy gaze at the stern-faced military man standing before the hearth. "The general and I were . . . um . . . partnered for a charade."

"Ah, yes," her father said absently, then turned back to his business with the brandy.

He handed the snifter to Huntley as Eliza slipped onto a straight-backed chair near the low-burning fire.

"What have you heard of our classmate Scrope Davies?" General Huntley asked, moving to seat himself in a comfortable overstuffed chair, one long leg crossed over the other.

Sir Richard lounged against the mantelpiece, also sipping from a glass of brandy.

Eliza thought her father looked quite handsome this afternoon in a pair of biscuit-colored pantaloons and a navy coat with brass buttons.

"Scrope became a fellow at Cambridge," her father was saying, "and later entered King's College. Believe he passes most of his days now at the gaming table." Sir Richard laughed. "A remarkable story circulated a few years back about ol' Scrope. Appears he was betting against a young man who'd just come into his majority and was about to be married . . ."

Eliza's ears perked up. The conversation turning to marriage so quickly! How very opportune! She leaned forward, alert for opening.

". . . after the poor fellow'd lost round after round, he grew quite overset over his great losses," Sir Richard continued. "Scrope finally took pity on him and quite gallantly gave him back all that he'd lost; all except a tidy little *dormeuse* that was fitted up with a bed."

Huntley grinned. "Which I presume Scrope still sleeps in?"

Sir Richard nodded. "Says when he travels in it, he sleeps better for having acted rightly."

Both gentlemen laughed, looks of fond remembrance settling on their faces.

"What happened to the young man?" Eliza asked brightly. "Whom did he marry? I expect he made a *proper* match."

Both men turned quizzical gazes upon her.

Presently Sir Richard said, "I don't recall whom the young man married, Eliza."

"Hmmm. Well, then . . . whom did Scrope marry?"

Still gazing at his only daughter, Sir Richard's brow furrowed. Then, without venturing a reply, he turned back to his guest. "I understand 'Teapot' Crawfurd was appointed to the Hussars."

Huntley nodded. "Crawfurd was foremost in the charge at Orthes in Spain. Performed quite splendidly, he did. Damn shame about . . . er"— a gaze cut toward Eliza— "beg pardon, Miss Foxburn." He cleared his throat. "Nasty shame about Crawfurd's brother. Lost his life at Waterloo."

Sir Richard exhaled a sigh. "We lost far too many brave men to this war. Damn shame about all of 'em." He offered no apology to his daughter for his own profanity.

A contemplative pause followed the pronouncement, which Eliza shattered by addressing the general. "You were quite fortunate to have escaped injury, sir."

Huntley nodded thoughtfully. "Indeed, although I had one very close call."

"Oh?" Sir Richard's interest was piqued.

"Was the fourth day after Waterloo, after we'd arrived at Peronne."

"Heard of it." Sir Richard nodded. "Township that boasted it had never been taken by the enemy."

"The very one. Although Wellington was determined to take it. We commenced proceedings by battering the gates with a strong round of artillery, to which the little village responded quite heartily. In fact, the first shot fell beneath the belly of the Duke's own horse."

"Oh, my!" Eliza exclaimed.

The general glanced in her direction, his penetrating gray gaze having much the same effect on Eliza as it had that night at Lady Villiers's dinner party when they first met. "Wellington's mount was obviously frightened," he said, "but beyond the scattering of stones and pebbles in all directions, no real harm was done."

He shifted his weight on the chair. "Quite soon afterward, however, I was certain I'd been hit, but"—the general's well-shaped lips curved into a smile—"turned out a ball had merely struck my breeches pocket and a half dozen five-franc pieces broke the force of the blow!"

Sir Richard's hearty laughter joined the deep rumble that gurgled up from the general's throat.

It was the first time Eliza had heard the general laugh aloud. She warmed to the pleasant sound. Her feminine trill soon mingled with the gentlemen's.

Still, despite her enjoyment of General Huntley's stories, she was becoming quite impatient to steer the conversation in the direction of her choosing. This could very well be her only opportunity for an ally in her quest to enlighten Papa. He simply must hear the great man's views on the Important Matter of marriage. He *must!*

When the gentlemen's amusement died away, she seized the moment. "I expect Lord and Lady Torbett were quite appreciative of your efforts on Lady Constance's behalf, were they not, General Huntley?"

He looked up. "I couldn't say, Miss Foxburn."

"You are being far too modest, sir. Of course, they were." She smiled charmingly at the handsome officer. "Do apprise Papa of the situation. I confess I told him very little of it."

"What's this?" Sir Richard asked.

General Huntley cleared his throat. "Lord Torbett and I were unable to dissuade the young couple from their plan to marry."

"Ah." Sir Richard's blue eyes began to twinkle. "I daresay I have been giving some thought to taking the plunge myself."

Though the conversation was not going quite as she'd planned, Eliza was elated once more. She quickly charged in with, "I am certain the general would be interested in hearing about Miss Heathergill, Papa."

It was her father who now regarded her quizzically, though he did not remark on the oddity of her request. Instead he addressed Huntley. "Perhaps you'd like to meet the young lady; she is most extraordinary."

The general nodded politely and seemed about to speak when they were all interrupted by Briggs and Mrs. Allen, who advanced into the room carrying between them a steaming pot of tea, cups and saucers, plates, and a platter piled high with assorted cakes, tarts, and, Eliza noted with pleasure, a goodly number of sandwiches.

After everyone had been served and were munching away on the sandwiches and cake, Eliza, who was growing quite anxious now over the lack of conversation on the subject she wished dearly to address, began afresh, "Well, I for one, think it quite unwise of Lady Constance even to consider marrying Lieutenant Langston."

Both men cast puzzled glances her way, then suddenly, General Huntley sprang to his feet as if he'd been shot. In one hand, he held up a bun that seemed to have . . . a tail.

"It appears I have found your mouse, Miss Foxburn," he announced in quite a somber tone.

Eliza stared with disbelief at the bun in the general's hand. Indeed, it did have a tail, and two pointedly little ears.

"Ee-e-ek!" she cried, and in her haste to scramble to the safety of the chair upon which she sat, overturned her own teacup and sent the china plate in her lap clattering to the floor, where it and the delicate teacup splintered into a million pieces. *Papa, do something!*"

"Briggs!" Sir Richard bellowed. Also on his feet, he reached for the odd-looking bun and, holding it aloft, met the elderly retainer midway across the room. In his arms, Briggs was carrying the gray-and-white cat Sailor. "What is the meaning of this?" Sir Richard demanded.

Spotting the sandwich, Sailor made a lunge and caught part of it—the part belonging to the tail—between his teeth. With the small gray mouse dangling from his mouth, the cat flew toward the outside door but upon finding it not open, whirled about and, with a wild look in his golden eyes, began to dart madly about the room as if he feared someone might snatch his prized catch away.

"Sailor!" shouted Eliza. Having collected herself, she scrambled to the floor and ran toward the same door Sailor had found not open. "This way, boy! Come quick!"

In a flash, Sailor streaked back across the room and once again, disappeared through the door Eliza had flung open for him.

A collective sigh escaped all in the drawing room who'd witnessed the unusual spectacle.

It was Briggs who broke the charged moment of silence with, "Beg pardon, sir. Seems I got Sailor-boy's sandwich mixed in where it don't ought to be."

"Oh, Briggs . . ." Eliza sank onto the sofa, her dark locks shaking with chagrin. General Huntley would think them all daft.

During the excitement, Sir Richard had exited the room and now came striding back in with a housemaid on his heels, whom he set to cleaning up Eliza's spilt tea and broken teacup and plate. General Huntley had moved to stand near the mantlepiece, his long gray eyes more alert now than Eliza had ever seen them.

When the housemaid had at last swept up the mess, and Sir Richard had again taken a seat, Eliza tried once more to broach the topic she was determined the three of them would discuss that afternoon.

Inhaling a deep breath, she worked to stay calm. "General Huntley has quite strong views on marriage, Papa," she began evenly. "Do tell Papa what you told me about Lieutenant Langston and Lady Constance, sir."

The general again looked befuddled. "I confess, I do not recall what I said on the subject, Miss Foxburn."

Eliza was very near to exploding now. "You said you thought it vulgar!" she blurted out, her high-pitched tone quite agitated.

Sir Richard chuckled. "I rather expect Lord and Lady Torbett agreed with you on that head, eh, Huntley? Pup had aspirations, did he?"

"Indeed, he did," the general agreed most heartily. "I daresay love can cause a young man to go quite off his head."

A young man! Eliza thought bitterly.

Still, she managed to curb her temper and say somewhat primly, "I daresay I think it quite foolish of Lady Constance to even consider marrying Lieutenant Langston, wouldn't you agree, General Huntley? He, being so far . . . beneath her."

This caused Sir Richard's blue eyes to cut 'round suspiciously.

"Are you saying you would not marry a soldier, Miss Foxburn?" the general asked innocently.

"Well, I . . . I—"

"Eliza has given no thought at all to marriage," her father interjected pointedly.

Eliza's eyes rolled skyward as, once again, she felt the conversation slipping from her grasp. She had to do *something* to keep it on course!

But, what?

Suddenly, her blue eyes snapping, she sprang to her feet. "That is not true, Papa! The fact is, I . . . I . . . am affianced to"—she cast about for something *shocking* to say, and found it—"to . . . General Huntley!"

CHAPTER 6

"AN UNEXPECTED OFFER"

Both gentlemen stared at Eliza as if she'd taken leave
of her senses. Eliza couldn't help wondering the same.
What on earth had made her blurt out such an absurdity?
Not in her wildest imaginings could she have conjured up
such an outrageous thing! Betrothed to General Huntley?
It was not outrageous, it was laughable!

But . . . no one was laughing.

"I was given to understand that you and Huntley had
only just met, Eliza," Sir Richard said, his incredulous gaze
traveling from his daughter to Huntley and back again. "I
had no idea that the acquaintance had . . . had . . ." His
astonished voice trailed into oblivion.

Eliza turned a wide-eyed gaze on the tall military man,
whose stunned features looked anything but bored now.
Of the three of them, she expected General Huntley was
more accustomed to surprise maneuvers. Still, despite his
vast experience in strategy and such, he appeared to be
experiencing considerable difficulty recouping from this
unexpected blow.

She watched him gulp, then in a somewhat halting voice,

he said, "Y-Your daughter and I met . . . er . . . that is, we first became acquainted—"

"Two years ago!" Eliza interrupted, her tone quite shrill. "At . . . my come-out ball!"

Sir Richard turned another bewildered gaze upon his daughter. "At your come-out ball?" he repeated incredulously.

"Yes." Eliza nodded vigorously. "Ummm . . . whilst you and Lord Hamilton were gone. You recall, Papa, you left my party early. General Huntley arrived quite late in the company of . . . of . . ." She looked a question at Huntley.

He gulped again. "The . . . Duke of Wellington," the great man supplied weakly.

Although his inflection made the reply sound a bit like a question, Eliza nonetheless nodded with decision, her blue eyes growing quite large and round.

"The Duke of Wellington?" her father sputtered.

"Yes!" Eliza cried, and despite her pounding heart and quickened breath, added, "Mama and I were quite sorry that you were not there to meet him." She turned another wild gaze upon her accomplice. "General Huntley asked me to stand up with him and . . . and we have been corresponding ever since. Secretly. Secretly corresponding. Yes, yes that's it."

Sir Richard frowned. "Can this be true?" he demanded.

"Of course, it's true, Papa." Eliza willed a shaky smile to her lips and hastened to cross the fingers of one hand that was hidden in the folds of her long skirt. She turned a lopsided grin upon the still-stunned features of General Huntley. "The . . . the general and I were . . . quite taken with one another," she added.

"No, no, I mean, can it be true that the great Duke of Wellington attended one of our *soirées* and I was not apprised of the fact until now?" her father demanded.

Eliza's chin shot up. "Well, perhaps you can appreciate now how very scandalized Mama and I were that you were not present when he, I mean, when *they* arrived." She folded her arms across her middle and glared reproachfully at her father.

It quite took her by surprise when she heard Huntley's voice chiming in. "The Duke was a bit put off by it, as well," he said evenly. He cast a quick glance at Eliza as if to seek her approval of his clever fabrication.

Approval which she willingly gave, in the form of a small satisfied smile and an almost-imperceptible nod. The general glanced back at Sir Richard.

"Where were you, by the by?"

"My whereabouts do not signify!" Sir Richard bellowed. "What matters at the moment is this . . . is that you . . . the Duke of Wellington? Well, I'll be demmed!" His dark head shook with amazement. "Two years ago, ye say?"

The small smile still in place upon Eliza's lips, she nodded decisively at her parent. "Indeed. Two years. Two *very* long years. I daresay the general and I have come to know one another quite well in that length." Her blue eyes again sought Huntley's. She thought the general appeared to have regained himself rather nicely and was performing this charade as admirably as he had that night at Lady Hamilton's.

Sir Richard exhaled another astonished breath. "And 'ye never once let on," he marveled. "Did your mother know?"

Eliza was still looking at Huntley, unaware that something in her gaze was begging him to continue, to follow her lead, to see this thing through to the end, despite the fact that she could not yet tell him what it meant. Yet, when she caught a hint of hesitation and wariness flicker in the depths of his gray eyes, for a split second she considered bringing the proceedings to a halt before the falsehood grew so big no one could possibly unravel it. Another part of her, however, hoped the lie was of such magnitude that it, alone, might achieve what she, and General Huntley, had been unable to do—convince Papa that very *old* gentlemen ought not to marry very *young* ladies.

An intense look in her sapphire blue eyes, she silently begged Huntley to trust her. As she watched his mouth harden and a ripple of tension clench his jaw, she hoped the subtle response meant he would not betray her . . . not yet anyhow.

Her gaze swung back to her father. "No," she said simply, and truthfully, "Mama did not know."

"Well!" Sir Richard said with decision. "Now, I am convinced that you are being truthful with me, Eliza. Your mother would never have permitted such a clandestine liaison to continue. Would never have permitted it."

"If you have objections to our betrothal, sir," General Huntley suddenly interjected, his rather hopeful-sounding tone giving Eliza a moment of concern, "you have only to say the word, and I will—"

"No, no." Sir Richard held up a hand. A considering look on his face, he began to pace up and down. "Come to think on it, I believe you and Eliza do suit. She's a good deal like me, you know. Impetuous, headstrong." He leveled a look at Huntley.

Cool gray eyes cut toward Eliza, and a brow cocked. "Indeed."

She sheepishly ducked her head as her father continued. "Her mother attempted to school those traits out of her, but it is quite clear she failed miserably." A satisfied gaze encompassed both his daughter and General Huntley. "The betrothal stands."

A charged moment of silence followed Sir Richard's pronouncement. During the interval, Eliza dared not look at General Huntley, or her father, lest the trepidation building inside her spoil everything.

She exhaled a small sigh of relief when her father reached to shake his boyhood friend's hand.

"Welcome to the family, Huntley!"

A small squeak of alarm escaped Eliza.

She was certain she also heard a similar sound coming from the great general's lips, but despite his obvious shock and possible displeasure, he managed to say, "Thank you, sir."

Eliza wondered if she ought not to move a bit closer to her betrothed, or perhaps even to embrace him? That thought caused an unwelcome quiver of . . . of something unsettling to travel up her spine, but she put the oddity down to sheer nervousness. After all, she'd just fabricated the most scandalous tale of her entire life!

Not given to lying, Eliza knew she'd be unable to sleep a wink that night, or perhaps any other night until the truth came out. But, if the charade accomplished what she intended, well, perhaps in this case, the means justified the end.

At the moment, not a single thought of the *other* matter Eliza hoped the charade might also accomplish—that of allowing her to travel to Paris unfettered by worries over her father's marital state—entered her mind.

"Well, then," Sir Richard added jovially, still addressing his future son-in-law, "I expect we have a bit of discussing to do—dowry, allowance, the like. If you'll accompany me to my study, Huntley, we'll put these tedious matters behind us."

The pounding of Eliza's heart intensified as she watched her father and the tall, dark-haired man, handsomely turned out in the crimson coat and gold braid, head down the corridor to the Foxburn study.

Since it was far too soon for there to be papers to sign, the betrothal could not yet be considered official. Therefore, Eliza reasoned she'd be accorded the necessary time in which to explain the faradiddle to Huntley and cry off before the lie was further compounded. In the meantime, she prayed the general would be successful in bargaining for a long betrothal. A *very* long betrothal.

Suddenly, the funny fluttering feeling in her stomach made itself known again. She put it down to the intense guilt she felt over hoodwinking her father. What else could it be? She and General Huntley both knew the betrothal was false. He was far too old a man for her, and that's all there was for it.

Wasn't it?

Afternoon tea typically did not alter one's life in so dramatic a fashion, General March Ashford Huntley thought, as he descended the steps in front of the Foxburn town house a half hour later and climbed into the carriage lent him by the British government for his use whilst in London.

After instructing the driver to deliver him to the Clarendon Hotel, where he and a number of other officers were quartered, he settled back to wait out the mile-long ride, which, depending upon the heavy traffic in Town at this hour, could take anywhere from a quarter hour to forever.

A few moments later, Huntley realized there was far too much on his mind for relaxing to be a viable option. He supposed he should be grateful that his longtime friend, Richard Foxburn, had not mentioned announcing this unexpected "betrothal" in the London newspapers just yet, or that his "intended," Miss Foxburn, hadn't fixed upon a date for the nuptials.

His head shook again with astonishment over the thicket he'd unwittingly landed in. What lunacy had possessed the little chit to say what she did, he wondered? The two times previous that he'd been with Miss Foxburn, she seemed quite level-headed and intelligent. Not at all caper-witted or given to flights of fancy.

Her strange action today had caught him completely off guard.

As tea parties went, this one had been the most unusual fare he'd ever been served up. The surprises had begun even *before* he discovered the mouse sandwich on his plate.

It had begun the other night at the Hamiltons' when Miss Foxburn had invited him to call upon her father, and continued today, when she'd expressed the hope that he'd offer Richard some advice or other. He'd expected to learn that his boyhood friend was in some sort of trouble, but Richard seemed in fine fettle, so that couldn't be it.

He chuckled to himself. It was becoming quite obvious that Richard Foxburn and his pretty little daughter were cut from the same cloth.

Richard had been a real cock-of-the-school at Eton, his mischievousness landing him in trouble with the headmaster more than once. But, he was a likable chap and had a good many friends. He and Huntley had not been terribly close chums, however, Richard being not only a few years older than he, but for the most part, keeping company with those of his own ilk, in other words, the sons of dukes and earls.

Huntley was more the scholar, paying closer attention to his studies than he did to larking or the ladies. He'd graduated with honors and used the money he'd earned working as a clerk in a law office to buy himself a commission in the army. He'd served in the military ever since, and until today had not laid eyes on Richard Foxburn in over two decades.

It had not occurred to him that Foxburn might wonder at his sudden appearance in his drawing room today. Richard was as unpredictable as they came and would not question the same trait in anyone else. Huntley had only called upon his onetime friend because Miss Foxburn had asked it of him. He wasn't certain now why he'd felt compelled to honor the young lady's request. He just had.

Still puzzling the oddity over, his lips began to twitch again. Miss Eliza Foxburn was a taking little thing. She had the most expressive blue eyes he'd ever seen, except, of course, in her father's face. The two favored one another a great deal. The sapphire blue of their eyes reminded Huntley of the deepest part of the Mediterranean on a sunny day, although the analogy had never struck him when he thought of Richard.

They both had dark curly hair, as black as pitch and as shiny as a raven's wing. And this afternoon, as well as the other two times Huntley'd been in Miss Foxburn's company, he'd had to stifle an unsettling urge to stroke hers. Which was another thing that had never occurred to him where her father was concerned.

Obvious as well to Huntley was that Miss Foxburn had inherited her father's quick wit and composure under fire, which, being a military man, was a trait Huntley not only recognized but greatly admired.

He did not believe the tale she'd blurted out today was preconceived; the falsehood had spilled too haltingly from her lips, but once she'd started it, the story had seemed to spin out of control and ended up being quite convincing. Huntley'd been almost convinced of the truth of it himself! Of course, Miss Foxburn had borrowed heavily from the real-life drama she'd recently witnessed in the lives of Lady Constance Torbett and her *amour*. But, nonetheless, she'd done a credible job of fabricating under fire.

The question was, what did she hope to accomplish by today's charade?

He mulled the matter over a bit longer, but failed to come up with anything plausible to explain it.

Eventually, his thoughts settled again on the young lady herself. Despite the vast difference in their ages, he had to admit there was something about Miss Eliza Foxburn that he found immensely alluring, though he was hard-pressed actually to name it. He was certain she was as innocent as a girl of her tender years ought to be. She was not a flirt, and, so far as he could tell, she exhibited none of the shameless artificiality that some women skillfully used to manipulate men into doing their bidding.

No, Miss Foxburn was quite guileless, and she had a charming way of looking to him as if she . . . *needed* him to rescue her. He'd not had much experience in rescuing damsels in distress . . . but, for some reason, he found it not an unattractive prospect.

Continuing to mull the strange situation over, he absently glanced out the coach window. The carriage had just entered fashionable Bond Street, which he knew to be off-limits to proper young ladies. And yet, he caught sight of a group of four or five pretty young girls, each attired in pastel-colored muslin gowns, and twirling ruffle-edged parasols, strolling carelessly down the boulevard. Trailing behind them was a parade of five or six young military men. As if they hadn't a care in the world for their reputations, the girls were tossing their heads and giggling flirtatiously with the soldiers.

It struck Huntley then, that that was precisely the sort of behavior he'd never expect to see from Miss Eliza Foxburn. She was *too* refined and contained to act in such a frivolous fashion.

And yet . . . her behaviour today certainly put that theory to a test.

Why had she wished to attach herself to him, he wondered, again and again. There had to be a logical answer for it; he just could not think what it might be.

Duty, of course, demanded that he not dispute the young lady's word, at least, not for the moment. To contradict her at this juncture, or to call her a liar, would serve to needlessly sully her reputation. And Huntley would never do that.

As he continued to stare at the passing blur of busy London streets, he toyed with the idea of actually settling into the life of a country squire . . . with his pretty young bride, Miss Eliza Foxburn, at his side.

That unlikely thought caused him to squirm a bit on the coach bench, though again he couldn't say why it affected him thusly.

As a young man, March Huntley had only once fancied himself in love, but the infatuation was short-lived and ended soon after his company had vacated the military post where he'd been briefly stationed that sultry summer. Beyond the usual dallying with the fair sex that most men engage in, he'd never felt compelled to travel that emotional road again, at least not to completion, meaning he'd never told a woman he loved her, or proposed marriage.

In all honesty, he had no objection to taking a wife. Not at this point in his life. He was not a young man, by some standards, but at eight and thirty he was also not over the hill. And with the war finally at an end, he had the option now of leaving the military, or of retaining his commission and accepting a peacetime command. He'd about decided upon the latter, but were he to change his mind, and retire instead, his pension and stipend, coupled with the modest fortune he'd inherited from his long-dead parents, would be more than enough to provide adequately for a wife and family.

He owned a sizable farm and acreage in the north of England, just beyond Chester. A younger brother, Jan, was looking after it, and another brother August, lived also on the estate. His three sisters had all married and were now scattered to various parts of the island. The family was not a particularly close one, not owing to animosity on anyone's part, but simply the natural manner in which their rather nondescript lives had unfolded.

His thoughts settled again on Miss Eliza Foxburn. She had mentioned no brothers or sisters, and beyond remarking that his wife had recently passed on, Richard made no mention of other children either. Which . . . gave him no clue whatever to the perplexing problem at hand. Miss Foxburn had simply blurted out the ridiculous pronouncement for some reason that Huntley was not yet privy to.

Exhaling a long breath, he decided it best simply to dismiss the hoax. When the truth finally came out, as he was certain it would, there would be an end to it. The honorable thing for him to do now was to remain silent and wait until the young lady took him into her confidence.

He only hoped the truth emerged before the wedding invitations did.

A wry grin on his face, he leaned his head back on the coach bench . . . but found that the vivid image of sapphire blue eyes looking to him for help just would not go away.

CHAPTER 7

"A PICNIC"

That she desperately wished to go to Paris and that she could not go unless she was certain her father would not marry in her absence, was the sole reason Eliza latched on to to explain her rash behavior in the drawing room that afternoon.

From an upstairs window a few minutes ago, she'd anxiously watched as General Huntley left the house. Moments later, her father had come to her with a smiling countenance and again offered his congratulations on her fine choice.

Fine choice, indeed!

Eliza's dark curls shook dismally as she flung herself across her bed. Whatever was she to do now? Lady Villiers had said she wished to leave for the Continent inside a week. How was she to dissuade Papa from the course he was set upon *and* explain her actions to General Huntley in that short length?

The following morning at breakfast, she was still in a dither over the troublesome matter when her father cheerfully announced, "I think the four of us should spend the entire day together."

"The . . . four of us?" Eliza repeated numbly.

Her father nodded as he helped himself to a second serving of kidney and buttered eggs. "With Ivy soon to become your stepmama, I think it high time the two of you became acquainted with one another." Setting the platter down, he raised twinkling blue eyes to his daughter's rather wan face. "I am quite looking forward to having a war hero as a son-in-law," he added.

Eliza winced. "But . . . what shall we do? I-I mean, for an entire day?"

"What shall we do? Why"—Sir Richard shrugged— "anything that strikes our fancy. What would *you* like to do? Better still, what would Huntley like to do? I expect by now you know him quite well. Two years of corresponding ought to have taught you a great deal about the man. Pray, what are his interests? Outside the military, that is."

He paused, and when no answer was immediately forthcoming, he went on. "I took the liberty of sending notes to both Huntley and Miss Heathergill last evening apprising them of my plan. Ivy consented at once, and Huntley's reply was delivered above half an hour ago. Said he was quite looking forward to the diversion. That he'd be delighted to accompany us wherever we wished to go."

"He . . . did?"

"Of course he did! Why would he refuse? I should think you'd be equally as delighted over the prospect of spending an entire day in your betrothed's company. After conducting a two-year courtship by letter, I should think anything would be preferable to that! Come to think on it, I can't imagine why you haven't been all a-twitter to see more of your young man than you have of late. Why, you've been a virtual recluse this past week."

It was on the tip of Eliza's tongue to blurt out that she was not a recluse, that even now she had plans to travel to Paris. But her father was sure to wonder why, after suddenly announcing her engagement, she would suddenly nip off to Paris. Oh, what a bumblebroth she'd landed in!

"Well?" Sir Richard demanded.

"Well, what?" Eliza returned, her chin tilting up stubbornly!

"Why are you not a-twitter over the opportunity to see your young man openly?"

"The prospect ... pleases me," she lied. Again. Or, perhaps she wasn't lying this time. Oh, bother! She had no time to refine upon that now! "I am quite pleased finally to meet Miss Heathergill," she said with conviction.

Which was *not* a lie. She very much wished to meet the young lady, if for no other reason than to add additional items to her arsenal of reasons why Papa should not marry her!

"So, what are your suggestions for the day's entertainment?" Sir Richard asked again. He reached for his coffee cup and, after draining it, picked up the silver pot at his elbow and refilled his own cup.

"A ... picnic luncheon might be nice. In Green Park, or on the banks of the Serpentine."

"Ah. I see we are of the same mind. I, too, had thought a picnic would be pleasant and to that end, have already instructed Mrs. Allen to prepare a basket. I expect Ivy will wish to bring along some delicacy or other from her father's store."

"Oh, Papa, must we go there?" Eliza protested. *What would General Huntley think of them?*

Sir Richard looked at her levelly. "I had thought also to introduce Huntley to Mr. Heathergill. We are all to be in-laws, after all."

Her face white with mortification, Eliza sprang to her feet. "Oh, Papa, no! I cannot do it."

Her father continued slowly to eat his breakfast. "Cannot do what, Eliza?"

"I . . . Oh!" Frustrated tears welled up in her eyes, but sheer determination kept them at bay.

Sir Richard was eyeing his daughter intently. "You'd best go and change your clothes now, Eliza. Huntley will be along shortly, and we shall all go together to collect Miss Heathergill." He turned back to the delicious food on his plate. "There's a good girl."

Eliza darted from the breakfast room and scampered up the stairs to the safe haven of her bedchamber. The preposterous announcement she'd made the previous afternoon had shocked her as much as it had anyone. That natural consequences—such as having to actually spend time with her "betrothed"—would result from the disclosure had not entered her head.

She had no desire to further her association with the elderly man!

Did she?

Of course, she didn't! She and the general were as unsuited for one another as Papa and Ivy were!

But her father seemed quite taken with the idea of their marrying. Which, as she was casting about yesterday for something to jolt him to awareness, was an eventuality she could never have foreseen. When she'd blurted out the scandalous pronouncement, she'd simply thought to use her secret "tendre" for General Huntley as a bargaining tool—she'd give up Huntley if Papa'd give up Miss Heathergill.

She should have known that Papa's reaction would be anything but what she expected. Papa never did what was expected of him.

General Huntley's reaction, however, did, and did not, surprise her. That he'd said nothing to the contrary yesterday did not come as a surprise. He was a gentleman, and his cool composure in the matter attested to that fact. That he was continuing now to go along with the ruse, without demanding an explanation from her, was another matter altogether.

What that meant, Eliza could not begin to hazard a guess.

The gentleman deserved an explanation, certainly. But, he was Papa's friend, and, despite his views on marrying outside one's class, he might think her ideas on a May-December union quite ill-founded, as apparently her father did.

She did not know which way to turn now, to apprise Huntley of the truth, or to let well enough alone and hope that, before she found herself wed to an elderly gentleman not of her choosing, she'd have the necessary time to show her father, once and forever, how foolish he looked with a nineteen-year-old girl on his arm.

Rap-rap-rap!

"Miss Eliza!"

The sound of Briggs's voice coming from the corridor outside her bedchamber snapped Eliza from her reverie. She turned from her position before the little dressing table in her room and called somewhat irritably over one shoulder.

"What is it, Briggs?"

"Your papa wishes me to inform you that your gentleman caller has arrived, Miss Eliza. His nibs and the general be awaiting ye in the drawing room."

"Thank you, Briggs."

Eliza pulled herself upright and hurriedly began to unfasten the hooks marching down the back of her morning gown. On the way to the clothespress, she tugged at the bell rope, summoning Betsy to come and help her change.

When her abigail arrived, she helped Eliza into a pretty new afternoon costume that had been delivered only the day before. The long slim skirt and scooped neckline of the pale pink dimity gown were decorated with tiny embroidered rosebuds. A lightweight pink serge pelisse, and long-billed bonnet completed the ensemble.

After drawing on her gloves, Eliza reached for her pretty

new bonnet and nestled it atop her dark curls. Patting them into place, she preened before the looking glass.

Would General Huntley like her new gown, she wondered, then drew herself up short. What did it matter what he thought, she demanded of herself sharply.

She snatched up her reticule and headed for the drawing room and the two gentlemen who awaited her there. She fervently hoped before the day was out she'd be struck with another brilliant idea that would finally set things to rights and allow her to make the trip to Paris worry-free.

In the carriage, on their way to the Heathergill home, located in the burgeoning neighborhood of Chelsea, Sir Richard kept up a lively discourse with his friend, General Huntley. The gentlemen's conversation touched briefly on everything from Huntley's final campaign at Waterloo— that Sir Richard had read a fresh account of only that morning in the *Times*—to the current whereabouts of the Duke of Wellington, whom Sir Richard confessed he had not yet got over not meeting.

Eliza squirmed when her father mentioned the great duke. She fervently hoped that her father *never* met the man!

". . . am quite looking forward to introducing you to Heathergill," Sir Richard was saying to the general now. "Fine man. Got a good business head on his shoulders. And charitable, too, I daresay. He and a Mr. John Trotter have hatched a plan to open a new shopping bazaar in Soho Square. Motive behind the scheme is to aid poor widows and the daughters of men lost in the war."

"That so?" Huntley replied, nodding both his approval and interest.

"What sort of shopping bazaar is it to be, Papa?" Eliza forced a question from her lips. Thus far, she'd had very little to say this morning and she did not wish the general to think her ill-tempered or sullen . . . besides, the idea did arouse her curiosity. She liked to shop as much as the next young lady.

Sir Richard glanced at his daughter. "I have been given to understand that the area will be divided into individual stalls," he said, "which are to be let at a pittance a day to craftswomen who have wares of their own making to sell."

"Ah." Huntley again nodded his appreciation. "A splendid idea. Should provide a good deal of help where a good deal is needed."

"A considerable amount of the credit belongs to Ivy," Sir Richard put in, more than a trace of pride in his tone. "Young lady is taking a genuine interest in the project."

"I am quite looking forward to meeting your betrothed."

Foxburn turned a solemn gaze upon his friend. "Truth is . . . it's not yet official between us."

"Beg pardon?" Huntley's head tilted forward.

Eliza's ears perked up as well. Until now, she'd had the impression that her father had already offered for Miss Heathergill. Sitting up a bit straighter on the bench, she fastened an alert gaze upon her father's face.

"I've not yet presented my suit," Sir Richard clarified.

"Ah." Huntley nodded.

"Which is not to say I do not have strong inclinations in that direction," he added hastily, his blue eyes beginning to twinkle again. "Guess I'm a bit more cautious than you, eh, Huntley?"

The dashing officer in the crimson coat and gleaming Hessians cast a quick look at Eliza. She thought she caught the flicker of a smile on his stern lips, but could not say for certain. His eyes, however, locked with hers for a long moment, and there was no mistaking the solid warmth she beheld there. Despite her discomfort over the deception she was fostering, Eliza's features relaxed into a small answering grin. Perhaps Huntley was not too terribly angry with her, after all.

When next she heard the general say, "I find your daughter quite enchanting, Foxburn," her lips parted into a charming smile.

Feeling her cheeks suddenly grow warm, however, she looked away at once. Was the general merely being gallant, or . . . what? She vowed to find a way to speak with the gentleman alone today. Though she'd best weigh what she told him, she reminded herself. He was her father's friend, after all, and she did not yet trust that he would not reveal her deception to Papa.

She was grateful when nothing further was said on that charged subject, for just then, the Foxburn carriage drew up before a large four-story red brick town home. The well-kept garden in front was enclosed by a white wrought-iron railing and a highly decorated gate. Neat flower boxes on the ground floor and upper stories brimmed with red and gold autumn asters and cheerful marigolds. Most windows on the upper floors, Eliza noted, sported individual balconies.

It was a *stunning* home, unlike anything she could have conjured up for a lowly tradesman and his family to live in.

Eliza had assumed the primary reason Miss Heathergill wished to marry her father was to lay claim to his modest fortune and become the mistress of their home in fashionable Mayfair. Truth was, the Heathergill mansion quite put the Foxburns' three-story town house to shame!

Eliza was still staring up at the impressive facade, complete with large statuary lions flanking each side of the spacious marble portico, when she realized that both men had already stepped to the ground and were each extending a hand to assist her down.

Sir Richard's lips were twitching. "It is clearly evident that you are impressed, my dear," he said, as Eliza absently took his hand and allowed him to help her to the ground.

Once there, a quick glance at Huntley's somewhat crestfallen face told her she may have chosen unwisely. She looked away lest he become aware that she'd noted the trace of hurt clouding his eyes.

Surely the gentleman was not harboring romantical notions about her!

A prim-faced butler, properly dressed in black, showed them into a large, carpeted drawing room, that, Eliza also noted, was as tastefully decorated as any belonging to the most *tonnish* of her acquaintances.

The furnishings were of the first stare, many pieces in the new japanned style with decorative touches of gold leaf. In a far corner sat a curious square table upon which rested an assortment of cone-shaped spools of thread and an odd-looking tambour frame of sorts.

"Ivy makes lace," her father told her simply.

"Makes . . . lace?" Eliza murmured.

She had moved to inspect the table and the clamped wooden frame when the sound of approaching footfalls on the highly polished floor of the corridor claimed her attention. She whirled about, every fiber of her being alert with interest to meet the young lady who had so thoroughly captured her father's heart.

Heading across the carpeted expanse of drawing room were two women of nearly identical height. Eliza's gaze passed right over the elder one, whom she assumed to be Mrs. Heathergill and who, she now realized with a start, would be about the same age as her own mother and, were she a widow, infinitely more suited to be courted by her father. The woman's daughter merited a far closer inspection.

The young lady was a good bit taller than Eliza, who at only five feet one inch was rather petite in stature. She had thick honey brown hair, dressed in the latest style, with a fringe of curls across her brow and soft tendrils dangling over each ear. Her skin was rich and creamy, with a lovely pink blush to her cheeks and full lips. Taken all together, Eliza had to admit, Miss Heathergill was quite an attractive young lady.

She had so hoped the girl would look every bit the part of the "golden dolly," a derogatory term used to describe

the ambitious daughters of some tradesmen who made it
their life's work to wed gentlemen of the aristocracy and
consequently elevate themselves to the rank of "Lady."
Ivy Heathergill was as handsome and refined-looking as
any of Eliza's young lady friends.

Sir Richard had already moved to Miss Heathergill's side
and Eliza watched spellbound as her father scooped up
the girl's gloved hand and wrapped her fingers possessively
over his arm.

With a proud look on his face, and an even prouder lilt
to his tone, he heartily proclaimed, "Eliza, Huntley, may
I present the lovely Miss Ivy Heathergill"—he turned to
wink affectionately at the young lady's mother—"and the
equally lovely Mrs. Heathergill."

Both women turned smiles on the handsome man now
walking between them. Ivy's smile, Eliza noted with a sinking heart, only made her pretty face prettier.

"Ladies," Sir Richard said, drawing nearer to Eliza and
Huntley, "this is my daughter Eliza . . . and her betrothed, a
longtime acquaintance of mine, General March Huntley."

Eliza started. She hadn't expected her father to make
their betrothal public knowledge yet. It also struck her
that, until now, she hadn't realized that General Huntley
had a first name, let alone what it was.

"I am so pleased finally to meet you, Miss Foxburn,"
Ivy Heathergill was saying. The melodic sound of her voice
and perfect modulation also surprised Eliza, it telling her
the girl had received a privileged education.

"And I you, Miss Heathergill," Eliza murmured politely.

As Ivy stood smiling down at her, Eliza noted the rich
sea-green color of her eyes. She really was *quite* lovely.

"Your father has told me a great deal about you," Ivy
continued. "I have so looked forward to meeting you,"
she added, then turned a charming smile on Eliza's papa.
"I was thrilled to receive Sir Richard's note last evening
suggesting we all spend the day together."

Eliza forced a small smile to her lips, and, gazing steadily at the young lady, said, with no hint of malice in her tone, "I too, was delighted at the prospect, Miss Heathergill."

Their pleasantries exchanged, the young ladies looked toward the other members of the party, and in turn, spoke polite words of greeting to each of them.

"Eliza is quite taken with your lace-making apparatus, Ivy," Sir Richard said. "Why don't you show her how it's done?"

Miss Heathergill's face lit up. "I'd be delighted to demonstrate the process for you. Come."

With Ivy in the lead, they all strolled in that direction.

"I daresay watching those spools fly through the air—" Sir Richard said, with a laugh, "—is quite hypnotic.' "

"Ivy is very talented," her mother interjected proudly.

"Oh, Mother," Ivy demurred, as she slid onto the pretty little chair, upholstered in a costly-looking embroidered fabric, that was drawn up before the table.

An interested look on his face, General Huntley had already taken up a position to one side of the frame. "When in Brussels, I observed a number of lace-makers at work in the shops lining the Grande Place," he said. "I had meant to purchase samples of their work as gifts for my sisters but never seemed to have the opportunity."

"You have sisters?" Eliza inquired curiously, then bit her tongue. During a two-year correspondence with the general, she should have learned whether or not the man had sisters! She flung a hasty look at her father, hoping he had not caught her *faux pas*.

Fortunately, or perhaps not so fortunately, her father was leaning over Miss Heathergill's shoulder, his rapt gaze fixed on her delicate hands as she removed her gloves and took up the long wooden spools that were tightly wound with delicate strands of fine white thread.

General Huntley turned to address Eliza. "Come and stand near me, Miss Foxburn," he said gently, a hand urging her toward him. "This is quite a good vantage point from which to view the operation."

Breathing a small sigh of relief, Eliza did as the hand-some man asked.

Once Miss Heathergill had grasped the spools and looped the strands of thread through her fingers, suddenly thread seemed to fly in all directions at once. The rapid clacking sound the wooden spools made did, indeed, become hypnotic to the ears, as did the rhythmic motion of Ivy's competent hands.

Entranced, Eliza watched as the whisper-thin threads, shimmering in the sunlight that poured from the long mullioned windows behind Ivy's right shoulder, began magically to form a pattern before her very eyes. First came a rose, and then a bird, encircled by a wreath of leaves, with lacy ripples and crests forming all the while along the outer edges. It was a fascinating procedure!

The small group watching fell silent with almost reverential awe. At length, Miss Heathergill let the threads go lax, and, when the motion of her hands slowed to a stop, she gently laid the spools aside and turned a sweet, smiling countenance upward. "There," she said, as if she'd done nothing more complicated than turn a simple hem in a hanky.

Spontaneous applause erupted from both Eliza's father and General Huntley.

"Splendid!" cried Sir Richard, a bit too enthusiastically for Eliza's liking.

For pity's sake—her lips thinned—he was acting as if Miss Heathergill were the only lace-maker in the world!

Eliza had to admit the girl was quite talented, however, and not wishing to appear unkind, she bent to more closely examine the handiwork. "The pattern is quite lovely," she murmured.

"Thank you," Ivy replied sweetly, the smile still upon her lips as she rose to her feet. She stepped around the table and moved to a pretty japanned sideboard, where she retrieved a small package wrapped in pale pink tissue paper. "I'd consider it a honor if you'd accept this small gift from me, Miss Foxburn."

"Oh." With all eyes trained on her, Eliza felt a good bit ill at ease. All the same, she accepted the package and curiously turned back the tissue paper. Within lay a generous length of the loveliest double-edged lace she had ever seen.

She fingered the delicate fabric gingerly, then turned a fixed little smile upon the eager-eyed Miss Heathergill. "It's exquisite," she murmured.

"Thank you, Miss Foxburn. I had hoped you would like it."

"Indeed, I do. Very much. Thank you."

"Are you not having several new gowns made up for yourself, Eliza?" her papa asked.

"Yes." Eliza nodded.

Sir Richard reached to stroke the fine tatting. "This should serve as an excellent adornment for one of them."

Eliza's features softened. "Yes, Papa, it will. Thank you again, Miss Heathergill."

"Ivy. Everyone calls me Ivy."

Eliza said nothing for a moment. She had no wish to become bosom bows with the girl, though, in all fairness, she knew very well that had she met Miss Heathergill in Lady Villiers's or Lady Hamilton's drawing room, and had *not* known that she was a tradesman's daughter, she'd have warmed at once to the sweet-tempered young lady.

"You may call me Eliza," she finally murmured.

A small fraction of the tension between the two young ladies dissolved. The collective sigh of relief emitted by the elder members of the party attested to their acute awareness of its presence.

"Well, shall we all head for the country?" Sir Richard asked jovially. "I, for one, could do with a bit of sustenance before too very long."

"Could I offer you something now?" Mrs. Heathergill said at once.

"Thank you, no, madam. I am certain Mrs. Allen has prepared quite a hearty luncheon for us."

Mrs. Heathergill stepped to yet another sideboard and returned, carrying a large wicker basket chock-full of a wide variety of rich, ripe fruit, some of which, Eliza noted, were long out of season in England.

"Ivy's father wished to contribute something to the repast." She handed the heavy basket to Sir Richard. "He had business in the city this morning but had this sent 'round for you."

"Ah." Sir Richard inclined his dark head in acknowledgment of the fine offering. "You will thank Mr. Heathergill for us. I had hoped to introduce Huntley to him. Perhaps another time."

"Yes. Another time. I expect the four of you will have a lovely day."

"I had thought we might explore the ruins near Ornsbee," Sir Richard said, "then perhaps, take tea in the village. You mustn't worry if it is a bit late when we return to Town." He winked rakishly at the older woman.

"Oh, I shan't worry a bit, Sir Richard! I never know a moment's concern when Ivy is with you. She is quite fond of you."

Ivy's sea-green eyes widened. "Mo-ther!"

One of Eliza's arched brows quirked. Perhaps the younger woman did not have aspirations, but it was quite clear her mother did. With a disdainful sniff, she thrust her chin up and stepped past the girl to stand near her father.

Who seemed not to notice. "Step lightly, ladies," he said jovially. "The great outdoors beckons."

Once they had all settled in the carriage—Eliza and Huntley facing her father and his companion—it set off down the street at a spanking pace. The gentlemen fell again into conversation.

Eliza could not help noting that Miss Heathergill seemed quite enthralled by whatever her father had to say. She winced when he again casually reached for her gloved hand and draped it affectionately over his arm. It shocked her to see Ivy inch even closer to him on the coach bench. How very forward of the girl!

Seeing her father with this woman, who was little more than a schoolgirl, really, was even more difficult than she'd thought it'd be. Still, in all fairness, she had to allow that she hadn't yet found anything remarkably disagreeable about her.

Miss Heathergill looked quite stylish in a pale lavender sprigged muslin gown with a wide sash tied beneath her bosom. She looked every bit as fashionable as any of Eliza's young lady friends. Even more so, considering the wealth of handmade lace embellishing the neckline of her gown and the inside edge of her bonnet. There was even a delicate edge of it trimming her gloves.

"I could do up a pair for you, if you'd like me to, Eliza."

Though the words were spoken in a soft tone, that they were directed straight at her startled Eliza. It was obvious the girl was trying very hard to befriend her. Still, the cool blue gaze Eliza lifted to Ivy's face was decidedly aloof.

Miss Heathergill's father might have untold wealth, but that did not elevate the family to a position of prominence in society, or make Ivy a suitable candidate to wed her father. Eliza felt compelled to keep her guard up. It was her duty to look after Papa.

"That is very kind of you, Miss Heathergill," she replied coolly. She ignored the imploring look that appeared on the young lady's face at her refusal to use her given name. "But I shouldn't wish to impose."

"It would be no imposition, Eliza," Ivy said hastily. "I would be most happy to do it. I have no sisters and"—a sad little look flitted across her face—"few close female friends in London," she added, looking away.

Glancing back up, Ivy's sea-green eyes were once again warm and her voice strong. "My aunts also make lace, you see, so it is of no consequence when I present them, or my cousins, with lace-edged caps or shawls or gloves." She gave a little laugh, which caused Sir Richard to glance her direction. "It would be a treat if you'd allow me to make something pretty for you."

"You young ladies getting acquainted, are you?" Eliza's papa asked. His tone bespoke his pleasure that all was going well in that quarter.

Ivy turned toward him. "I have offered to do up a pair of lace-edged gloves for Eliza." One hand indicated the delicate trim on her limerick gloves.

"Ah." His full lips curved into a pleased smile. "You are a clever girl, Ivy. Did I not tell you she was clever, Eliza?"

"Hmmm."

"Father thinks I should offer my lace for sale in one of the stalls in Soho," Ivy continued, "once the bazaar has opened."

Fresh alarm stabbed Eliza. *How would she bear it if her father married Ivy and her own stepmama became a tradeswoman?* "Do you really think that a good idea?" she cried. "I mean . . ." Her voice trailed off.

Ivy looked a smile at her. "Father assures me it will be quite proper. Mr. Trotter, who is the chief benefactor of the project, told us the other evening that he means all the stall holders to supply references attesting to their high moral character, and he has drawn up a list of strict rules to govern all the young ladies who serve in them. I shan't need to have a care for my reputation, if that is your concern."

Eliza fell silent, but beside her, General Huntley took it up.

"I think the bazaar a splendid idea, Miss Heathergill. There are a good many widows and daughters who will benefit greatly from the additional means of support. The loss of their menfolk left many of them with nothing. I find your father's concern for these families quite commendable." He paused, then added, "With your permission, I should like to have my secretary write to several widows that I know of who are excellent craftswomen and who I am certain would be eager to participate."

"That would be wonderful, sir. Neither Father nor Mr. Trotter would have the least objection."

"Heathergill indicated to me that it would be some months before the building is ready," Sir Richard remarked. "I expect there are still stalls aplenty to let."

"Indeed, there are," Ivy said eagerly.

"I have lent my support to the project," Sir Richard told Huntley, "financially speaking. Heathergill and the other investors anticipate Soho Square to become quite a popular shopping place with the *ton*. There are already a number of fine craftsmen located in the district. Chippendale's is in St. Martin's Lane, and there are several French jewelers and Swiss watchmakers in Church Street."

"Don't forget the perfumery," Ivy said, with a merry laugh.

Sir Richard chuckled and gave her hand, still draped over his arm, a warm squeeze. "Ivy is quite taken with the stuffed bear in Atkinson's doorway." He glanced toward Eliza. "I recall you were fascinated with the beast when you were a child, Eliza."

She nodded tightly. "Yes, I was." As a little girl, she had quite enjoyed going to the famous perfumers with her mother. The bear was meant as an advertisement for the shop's principal product, bear grease for gentleman's hair. Papa used it.

The talk turned to other things, and, at length, the carriage entered the pretty park just beyond the little village of Ornsbee.

With Ivy and Eliza looking on, both gentlemen, assisted by the two Foxburn footmen, who had ridden the entire distance clinging to the rear of the carriage, spread a patterned rug on the ground at the base of a huge sycamore tree. On a small table, they spread the luncheon out.

It was a lovely autumn day, with a light breeze wafting

through the trees and a cobalt blue sky lazily dotted with puffy white clouds. The tree's leafy branches provided a shady canopy from the bright sun overhead.

The silent footmen filled four crystal goblets with sparkling red wine and brought it and the plates, laden with slices of cold chicken, wedges of cheese, and a crisp garden salad to the foursome, who had arranged themselves expectantly on the rug.

Quietly munching on her food, Eliza noted that Ivy seemed to fuss over her father, much as her mother had done, seeing that he had plenty of whatever he wanted and noticing when his wineglass grew empty.

Eliza had so wished to find a great many things to dislike about Miss Heathergill, but the truth was, she had uncovered nothing, beyond the obvious—that she was far too young to wed him and that her father was a common merchant.

She gazed unabashedly at the girl. Papa had failed to mention how very talented she was . . . or even how pretty. She looked quite appealing now with the sunlight dappling her rosy cheeks and scattering droplets of pure gold onto her shiny brown hair. Eliza could plainly see why her father was drawn to her. Ivy Heathergill was warm, sweet-tempered, and, although Eliza was loath to admit it, *very* likable.

Eliza wished she might pull down the thick barriers she'd erected between them . . . but something just would not let her do so. Not yet anyway.

When the meal had concluded and the two footmen had carted away the soiled plates and utensils, the pair of gentlemen, their stomachs full, appeared content simply to lounge about upon the rug.

General Huntley lay stretched out on his side while, across from him, Eliza's father leaned comfortably against the tree's massive trunk. The young ladies, their legs drawn up beneath their long skirts rather resembled fresh summer flowers, one pink, one lavender, nestled between the men.

Suddenly, it occurred to Eliza that this was the perfect opportunity to demonstrate the vast difference between the ages of the men and the women. *She* felt quite energized after consuming the hearty luncheon and reckoned the same was true for Ivy. But the men ... she gazed calculatedly at them ... well, suffice to say that youth hardly required a nap after a meal.

Her dark head cocked to one side, she sprang to her feet. "I should like to explore the ruins now, Papa." She turned and gazed with interest at the stone configuration some hundred yards beyond them. "Shall we go and see what lies beyond that crumbling wall?"

A charming smile on her lips, she stretched a hand toward her father. "Come along," she said brightly, "we mustn't waste our glorious afternoon napping!"

Sir Richard lifted a lazy gaze upward and seemed about to protest when, across from him, Huntley hauled himself to his feet.

"Up you go, Richard," he said. "The ladies can hardly go exploring without us. I, too, am curious to examine the old abbey." He glanced at Eliza. "Suppose there is any truth to the legend surrounding it?"

"I haven't a clue, but it will be great fun finding out. Do get up, Papa!"

Between them, Ivy had not yet risen to her feet. "If you'd like to rest a bit longer, Richard," she said soothingly, "I shall be happy to keep you company."

Eliza's eyes cut 'round sharply. Was Ivy contriving to be alone with her father, or was she genuinely concerned for his well-being?

"You youngsters run along," Sir Richard said, a teasing grin lifting the corners of his mouth. "Ivy and I prefer to stay right here in the shade."

"We'll be along in a bit," Ivy said firmly.

Eliza cast a sidelong glance at General Huntley. Sud-

denly, she realized that being alone with the handsome
older man felt . . . quite discomforting.

   Huntley noted the alarmed look on Miss Foxburn's face
and smiled inwardly.
   He was enjoying this outing immensely.

CHAPTER 8

"CORNFLOWER BLUE EYES"

It had not taken Huntley long today to ascertain the truth: Miss Foxburn had strong objections to her father's marrying Miss Heathergill. He wasn't certain which she found most objectionable about the young lady, her age—or lack thereof—or the fact that Mr. Heathergill was in trade. How *he* figured in the picture was still a mystery.

As to the other, he assumed Miss Foxburn's mother had schooled her daughter well in the proprieties. Perhaps Eliza feared that her father's association with the trades-man and his family would adversely affect his standing in society, or quite possibly even her own chances for making a good match.

Aware of the *ton*'s proclivity for superficiality, Huntley reasoned the latter could very well prove to be true. On the other hand, in the wake of the French Revolution, class distinctions even in England were growing dimmer every day. With the world changing so rapidly, he person-ally doubted that Sir Richard's marriage to the wealthy tradesman's daughter would have that much effect on his own child's future.

Unfortunately, the same had not been true when Huntley's mother was a girl. She, like the privileged Lady Constance, had turned a deaf ear to wise counsel and married well beneath herself.

Huntley's father had been a hardworking country squire who'd fallen in love with the fragile Lady Rosalie the minute he'd laid eyes on her at a country ball in the county where Huntleys had resided for generations.

After the pair wed, Lyle Huntley used his new bride's dowry to substantially increase his holdings. Soon, the lovely Lady Rosalie grew less and less enchanted with the harsh reality of the life she'd chosen. Kept constantly with child, the delicate beauty soon discovered that taking care of her demanding husband and their growing family was a daily sunup to sundown grind.

March had been firstborn, and as soon as he was six, had been put to work alongside his father and the estate's dozen or so tenant farmers, whose own wives and sturdy sons annually planted and harvested the rich corn.

As the years went by, everyone on the estate flourished except March's mother. Ten years and six children into her misbegotten marriage, the young woman, exhausted and spent, was carried aloft while giving birth to a seventh babe.

March determined then, after years of quietly listening to the bitter battles between his parents and watching his beautiful mother wither away and finally die, never to stray too far from his own class.

Although he had good reason to feel as he did, he did not believe Miss Foxburn's concern for her father was as well grounded. Foxburn was a grown man, whose first marriage had been all that was proper. If he loved Miss Heathergill now and wished to marry her, Huntley could see no reason why he shouldn't.

But he could understand how the innocent Miss Foxburn might think otherwise. She was still young and idealistic. Her views of the world were limited to what her parents, and most particularly, her mother had taught her.

By seeking him out, perhaps she merely hoped to elicit his aid in turning Richard from his pursuit of Miss Heathergill. He recalled her reminding him only the previous afternoon in the drawing room that he had said Lieutenant Langston's aspirations to wed Lady Constance were vulgar. Was that why she had turned to him for help? She might simply have asked, he thought. To affiance herself to him seemed doing it up a bit.

Still, despite her rash action, he admitted, he was quite enjoying the small diversion.

It'd been years, nay decades, since he'd experienced a lazy afternoon such as this one—fraught with none of the tension of the battlefield, no anxiety straining to hear the first bullet fired, or charging into battle the second the shot rang out, wondering all the while if, by day's end, a stray slug or razor-sharp sword would pierce his heart or brain. Today's peaceful pursuit was indeed a welcome relief.

And—he glanced now at the delicate dark-haired beauty walking silently alongside him in the tall grass—observing this simple tug-of-war between the wills of father and daughter was like child's play to him.

Miss Foxburn looked quite charming today in her pretty pink sprigged muslin gown, a wide pink sash tied beneath her small breasts. She had on a rather odd-looking—odd-looking to Huntley, that is—long-billed bonnet with a frilly edge and a crisp pink bow tied over one ear. An indulgent grin played at his lips. She looked as young and fresh to him as a newborn babe.

Most of the women he'd come in contact with in the glittering ballrooms in Paris, Vienna, or Brussels were seasoned veterans at multiplicity, their painted faces hiding ulterior motives that ranged all the way from secret espionage aimed at furthering their husband's military careers to the simple desire for a clandestine assignation with a high-ranking officer.

"I have plans to go to Paris, you know," Miss Foxburn announced suddenly. Still tramping through the tall grass, she had spoken without looking directly up at him.

"Oh?" Huntley responded. This was an unexpected disclosure, but then, everything he'd encountered thus far about Miss Eliza Foxburn fit that category like a glove. She was very like her father in that regard. One could never be certain of anything where Richard Foxburn was concerned.

He decided that rather than try and draw her out, he'd simply wait and let her reveal whatever she chose to him of the perfidy she was forwarding.

"Lady Villiers has asked me to accompany her and Jane there. We are to leave inside the week."

"You've apprised your father of the plan, have you?"

After a pause, he thought he saw her shake her head. All he could see of the action was the gentle sideways motion of the long bill of the bonnet that jutted forward from her face.

He knew a sudden urge to fling the silly hat away so he might feast his eyes on the shiny black silk of her hair. As it was, only a few dark tendrils had managed to escape the confines of the close-fitting bonnet and now floated free whenever a light breeze wafted past.

"Papa doesn't know yet," she said simply. She surprised Huntley then by turning to look up at him.

His eyes locked with her sapphire blue orbs, the rich color putting him in mind of the startling blue summer cornflowers he'd picked for his mother as a boy in the eager hope of coaxing a smile to her pale pink lips.

"Is it your wish that I tell him?" Huntley asked at length.

She was still gazing up at him, and again the look of innocent appeal in her eyes tugged at his heart. "Would you, sir?"

Huntley gulped down an unseemly urge to draw this innocent beauty into his arms and . . . and kiss her! Despite the inappropriate thought, however, he managed, in quite a calm tone, to say, "I doubt Richard would have any objections to the trip, taken as it were in the safe company of Lady Villiers and her daughter."

She ducked her head, but not before he caught the crestfallen look that clouded her pretty features. He had disappointed her! The pang he felt was akin to watching his own sweet mother sigh once more with resignation when his father's pinchpenny ways denied her yet another small pleasure.

"I thought it would be best if the news came from you," Miss Foxburn murmured.

"Ah. As your betrothed," he replied, having for the moment forgotten the vital role he was playing in this real-life drama.

She nodded, then directed another imploring gaze upward. "I am *dying* to go to Paris, sir. I have never been anywhere. I have never done anything even remotely outrageous, and I fear that if I do not take advantage of this opportunity, I shall never be accorded another."

"Do you not think becoming affianced to me something of an outrage?" Huntley asked, before he'd considered the forthrightness of his words.

When she ducked her head again, he heard, rather than saw, the sheepish grin that that remark elicited. "I do owe you an explanation, sir," she said softly.

They had now reached the foremost crumbling wall of the deserted old abbey, and he took her arm to assist her up and over the ragged stone steps that remained. They entered what looked to have once been the ancient vestibule, although all that now stood of it were jagged remnants of two of the outside stone walls. A narrow stone staircase led the way to the bell tower, from which, legend had it, the bells still tolled on the anniversary of the blinding of a young shepherd whose jealous ladylove had gouged his eyes out with his own staff when she caught him looking with admiration upon another pretty maid.

It was said the young man's spirit haunted the abbey, that he spent his days polishing the bells, and that, on occasion, when he caught sight of an especially handsome maiden, he, himself delightedly rang the bells.

What had once been intricate stained-glass windows in the abbey walls were now nothing more than twisted iron fingers reaching toward the heavens, the colored chips of glass having long since been carted away by thieves or vandals. The clear blue sky overhead comprised the ceiling of the ruin.

Huntley guided his charge to a stone ledge beneath one of the gaping holes in the weathered stone wall.

"We've plenty of time before your father and Miss Heathergill arrive. Perhaps you'd like to apprise me of your plan," he suggested, once she'd settled herself comfortably on the ledge and he'd taken a seat beside her.

During the few moments that elapsed before Miss Foxburn began to speak, Huntley became keenly aware of her feminine presence, the soft flutter of her gown against his buckskin-clad leg, the gentle rise and fall of her breasts as she drew breath.

At length, she began to speak, her soft voice reminding him again of the gentle tone of his own dear mother's voice. "I had hoped that by seeing us together, that ... Papa might realize how ... foolish he looks with Miss Heathergill."

When she turned to gaze up at him again, Huntley detected within those alluring blue depths the faint hint of an apology.

"Not that I think you are ..." Her long dark lashes fluttered against the smooth silk of her cheeks.

The stern set of Huntley's lips softened. "I am beginning to understand your ploy, Miss Foxburn. You feel that both your father and I have too many years in our dish to render us suitable for you young ladies." He paused. "Still, I fail to see the connection between your desire to come

between your father and Miss Heathergill and that of traveling to Paris."

"Because, sir," she said heatedly, "I cannot go to Paris
unless I can be certain Papa will not marry Miss Heathergill
in my absence!"

"Ah. And you had hoped I might dissuade him, and
thus save you the disagreeable task?"

She nodded, her trusting blue eyes again quite round.
"Surely you cannot think theirs a wise match, sir. They are
as unsuited as . . . as you and I are. Even more so, considering Mr. Heathergill's occupation," she added, a slight tinge
of derision creeping into her tone.

"You do not believe your father capable of making his
own decision in the matter?"

"You do not know Papa as I do, sir. Papa is forever
landing in the basket!"

Huntley could not stifle a grin. Foxburn was, indeed, a
wild card, though it had never occurred to him that he
needed a keeper. He cast a sidelong look at Eliza. That his
pretty little daughter might require looking after, however,
was another matter altogether. "A week is a very short time
in which to accomplish all that you wish, Miss Foxburn,"
he replied gently.

She turned to gaze up at him once more. "Not if you
help me, sir. Papa will listen to you. You are very knowledge-
able and . . . quite brilliant."

Huntley felt another smile tug at his lips. How could he
not be swayed in the face of such fierce admiration and
trust? After a length, he said, "I can offer no assurances,
Miss Foxburn, but I will do what I can."

"Oh, thank you, sir!" she cried. She gleefully clapped
her small hands together. "You have convinced far more
formidable foes than Papa! I am certain you will succeed
in this!"

Huntley experienced a fleeting moment of exhilaration.
It was the same feeling he'd sought those many years ago

when he'd tried in vain to please his despondent young mother.

They settled into companionable silence for a spell, Huntley again enjoying the peaceful tranquillity of the setting. He lifted his chin to catch a whiff of the sweet fragrant air, or . . . he turned his head slightly, was the pleasant aroma of wild roses perhaps the sweet-water worn by Miss Foxburn? He couldn't be certain.

When a playful breeze danced through the open-air abbey, it lifted the gossamer hem of her sprigged muslin gown. Glancing downward, he enjoyed the sight of her trim ankles visible above the pale pink ribbons that held her dainty slippers in place.

How very far removed he was from the war-ravaged cities in Europe where he'd spent the past dozen or more years of his life.

Presently Miss Foxburn said, "Tell me about your sisters, General Huntley."

Huntley settled back comfortably. "My given name is March. Perhaps when we are in your father's presence, our sham might be furthered if you'd address me less formally. With your permission, I shall call you Eliza."

She smiled up at him. He noted for the first time the charming pair of dimples deeply etched into her silken smooth cheeks. The sight enchanted him.

"I think that quite a good idea . . . March." Her sweet treble had an almost saucy lilt to it. When suddenly she giggled, and her blue eyes began to twinkle, Huntley thought again how very much the little minx resembled her father. "I have never known a man named March before," she added, her dark head at a flirtatious tilt.

Suddenly, Huntley wished to simply stare at her, so captivated did he feel by her charming fresh-faced beauty. Instead, he said, "My siblings and I were named after the months in which we were born. My father had wanted a dozen children, one for every month of the year. I am the eldest. I have a brother January, whom we call Jan, and another brother August."

"How very fortunate you were not born in May, or June!" she exclaimed, a look of astonishment on her pretty face.

Huntley grinned. "I admit that has often occurred to me. As it was, I barely escaped having to go through life being called April. My birth date is the thirty-first of March."

Another laugh spilled from her lips. The merry sound quite delighted Huntley. He told himself he'd best keep his guard up, lest this delightful young lady worm her way into the dusty chambers of his thirty-eight-year-old heart.

"When I entered the army, I requested of my superior officer to be allowed to use my middle name, Ashford; but as there were already two soldiers by that name, my request was denied. I have been March ever since."

"And your sisters? Let me guess . . . *they* are May and June."

"And April. She and May are twins."

Eliza's blue eyes widened. "How could that be?"

"Last day of the month again." Huntley chuckled. Grinning, he realized that despite the vast difference in their ages, he actually felt quite relaxed conversing with Miss Eliza Foxburn. "April arrived at two minutes before twelve, May a few minutes after."

"Which day do they celebrate as their birthday?"

"They each insisted on their own day. April thirtieth and May first."

"Were there no more children after that? No December or February?"

"September." His voice grew solemn. "The babe died. As did my mother."

"Oh." Eliza's gloved hand reached to cover his much larger one. "I am so very sorry, sir. Losing one's mother is quite distressful. Were you . . . just a boy?"

"I was ten."

"Is your father . . . ?"

His dark head shook. "He passed on soon after I entered the army. My brothers now look after the farm."

After a pause, Eliza said, "I wonder that you never married."

Huntley exhaled a long breath. "I have been far too busy winning the war, my dear. Just as you feel you must look after your father, I feel it my duty to look after England."

Eliza's pert nose tilted up, and again in an almost-saucy tone, she exclaimed, "Well, you have done a splendid job of that, sir! On behalf of the entire kingdom, may I express my countrymen's sincerest gratitude!"

There was something in the child's twinkling blue gaze that again made Huntley nearly forget that the slip of a girl beside him was young enough to be his own daughter and . . . but, at precisely that moment, the muffled sound of voices and footfalls on the bare stone floor of the deserted abbey interrupted them.

CHAPTER 9

"FOR WHOM THE BELLS TOLL"

Eliza could not bite back the wide smile that lit her face as she turned to watch her father and Ivy approach from across the vestibule. Not even the fact that as she walked both of Ivy's arms were curled possessively over Sir Richard's was enough to dampen Eliza's spirits.

General Huntley had agreed to help her! And the fact that Papa had not yet offered for Miss Heathergill meant that with Huntley's help, this could very well be Papa and Ivy's last day together.

Springing happily to her feet, Eliza exclaimed, "Are you feeling better, Papa? Shall we climb to the top of the tower now?"

Sir Richard took in the bright smile on his daughter's face. "You and Huntley have a nice coze, did you, sweetheart?"

General Huntley had risen also to his feet. "It has been quite pleasant, Foxburn." A grin twitched at his lips. "Though we've not yet heard the bells peal."

"Perhaps the shepherd was also napping," Ivy suggested

humorously. She directed a warm gaze up at her companion.

R-i-n-g . . . r-i-n-g . . . r-i-n-g.

The sudden, ear-shattering sound of the bells chiming in the tower sent a spine-tingling shudder through the four gathered in the vestibule.

Uttering a small cry of alarm, Eliza shrank back against General Huntley. When his strong arms encircled her small body, a fresh wave of apprehension rippled through her. Why was it that every time she was *this* close to the man, she suddenly felt that she could not draw breath? However, there was no time to refine upon the phenomenon now, for the instant the bells had tolled, her father had broken into a run and was already halfway across the vestibule on his way to the stairs.

"Papa, no!" Eliza cried. Wrenching from Huntley's embrace, she darted after her father.

"There'll be no stopping him if he's determined to climb to the top," Ivy said matter-of-factly. Still, she lifted her shirts and also hastened in that direction.

"We must stop him!" Eliza exclaimed. She flung a helpless look at Huntley who, also on the run, scooped up Eliza's hand and the pair of them, as well, set out after Sir Richard.

As they drew near the stairwell, Ivy said, "I confess I am also quite anxious to discover who is ringing the bells."

"Well, I am not anxious to see Papa hurt, or trampled, or thrown to his death from the tower!" Eliza snapped.

"I expect it was only a harmless prank," Huntley interjected calmly. "The bells were probably rung by a village lad who saw us picnicking on the grounds and laid in wait 'til we'd all got here before ringing them."

Well ahead of them, Sir Richard was bounding up the stone stairs two at a time.

"Papa come back!"

"This is the only way to the Tower," Foxburn's voice

echoed back down the curved column. "The mischief-maker cannot escape us!"

Eliza turned a worried look on General Huntley. "What are we to do, sir?"

"Assist!" Huntley brushed past both Eliza and Miss Heathergill. Long legs carried him up the steep stairwell at lightning speed.

"Oh!" Eliza stamped her foot in frustration.

"I expect the men will be all right," the older girl said reassuringly."

"You cannot be certain of that!" Eliza cried. "Papa will not stop 'til he's caught the culprit and wrestled him to the ground. He takes no thought for his own safety! He is quite foolhardy!" Her agitated gaze flew from Miss Heathergill's calm countenance toward the shadowy stairwell where both men had disappeared.

"It is true Richard can often be capricious," Ivy replied quietly, "but despite his faults, I think him quite wonderful."

Eliza flung a contemptuous look at the taller girl. It was on the tip of her tongue to blurt out that her father would *never* marry her, so she might as well give up her quest to snare him but . . . something in the near-reverent way Ivy was gazing up at the tower stopped her.

Just then, the distant rumble of Sir Richard's voice arrested their attention. "Eliza! Ivy! Nip on up! Steps are perfectly safe!"

At once, Ivy began to ascend the narrow stairwell, an anxious Eliza close on her heels.

They'd gone but a few feet when Huntley's head popped round a corner. "View is excellent from the top, ladies."

He turned and led them the rest of the way up. Reaching the topmost riser, they stepped onto a small, open-air landing, enclosed by a waist-high ledge fashioned of roughhewn stones all around. Standing in the center of the clearing, both girls gazed curiously about, neither of them wishing to venture too close to the edge.

Above their heads, an ominous-looking double row of large bells hung from the centuries-old rafters. The bells did, indeed, look as if they'd recently been polished, for gleaming droplets of sunlight glanced brightly off them here and there. Long ropes attached to each of them dangled limply to the floor.

"Not a soul in sight," Sir Richard announced.

"And no other way up or down that I can see," Huntley mused. "Except . . ." He cast a glance over the side of the ledge nearest him . . . only to give a wordless shake of his head.

Foxburn's gaze followed Huntley's. He moved to the ledge and leaned quite far over. "Do you suppose . . . ?"

"Papa, do be careful!"

Ivy bravely edged closer to his side. "Perhaps we should go back down now, Richard."

"Is that a window?" Sir Richard asked. He leaned even farther over the edge in order to see better still. "I don't recall passing a window on the way up . . . do you, Huntley?"

Huntley's brow furrowed thoughtfully as he, too, leaned quite far over the ledge.

Eliza experienced a wave of alarm for the tall military man's safety, as well, but did not voice it. However, when her father stretched one arm and his lean torso even farther over the side, she cried, "Papa!"

"Fellow could almost reach the top corner of that window from here . . ." He inched even farther still.

"Papa!"

"Richard, do come back. You are frightening me."

Eliza cast a worried look at Ivy. The girl did appear quite anxious.

"Richard, please!"

"Toss me a rope, Huntley; I think I can reach . . ."

"Richard, *do* come back! *Please.* It isn't a bit important that we learn who rang the bells," Ivy added.

A second later, the dark-haired man pulled himself upright. Wearing an almost-contrite grin on his handsome face, he stood brushing the dust from the front of his waistcoat and jacket. " 'Spect you are right. Was a bit foolish of me to go chasing after a ghost, wasn't it?''

Eliza's bonneted head jerked 'round. If she hadn't heard it with her own ears, she'd not have believed it! Ivy had actually persuaded her father to take caution and he'd listened, *and* altered his course. It was most astonishing!

Huntley had also stepped away from the ledge. With an amused shrug, he said, "Whether it was a ghost or a village lad who rang the bells, the message was the same." He turned an indulgent grin on Eliza. "The bells were tolled because the boy had spotted a pretty maid."

Sir Richard's warm smile was fastened on Miss Heathergill. "Two pretty maids," he said.

That Ivy Heathergill had successfully persuaded her father to give up his dangerous quest did elevate Ivy somewhat in Eliza's estimation, but it was not enough to persuade her to give up her quest permanently to separate the pair.

Because the rest of the afternoon was spent in the company of the others, however, she had little time in which to think up a new plan or, if she had, to put it into action.

Over a late tea taken at a quaint little tearoom in the nearby village of Ornsbee, the two couples talked and laughed easily with one another over the ringing of the bells, each of them expressing his or her own theory over who might have been responsible for the phenomenon and how the feat was accomplished.

Though they were a tad less lively during the long drive back to London, they each, for separate reasons, proclaimed the day a resounding success.

* * *

Late the following morning, Eliza, still feeling uplifted over her promising talk with General Huntley the preceding afternoon, had just delivered her daily instructions to the housekeeper and Cook, and sent Briggs in search of Sailor—as he had not been seen since the mouse incident two days ago—when a footman appeared in the doorway of the small sitting room abovestairs, a calling card on a silver tray.

"A General Huntley to see you, Miss Eliza," the footman said, his eyes properly lowered.

"Oh!" Eliza's face lit up once more. "Show the gentleman into the drawing room, if you please. I shall join him straightaway."

She hurried to her bedchamber to remove her apron and run a brush through her dark curls. When she entered the drawing room a few seconds later, she was startled to find the handsome military man standing in the center of it, his face all but obscured by the largest, most glorious bouquet of fresh-cut flowers Eliza had ever seen.

"How lovely, sir! But ... what a pity"—her brow furrowed—"Papa is not at home!"

One gloved hand parted a path between a bunch of pink-tipped daisies and a soft mound of white and yellow mums. "The flowers are not for your father, Eliza. They are for you."

Her eyes still fastened on the huge bouquet, Eliza moved toward the uniformed man. "How vastly clever you are! The gesture will surely impress Papa. I shall make certain he knows that you delivered them in person, too." Still eyeing the colorful flowers, she breathed, "They are *very* beautiful, sir. My-y, I can't think when I have seen so many. I shall just ..."

She turned and hurried toward the French doors that led to the garden.

His hand still parting the posies, Huntley curiously

watched as Eliza flung open the double doors and stuck her head out.

"Br-i-g-g-s! Are you there?"

Me-o-w-w, me-o-w-w.

"Why, hello, Sailor-boy! I just sent Briggs to look for you. Now, where has he got to?"

Apparently hearing the cat's meow put Huntley in mind of the previous disaster involving the cat. He took a defensive step backward, but being unfamiliar with the placement of the furniture in the room, his backside collided with the edge of a small gaming table. Thrown instantly off-balance, he tried to compensate for the misstep, but that action caused one long leg somehow to become tangled up with those of a straight-backed chair he'd also not known was there.

"Oops!"

Eliza's head whirled about just as Huntley's long legs slipped completely from beneath him and the profusion of daisies, mums, cornflowers, hothouse carnations, and bright red roses plus assorted sprays of greenery were tossed helter-skelter into the air.

Perhaps thinking the flowers were butterflies, or birds that required chasing, Sailor had already flown past Eliza's skirts and was even now smack in the middle of the fray. As the rainbow-hued blossoms fell toward the floor, Sailor sprang upward to meet them, clapping his front paws together again and again in an attempt to catch a falling flower.

"Oh, dear!" Eliza cried. She ran toward General Huntley, who was already picking himself up off the floor. "Oh, dear," she said again, "I do hope Sailor wasn't the cause of . . ."

Hauling himself upright, Huntley jerked one glove off and set to slapping it against his thighs, his other hand picking at the daisies clinging to his chest and the primroses dangling from the damp sleeve of his crimson coat.

"Wasn't the cat's fault," he muttered irritably. "My own

damn—pardon me—clumsiness is to blame. Backed straight into the table on my own. No help from the cat."

At their feet, Sailor was sprinting from flower to flower, nose-diving beneath colorful piles of them, then peeking up at Eliza and Huntley from beneath his leafy cover.

Eliza began to laugh at both Sailor's antics and at the sight of the disgruntled general wearing fresh-cut flowers like medals upon his chest.

"I am so sorry, sir"—she tried in vain to choke back her mirth—"but you do look . . . quite funny!" Unable to push down the giggles bubbling up within her, she dissolved into peals of merry laughter.

Huntley's mouth hardened to a firm line as Eliza, consumed with giggles, sank to the floor, presumably to tidy up the mess. Instead, she scooped up a couple of blossoms and began to dangle them above Sailor's head. The cat rolled onto his back and commenced to swat wildly at the elusive petals with his front paws.

Watching the cat's spirited efforts, the hard set of Huntley's mouth softened, and he knelt beside Eliza. In seconds, he, too, was laughing aloud, his deep rumble mingling pleasantly with her high-pitched treble.

"Sailor likes you," she announced presently. She turned a twinkling blue gaze on Huntley. He was now teasing the cat with a near-shredded cornflower.

"I expect that means he'll be coming to live with us once we are married," he replied, in a near-absent tone.

"*Married!*" came a shrill female voice behind them. "What's this?"

Both Eliza and Huntley glanced up to find Lady Villiers bearing down upon them.

"Why, you little slyboots, Eliza! You never said a word to me about . . . come to that, neither did you, Huntley!" the older woman scolded. She cast a curious gaze at the sea of flowers, then one brow shot up. "No wonder I couldn't find Briggs. I see your bumbling butler was too busy upending flowers in the drawing room."

She turned and headed for a sofa, as a grinning Huntley assisted Eliza to her feet.

"I insist the pair of you tell me everything," Lady Villiers called gaily to them as she settled the cushions behind her. "And I want details! All of them, with nothing left out!" She turned an expectant gaze upward.

Eliza's heart sank. The last thing she wanted was for word to leak out among the *ton* that she and General Huntley were betrothed. Despite the strange comment he'd just made about Sailor living with them after they were married, they were *not* to be wed. They did not suit for precisely the same reason that Papa and Ivy didn't. Huntley was far too old for her.

Still, as Eliza slipped into a chair opposite Lady Villiers, she realized she had no choice now but to reveal the whole truth to her guest, which included the part about her father and Miss Heathergill. Otherwise, the sham she and Huntley were forwarding made no sense whatever.

"General Huntley and I are not to be married, Lady Villiers," she said straight out. She cast a quick glance up at Huntley, who had stepped to the mantelpiece and now stood leaning against it, one booted foot crossed over the other at the ankle. Eliza noted a somewhat troubled look marring his handsome features, but did not chance to wonder on the meaning of it. "We have merely been . . . pretending to be betrothed. For Papa's sake," she added.

Lady Villiers's brows pulled together in a frown. She flung a bewildered gaze up at Huntley, then back at Eliza. "For Richard's sake? What on earth can you mean?"

Eliza inhaled a long breath before plunging in. "Papa has been courting a young lady whom I believe to be quite . . . unsuitable for him, Lady Villiers. In the hope of exhibiting how . . . *very* unsuitable the young lady is, I thought to . . . contrive an *unsuitable* tendre of my own."

She turned another gaze on Huntley, this one carrying with it the hint of an apology. But because the troubled look on his face was beginning to trouble her, she looked quickly away. "You see, the young lady is . . . quite young and I thought that by linking up with General Huntley it would show Papa how foolish *he* looks going about with a girl who is little better than a twelvemonth older than I. General Huntley has quite graciously agreed not to betray my deception, and I . . . *we,* Huntley and I, beg your silence on the matter, as well, Lady Villiers. It would not do for Papa to learn the truth just yet."

"I see." Lady Villiers drew in a long breath. "Well . . . where does this leave us, my dear? I have been counting on you to accompany Jane and me to Paris."

"Oh, I have every intention of making the trip," Eliza hurriedly added. "Although I've yet to tell Papa about it. But, I shouldn't worry that he'll object. March has agreed that I should go and . . ." At her use of the general's given name, Eliza noted the look of surprise that flitted across Lady Villiers's face, but neither woman remarked upon it.

In his rich baritone, however, General Huntley put in, "Eliza and I have agreed that my permission in the matter is all that is needed."

Obviously still stunned by the couple's disclosure, Lady Villiers again murmured, "I see."

Huntley turned a thoughtful look on Eliza. "It just occurred to me, my dear, that it might serve if you invited Miss Heathergill along on the trip to Paris. Would remove her from your father's company, at least, for the time being."

Eliza's blue eyes brightened. "How clever you are, sir! I do declare," she addressed Lady Villiers in a gay tone, "General Huntley is the cleverest man I have ever met!"

One of Lady Villiers eyebrows lifted suspiciously.

Still addressing Eliza, Huntley added, "Such a trip would pose no financial burden to Heathergill."

"That is quite true," Eliza agreed.

"Heathergill." Lady Villiers tapped her chin with a gloved forefinger. "I don't recall ever hearing that name before."

"Oh, I do not doubt that, Lady Villiers. Miss Heathergill's father, Mr. Heathergill, is a"—her voice lowered to just above a whisper—"a ... common merchant. A grocer."

"Oh, my dear!" Lady Villiers drew back in shock. "I do, indeed, see your problem. Well," she added with aristocratic disdain, "I really do not wish someone of such low consequence to accompany our party to Paris." She sniffed. "One cannot be too careful, you know. I shouldn't wish *anything* to prevent my Jane from making a brilliant match. We must fix on another solution."

She paused to cogitate, then turned a questioning look on the general. Eliza also gazed up at Wellington's Master Strategist.

"Have *you* spoken to him, Huntley?" Lady Villiers asked. "I should think you, of all people, would be able to make Richard see reason."

"Make Richard see reason about what?" came a deep male voice from across the room. "I say, am I being talked about and not here to defend myself?"

Laughing good-naturedly, Sir Richard came striding toward them. He came to rest next to the chair where Eliza sat. "Afternoon, Lady Villiers." He nodded at Huntley.

"Good to see you again, old man." He bent from the waist to brush Eliza's now flaming cheek with his lips. "Hallo, Sweetheart."

Eliza gulped nervously, then bravely said, "Lady Villiers has invited me to accompany her and Jane to Paris, Papa. We were just discussing how it would look for me to suddenly trot off to the Continent so soon after becoming"—she gulped again—"betrothed."

"I readily gave my consent," Huntley supplied in quite a strong tone, considering. "All that remained was for you to do the same. We had decided it was ... uh ... up to me to ... um ... make you see reason."

"Ah." With an easy shrug, Sir Richard moved to a side chair and sank into it. "I've no objections, if you can

think of none, Huntley." He directed a wide smile at Lady
Villiers. "I confess these two quite took me by surprise.
Though I expect you and Jane were aware of Eliza's secret
tendre all along, were you not?"

A nervous squeak escaped Lady Villiers.

Sir Richard glanced toward the tall man leaning against
the mantelpiece. "Confess I couldn't be happier. Huntley
and I were schoolmates at Eton, you know."

"Umm . . . no, Richard," Lady Villers began, "I was
unaware that you and the general were the least acquainted
with one another. And . . . until moments ago, I knew very
little of . . . Eliza's tendre with the general."

That Lady Villiers seemed excessively uncomfortable did
not escape Eliza's notice. She hurried to say, "Our plans
are to leave for Paris within the week, Papa. In the interim,
March and I think it best not to formally announce our
. . . betrothal. You . . . have not told anyone, have you?"

Sir Richard shrugged again. "None besides the Heathergills." He paused, then in a somewhat halting tone, said
"I . . . expect you've nothing to fear from that quarter."

Eliza flung a speaking look at Lady Villiers and noted
with satisfaction both the lift of one eyebrow and the disdainful purse of the older woman's lips.

A second later, General Huntley cleared his throat. His
authoritative tone broke the stillness that had overtaken
them. "Upon your arrival in Paris, Lady Villiers, you would
be wise to present yourselves at once to the British
Embassy."

Lady Villiers turned a relieved look on the tall man.
"Indeed, we mean to do that very thing. Lord Villiers will,
of course, be along. I am given to understand that he is
quite well acquainted with our new ambassador, Sir Charles
Stuart. The Stuarts' daughter Charlotte is a dear girl."

"All of the ambassador's emissaries are quite helpful to
foreign travelers," Huntley replied firmly. "A number of
balls and receptions were in the planning stages just as I
was leaving the French capital."

Lady Villiers turned her full attention on General Huntley now. "I had quite forgotten you were so recently there, Huntley. Do tell me all that you can. I am most anxious to present Jane to all the right people."

Huntley shifted his weight, taking up the stance Eliza so vividly remembered from her first glimpse of the distinguished man—his legs wide apart, his gloved hands clasped solemnly behind his back. The older gentleman appeared every bit as handsome to her today in his scarlet coat with the gold buttons and wide gold lace. Her admiring gaze took in his thick dark hair and the striking wings of white that feathered outward from each temple. When her eyes dropped to his powerful shoulders and chest, she was beset once again by the strange fluttering sensation in her belly, only the feeling this time was even more unsettling considering the startling comment he'd made earlier regarding . . . Sailor coming to live with them after they'd married. What had prompted the man to say such a thing? she wondered.

"—the Duke of Devonshire is currently traveling in France," Huntley was telling Lady Villiers now.

"Oh, my stars!" that woman exclaimed joyfully. "What young lady, or her mama, for all that"—she laughed gaily—"would not wish to be presented to him?"

"The Duke is much sought after," General Huntley agreed quietly. He cast a guarded look at Eliza, though the implication of the look was quite lost on her. She was still gazing up at him with unabashed admiration. "At the one reception I attended where the Duke was present," Huntley went on, "I was most astonished at the vast number of young ladies vying for his attention. It seemed that every last one was reluctant to accept an offer to dance 'til she could be certain the Duke would not ask her. Only then did they agree to stand up with another."

"Any wonder!" Lady Villiers enthused, still quite a-tremor over this extraordinary bit of news. "The Duke of Devonshire is the most eligible bachelor in the kingdom

. . . and by far the richest. My!'' Her eyes rolled back in her head. ''What I wouldn't give if he and my Jane . . . Oh! do tell me all that you know of him, Huntley. I am determined to arrive in Paris prepared to do battle, as it were.'' She laughed quite heartily at her own small joke. ''The war may be over, but''—she continued to titter—''not all the spoils have been divided!''

Eliza smiled somewhat shakily at Lady Villiers's little joke, whilst Huntley merely cleared his throat again.

''Do go on, Huntley!'' Lady Villiers urged.

Huntley rocked back on his heels. ''I would also advise you to make yourselves known to Lady Aldborough. Though she does not move in quite the same circles as the Duke, she hosts very agreeable dinner parties.''

Lady Villiers pulled a face. ''I am not at all certain I should wish to meet her, Huntley. I have it on good authority Lady Aldborough can be quite plain.''

''That is true.'' Huntley nodded. ''The lady's wit can often be . . . unvarnished. But, she is acquainted with nearly all the European nobility. Gentlemen, most especially, find her entertaining.''

''Very well, then,'' Lady Villiers said with decision, ''I shall prevail upon you for a letter of introduction. Tit for tat, if you get my drift.'' She flung a speaking look at Eliza.

Huntley inclined his head a notch. ''I shall have my secretary draw up a letter at once, my lady.''

Lady Villiers clapped her hands together with glee. ''We shall have a glorious time, indeed, Eliza! Think of all the handsome, eligible gentlemen you and my Jane shall meet!''

Having merely listened to the above exchange, Sir Richard's brow now furrowed. ''I hardly think Eliza is in a position to—''

''You forget, Lady Villiers,'' Eliza spoke up sharply, ''that I am already spoken for.'' She cast a sidelong glance at the general, but was once again struck by the troubled look emanating from his long gray eyes.

"Yes, very well, then," Lady Villiers said primly. "You may do as you please, Eliza." She jerked a scrap of linen from her reticule and began nervously to fan herself with it. "But, I am quite determined not to leave Paris 'til my Jane is affianced! I am quite determined," she said again.

General Huntley suddenly felt as warm beneath the collar as apparently Lady Villiers did. That the adorable Miss Eliza Foxburn would soon be going about in Parisian society, without *him* to look after her, was a proposition he did not favor in the least.

Not the least.

CHAPTER 10

"A CHANCE ENCOUNTER"

When the conversation in the drawing room finally wound down, Lady Villiers took her leave, and Sir Richard and General Huntley retired to the Foxburn library, presumably to finalize the arrangements for the marriage settlement.

Feeling somewhat left out, Eliza made her way abovestairs to the small sitting room where she generally spent a good deal of her time, either reading or amusing herself at the pianoforte. But, because she didn't feel a bit like reading or playing music today, she merely sank onto the window seat that overlooked the street.

It occurred to her that she was suddenly not quite as a-tremor to travel to Paris as she was when Lady Villiers first proposed the trip to her a few days back. She told herself that her reluctance to leave the country just now was due to the fierce responsibility she felt toward her father. With Mama no longer around to look after him, someone had to protect Papa; otherwise, there was no saying where his unbridled actions would take him.

Her thoughts turned to the two men secluded now in

the library. And the odd comment one of them had made as he sat on the floor in the drawing room playing with Sailor a bit ago. What the meaning behind General Huntley's remark about the cat coming to live with them once they were married was, Eliza could not think.

But it did spark an equally odd question in Eliza's mind . . . what her life would be like if she were General Huntley's wife? Contrary to Papa, General Huntley was possessed of a steady, dependable nature. Therefore, she reasoned, he would never give his wife, or his daughter, a moment's cause for concern. The few times Eliza had been in his company, she'd always felt inordinately relaxed, not to mention safe and protected. Never once had she been on edge wondering what *Huntley* might say or do next. Equally comforting to Eliza was the sure knowledge that she could turn to him when she required aid or assistance and be certain of receiving intelligent, well-thought-out answers.

An unaccountable feeling of warmth stole over her. But, after a few moments of dreamy silence, Eliza shook herself. She was being silly, of course. In a few days' time, when Papa'd abandoned his infatuation for Ivy, she'd have no occasion to see General Huntley ever again.

That that thought caused an odd tugging sensation in the region of her heart unsettled her further. Whatever was wrong with her?

She endeavored to push the oddity aside, but found that thoughts of the handsome military man were not so easily dislodged. It was quite generous of him to bring her such an immense bouquet of fresh-cut flowers. In addition to being quite clever, he was also a very kind and thoughtful man.

When their daylong excursion had come to an end yesterday, they'd not fixed on another time to meet, so Eliza had been quite pleasantly surprised to find him awaiting her in the drawing room today. Although she did not think it opportune that Lady Villiers had arrived when she did and found them alone together. She only hoped that Lady

Villiers did not become so caught up in her lofty aspirations for Jane that she forgot the explanation Eliza and Huntley had given her regarding their "pretend" betrothal. She had not minded telling Lady Villiers the truth . . . but having the *ton* know all about it was another matter altogether.

Another long sigh escaped her. Perhaps she was worrying needlessly on that head. Unlike many less-principled tabbies of the *ton,* Eliza had never known Lady Villiers to betray a confidence. Eliza might better spend her time trying to fix upon a workable solution to the troublesome matter of Papa and Ivy.

From the direction of her father's library she could faintly hear the deep rumble of the gentlemen's voices. She wondered what they could be discussing now and how angry her father would be with her once he discovered she and General Huntley had deceived him?

Perhaps he would not be too terribly overset once he realized they'd had his best interests at heart. Fortunately, she and Huntley had been granted a few extra days in which to come up with a plan, since, as Lady Villiers was leaving, she'd told Eliza that Jane appeared to be coming down with a cold and they must delay their departure for Paris a bit.

"The air blowing across the Channel can be quite brisk, you know," she had declared.

Musing upon the possible courses of action she might take now, Eliza thought it had been quite a good idea of Huntley's to invite Miss Heathergill along on their trip. Ivy really was a charming young lady and with her lovely face and agreeable manner, she would have easily attracted *another* suitor in the glittering city of Paris. Perhaps even two or three.

The fact that Lady Villiers had instantly rejected the idea merely proved to Eliza that *her* feelings in regard to the matter were squarely on target. They all, including General Huntley, looked upon Papa's alliance with Miss Heathergill exactly as any self-respecting member of society would. Why her father could not see reason, Eliza could not think!

By the following morning at breakfast, although Eliza still had not come up with a viable plan of action, her gloomy countenance brightened visibly when her father announced that General Huntley wished to take her for a drive in the park that afternoon.

"Oh!" she exclaimed, with a smile. The prospect of seeing the general again so soon quite delighted her.

Last evening, she'd been as greatly troubled by recurring thoughts of the handsome military man as she had by worry over her father—with the result that she'd scarcely been able to fall asleep. Deep into the night, she'd finally crawled out of bed, lit a lamp, and begun to set down all the reasons she could think why he should *not* marry Ivy Heathergill. She was most anxious now to present the list to Huntley and ask if he had anything to add to it. The sooner they convinced her papa to terminate his association with the entire Heathergill family, the better.

"Said he'd call for you at five of the clock," her father was saying. "Appears Huntley is becoming quite an ardent suitor," he added, an amused twinkle causing his blue eyes to sparkle merrily.

Eliza's dark lashes fluttered nervously against her smooth cheek. Her false betrothal to General Huntley had not had nearly the effect on her father that she'd hoped it would . . . and it was having quite an odd effect upon her!

"Bringing you flowers yesterday was quite thoughtful of him," her father went on, his eyes fastened on her as he lazily stirred a lump of sugar into his coffee cup.

"They were, indeed, lovely," Eliza murmured. An impish grin began to play at her lips. "At least, they were before Sailor got at them."

"I believe Briggs managed to salvage a few."

"Yes, he brought them up to me. The carnations smelled especially sweet last evening." And were partly to blame for keeping her awake half the night, since *every* time she looked at them she thought of Huntley!

Sir Richard's gaze on his daughter's face remained intent. "Appears my old friend Huntley is quite taken with you."

Eliza chewed fretfully on her lower lip but said nothing.

"Well." Sir Richard drained his coffee cup, then dabbed at his mouth with a napkin. "I shall be out most of the day, as well as this evening. I told Heathergill about my plan for an electrifying machine. He has an idea on how to improve it."

"I thought you'd given up your experimenting, Papa," Eliza protested.

"Not at all. I am quite anxious to try it now with rods."

Eliza's lips thinned. "What does Ivy think of your . . . of this occupation of yours?"

Sir Richard shrugged. "Haven't asked her opinion on the matter." The smile on his face turned to one of immense satisfaction. "Though I daresay, Ivy seems to find nearly everything I do quite fascinating."

Eliza's chin shot up defiantly. "Well, Mama said electrifying can be quite dangerous and should not be played with as a toy!"

Her father leveled a long look at her. "There were times, Eliza, dear, when your mother's views could be quite dampening. Ivy is of a more tolerant bent. *She* understands that my experimenting brings me great pleasure." He rose to his feet, but before heading for the door, said in a breezy tone, "If you'd like to invite Huntley to stay to dinner tonight, you have my permission to do so."

Eliza's blue eyes widened. "But . . . what would he think if I were to ask him to stay to dinner and you not about? There would be no one to chaperone."

"I doubt he would think anything. The pair of you are to be wed, for pity's sake. You will be taking dinner together the rest of your lives. I see nothing improper in it now. Besides, Mrs. Allen and Briggs will be on hand.''

He fidgeted with his waistcoat. "I should think you would welcome a bit of time alone with your suitor, sweetheart.'' He bent to drop a fatherly kiss on Eliza's burning cheek. Then, with a rakish wink, added, "I quite enjoy the few minutes the Heathergills leave me alone with Ivy.''

Eliza's nostrils flared afresh, and her blue eyes snapped fury. Springing to her feet, she angrily flung the napkin in her lap to the table. "Why can you not see that Ivy is not the least bit suited for you, Papa?'' she blurted out. "General Huntley quite agrees with me on that score. And so does Lady Villiers!''

"Is that so?'' Sir Richard regarded his daughter coolly. At length, a dark brow lifted. "Only yesterday, Huntley informed me that he thought Ivy quite charming and sweet-tempered. I recall him saying nothing about her being *un*suitable.'' He continued to study Eliza, who stood with her arms folded obstinately across her small breasts, her chin elevated stubbornly. "I had hoped that after meeting Ivy, you would find her as agreeable as I do.''

"I do not find Ivy *dis*agreeable,'' Eliza retorted. "I find her disagreeable for *you!*''

"Ah.'' Sir Richard moved a few steps away from the table. Near the door, he turned to face Eliza again. "I have invited Ivy to accompany me to the theater on Thursday evening,'' he announced solemnly. "Drury Lane is open-ing for the autumn season, and because I thought the four of us had quite a jolly time together the other afternoon, I also took the liberty of inviting Huntley. On behalf of both of you, he graciously accepted the invitation.'' Moving into the corridor, he flung over his shoulder, "I will leave it to you to decide if you wish to join us or not.''

Her stomach churning furiously, Eliza watched her father disappear from the room. A scant second later, when once again she heard the sound of the double doors in the drawing room swoosh open but *not* close behind him, her lips thinned with near fury!

By the time Huntley arrived to collect her that afternoon, her elation over getting to see him again had had the effect of dissipating much of the anger and frustration she'd experienced that morning with her father. Further exciting her was the fact that during a solitary luncheon, she had been struck with a brilliant scheme that she could hardly wait to apprise Huntley of. She thought it quite rivaled anything Wellington's Master Strategist, or anyone else, for that matter, could come up with.

"Do you not think it a splendid idea, sir?" Eliza exclaimed, mere minutes after she and Huntley had set out for Hyde Park.

The pair of them were seated next to one another in a plush tilbury that actually bore the coat of arms of the royal family. Eliza assumed, and rightly so, that the Prince Regent himself had lent the carriage to the high-ranking army officer.

She'd felt quite elegant being handed into it by one of the liveried footmen that accompanied the equipage and who was now clinging to the rear of the well-sprung vehicle as it smoothly wheeled through the gates that marked the entrance to the enormous, shady park.

Though it was scarcely minutes past five of the clock, already a virtual parade of carriages and gigs were tooling along the wide thoroughfare, the tigers and gentlemen driving them having to stay alert in order to avoid colliding with the scores of other gentlemen, and even some ladies, promenading on horseback. The footpaths along either side of the roadway were thronged with other men and women all dressed to the nines, eager to see and be seen, as they leisurely strolled up and down.

It had been nigh on a year, or longer, since Eliza'd been in the park at the fashionable hour, and she'd quite forgotten the air of frenzied excitement and anticipation that accompanied such jaunts. Taking note of her surroundings today, however, was not uppermost in her mind. Her eyes remained fastened on the ruggedly handsome features of her companion as she breathlessly awaited his reply to her question.

"London is teeming with young men today, sir!" she added. "Just look about us now. The footpaths are crowded with young men in uniform, and I'll wager, the majority are *not* titled gentleman. They are younger sons and squires' sons; they hail from the provinces and farms and villages. They must all take a wife one day. Surely one of them would find the lovely daughter of a wealthy tradesman to his liking."

General Huntley nodded thoughtfully. "You may have hit upon the very plan that will succeed, my dear."

"But I cannot do it alone, sir. I shall need your help," Eliza added forcefully.

Huntley turned a sidelong gaze upon her. Miss Eliza Foxburn looked especially lovely today in a pretty blue-velvet afternoon gown, the neck and long sleeves trimmed in black braid. She had on a matching toque bonnet with a bright blue feather that curled fetchingly 'round her chin. The excitement shining from her round blue eyes had turned them an irresistible shade of deep sapphire. As usual, he found it extraordinarily difficult not to become lost in those alluring blue depths.

Her idea to host a party for Ivy Heathergill and invite only young men suited to that young lady's station was, indeed, an excellent one. That there would be no young men present that Eliza herself would find acceptable made the scheme that much more appealing to Huntley.

"I shall be most happy to assist in whatever way I can," he replied with conviction.

When that comment transformed Eliza's anxious gaze into the sweetest smile Huntley'd ever seen, his chest swelled to such a degree, he feared it might actually burst!

Damme, I am making quite a cake of myself over this little minx!
Equally astonishing to him was the fact that he'd never
felt quite like this before in his life, and, despite his
advanced years and vast experience in living, he felt equally
powerless to stop it! The chit's adorable dimples and tanta-
lizing blue eyes had him quite in thrall.

"You are the kindest man I have ever met, sir," she
gushed, her sweet countenance regarding him with guileless devotion. "I cannot tell you how pleased I am that we
met! It was surely fate that brought us together at Lady
Villiers's and again at Lady Hamilton's, do you not agree?"

Huntley attempted to swallow past the huge lump in his
throat that was threatening to suffocate him. "I expect our
acquaintanceship will prove fortunate for the both of us,
Miss Foxburn," he managed. Then, lest he make a complete fool of himself wallowing in the child's unabashed
admiration, he turned a cool stare upon the throng of
ladies and gentlemen promenading on the nearby foot-
path.

Still smiling happily, Eliza said, "I should think ten or
twelve young men should suffice, do you not agree?" Without waiting for him to reply, she added, "Our drawing
room is not terribly spacious, you know. It would hardly
accommodate more, especially if there is to be dancing."

Huntley's attention returned rapidly to her. "Dancing?
I assume you mean to invite sufficient young ladies to
partner the boys?"

Eliza chewed on her lower lip. "The bulk of the *ton* is
from Town just now. Of course, I shall invite Jane.
Although, it is doubtful that she will feel up to attending."

"Has Jane been ill?"

"Indeed." Eliza nodded. "You and Papa had already
retired to the library yesterday afternoon when Lady Villiers informed me that Jane has caught a cold. Our departure for Paris is to be delayed."

"Ah!" Huntley sat up a bit straighter. "Well, then . . .

we've a bit more time in which to plan our little soirée, haven't we?''

Eliza's eyes sparkled. "It will be a smashing success. I am certain of it!''

As the neat little tilbury, sporting the royal coat of arms, tooled about the park, Eliza and the distinguished military man beside her became quite lost in their own private conversation. So lost, in fact, that they scarcely noticed the vast number of curious looks and fixed stares flung at them from well-dressed passersby.

Not until the tilbury was forced to a halt amidst a snarl of traffic blocking the park's entrance on their second or third pass round it, did they glance up again.

"I say, is that you, Huntley?'' came a male voice from the interior of an elegant barouche drawn also to a standstill next to them.

General Huntley directed a look toward the open carriage. "Ah, taking the air I see, sir.''

Eliza glanced also toward the fashionable large vehicle drawn up beside them, but did not recognize the white-haired man who'd addressed the general, nor any of the other three gentlemen with him. Obviously from the vast number of ribands and medals upon their chests, they were military men and high-ranking officers. Each wore crimson coats with gold braid and lace, sparkling white breeches and gloves, and shiny black Hessians. All four appeared a good bit older than Huntley. The one who'd spoken seemed especially distinguished.

"You were invited to join us this afternoon, Huntley,'' said another of the men. "I can see now why the note went unanswered.'' He cast an appraising look at Eliza.

"Beg pardon,'' General Huntley murmured. "I was unaware a summons had been delivered.''

"No need to apologize,'' another chimed in. "Your young lady friend is far prettier than we are!''

At that the four men in the barouche laughed heartily. When the laughter had subsided, General Huntley

began politely, "Allow me to present Miss Eliza Foxburn,
your grace. This is the Duke of Wellington, Miss Foxburn.
Miss Foxburn's father, Sir Richard Foxburn, and I were
classmates at Eton," Huntley told Wellington.

Her heart in her throat, Eliza watched as with barely a
flicker of expression on his well-lined face, the great Duke
of Wellington inclined his snow-white head the veriest
notch. "Pleasure, Miss Foxburn."

After Huntley had presented the other gentlemen, a
Major General Priestley, Commander Lord Sharpe, and
General Meyers-Fraser, he again addressed the Duke.

"Miss Foxburn has asked my help is planning a soirée,"
Huntley said simply.

"Ah," Wellington muttered with obvious disinterest. "A
soirée."

During the small space of silence that ensued, Eliza
blurted out, "It is to honor . . . noncommissioned officers
and . . . um foot soldiers!"

At that, all four men turned to gaze at the young lady
who'd just spoken.

A tiny spark of interest appeared on the Duke of Wellington's war-weary face. "Foot soldiers, eh?"

"Hmmmm," Commander Lord Sharpe murmured.

"A novel idea," declared Major General Priestley. He
flung approving nods at each of the other gentlemen
seated in the carriage. At length, all four men again turned
expectant gazes upon Eliza.

With fear knotting her stomach and her cheeks suddenly
on fire, she wondered what on earth had prompted her
to blurt out such an absurdity? Deceiving her father was
one thing, but all out lying to the highest-ranking officers
in the realm was quite another! But, with every last one of
them looking to her for an explanation, she had no choice
now but to carry on with it!

"I-indeed. Most of the balls and receptions being hosted
by the *ton* are in honor of high-ranking officers . . . like
yourselves. Not that you do not deserve the accolades."

She grinned nervously at Huntley. "Indeed, you do! I . . . um . . . just thought it was high time someone heaped a bit of praise upon the . . . the common soldier."

The men's faces were each alight with interest now, all four of them nodding earnest approval over the exceptional plan.

"Splendid idea, Miss . . . er . . . beg pardon?" the great Duke muttered.

"Foxburn," Huntley supplied, his own voice a bit shaky now. "Her father is Sir Richard Foxburn," he said again.

"Indeed. Well . . . er, carry on, Miss Foxburn." Wellington directed another look at Huntley. "We've a regimental review at first light in the morning, General. Courtyard of St. James's. Presume I will see you there."

At precisely that instant, the elegant barouche jerked forward and disappeared from view in the cloud of dust churned up by the heavy spoked wheels picked out in red.

Eliza exhaled a huge breath of relief. "Oh, March!" she cried, not the least aware that in her agitation she'd used the general's given name. "Whatever do you suppose possessed me to blurt out such a piece of fustian?"

Huntley's chest had begun to heave with unrepressed mirth. "You are a good deal like your father in that regard, Eliza!" He threw his head back and laughed aloud. "Richard could fabricate the tallest tales of any lad in school. I shall never forget the time he nearly burned down Appleton Hall."

Eliza had also begun to laugh merrily. "Do tell me the story. I confess I hadn't heard that one."

Huntley again settled back comfortably as the neat tilbury also lurched forward. "Your father escaped punishment by telling the headmaster he was conducting a scientific experiment—" He again burst into laughter. "He wished to see if dirt would burn! It seems," he went on, the grin still playing about his mouth, "a hornets' nest was attached to a trellis on the porch and the damn—pardon me—the blasted hornets had been driving us all

mad. One day, Richard decided to remedy the situation
by sticking a lighted taper into the mouth of the nest and
burning the creatures out.''

"Oh, my!'' "Eliza exclaimed. ''That sounds exactly like
something Papa would do!''

"But he hadn't counted on the fierce wind that blew
up and sent great gusts of black smoke, and angry hornets,
I might add, straight into the house! The trellis caught
fire, as did the checkered curtains at the windows of the
headmaster's suite!''

"Oh!'' Eliza covered her mouth with her hands. ''Papa
never told us the tale. I expect he was quite embarrassed!''

"Embarrassed? Not Richard! But, he was obliged to continue with the 'scientific experiment' and turn in a lengthy
report on his findings . . . and *that* nearly undid him!''

They both laughed again. At length, Huntley drew out
a large white handkerchief with which he wiped the tears
of mirth from his eyes.

"I do hope my telling a falsehood to the great Duke of
Wellington does not land me in the basket!'' Eliza exclaimed.

"I doubt anything will come of your little fabrication,
my dear.'' Huntley folded up his handkerchief and tucked
it back into his coat pocket. ''You observed how preoccu-
pied the Duke was. Why, he scarcely recalled your name
two minutes after hearing it.''

"I expect you are quite well acquainted with him.''

Huntley nodded. ''After serving nearly fifteen years with
the Duke, there is very little we did not learn about one
another. Wellington is quite brilliant, but at times, he can
also be quite oblique. It is likely he has already forgotten
the exchange between us just now.''

"I do hope you are right, sir,'' Eliza murmured.

"Of course I am right!''

"All the same,'' she replied with a rueful smile, ''in
future, I really should endeavor to curb my tongue, else

you will think it is I who requires looking after, and not Papa.''

The general's only reply to that was a long, solemn look at his charming companion.

Eliza's smile faded. Sharing a laugh with General Huntley just now reminded her of how much fun she used to have with Papa. Beyond that, however, she was fast realizing that this elderly gentleman was not the least bit like her father.

And that alarmed her greatly.

CHAPTER 11

"A PERFECT PLAN"

"You met up with the Duke of Wellington in the park!"
Sir Richard sputtered, his elevated tone a mixture of dismay
and disbelief.

"Indeed," Eliza replied archly, although she could not
contain the playful smile tugging at her lips. "And I daresay
he remembered me," she added for good measure.

"Blast the luck!" exclaimed her father. "I knew I should
have taken Huntley up on his offer to join the pair of you
today."

"Well, you didn't . . . so, there it is."

The hour was late, and Eliza, having again found it
difficult to sleep, had padded down to the kitchen for a
glass of warm milk and honey. On her way back upstairs,
she'd encountered her father just returning home from
his evening at the Heathergills'. When he'd asked about
her drive in the park that afternoon with Huntley and if
she'd invited the general to stay for dinner, Eliza'd told
him their outing was quite pleasant but the general was
unable to stay to supper as he already had a previous
engagement.

Though Eliza had wondered where the gentleman was off to that evening, she hadn't pressed for an explanation and had instead settled down after a solitary dinner to concentrate on her party plans.

"The Duke thought my idea to host a party for . . . for General Huntley's foot soldiers quite a good one," she told her father as they walked alongside one another up the dimly lit stairwell.

"You and Huntley planning to host a party, are you?" Sir Richard repeated a bit absently, his mind apparently still mulling over the missed opportunity to meet the great Duke of Wellington.

Eliza nodded, then in a firm tone, added, "I mean to invite Ivy."

"Invite Ivy?" Her father's interest was again piqued.

Eliza nodded once more, her dark curls bobbing beneath her lacy nightcap. "Huntley is drawing up a list of young me . . . of the soldiers he'd especially like me to invite." She paused in the corridor before her own bedchamber, and asked sweetly, "You don't mind if we have the party here, do you Papa? I imagine as Huntley's wife, I will be expected to do a good bit of entertaining, state dinners and receptions, and whatnot. This will be good practice for me."

Her father smiled agreeably. "I think that an excellent idea, sweetheart. We've not had a soirée here since long before your mother passed away. You've my permission to do whatever you like. I'm especially pleased that you wish to include Ivy. You're a good girl, Eliza."

He bent to plant a quick kiss on her upturned cheek, then headed down the corridor to his own suite. "I daresay, I am especially looking forward to meeting the Duke!"

Eliza smothered a giggle as she entered her own darkened bedchamber. If Papa would like the great Duke of Wellington to come to their little party, then she would invite him! Who knows, he might surprise them and actually turn up.

* * *

Eliza awoke the next morning buoyed by her party plans. Immediately after breakfast, she set the small Foxburn staff to cleaning and polishing every mantelpiece, stairwell, and stick of furniture in the house. If the Duke and Duchess of Wellington were to come to their party, it would never do for something to appear less than its finest.

"Briggs," she called to the butler, who had just brought a fresh pot of tea to the small sitting room where Eliza was working, "you will please fetch the *Times* for me."

"The 'times', miss?" Briggs repeated, a puzzled look on his florid face. "The times for *what*, miss?"

"The *Times*, Briggs, the *Times!* I spotted an advertisement once for a fumigator, and I should like to hire the man. With Papa continually leaving the door in the drawing room ajar, it is quite possible the house is overrun with vermin. I shouldn't want any of my guests to be frightened by a mouse."

"I see, miss. A fumigator. Very well, miss." Cogitating the matter, Briggs shuffled off and returned a good bit later carrying a disheveled sheaf of newsprint that looked to have already been thoroughly read by someone.

Eliza was bent over a pretty little cherrywood desk in the corner, drawing up long lists of things to be done in preparation for the party.

"*The London Times,* Miss," Briggs said, then he added, "and your gentleman caller is awaitin' ye in the drawing room."

"Oh!" Eliza's dark head jerked up.

"Good morning, Miss Foxburn," General Huntley said. He popped to his feet from the chair upon which he'd been resting and, as she approached, reached into his coat pocket and withdrew a packet of paper. "I have compiled the list of names that you requested and thought it best to deliver them to you straightaway."

"Thank you, sir!" Eliza exclaimed. The general looked quite dashing this morning in his showy dress uniform of red, blue, and gold, sparkling white knee breeches and shiny black top boots. "How handsome you look!" she blurted out, then grinned sheepishly. "You must have just come from the palace. I recall Wellington mentioning a regimental review this morning."

General Huntley returned the smile, his long gray eyes actually appearing to twinkle. It occurred to Eliza that it had been quite some time since she'd observed the bored look, which he'd heretofore worn like a mask, on his rugged face.

"Indeed, I am just come from the palace. The Prince was present this morning, which, I daresay, added a good bit to the pomp and ceremony."

"The review must have been quite spectacular," Eliza said in an interested tone. "I expect the sheer number of soldiers in London at the moment is near to overwhelming." She recalled having attended a local military review once as a young girl when she and her parents had been visiting friends in Warwickshire. It was, indeed, an impressive affair what with the officers and soldiers, and even their horses, decked out in all their finery. "You must be exhausted. Would you care for a cup of tea, or perhaps a bite to eat, sir?"

Huntley smiled a bit tiredly. "A cup of tea would be greatly appreciated. I have been up since dawn, and do admit to a prodigious thirst."

Eliza crossed to the bellpull, then returned to a chair near where the general had been sitting. "Please, sir, do be seated," she said, settling herself.

In moments, Mrs. Allen answered the summons, and, after Eliza had given the housekeeper instructions regarding the refreshments, Eliza turned her attention to the list Huntley had handed her.

"There are twenty names," the general said. "If you wish me to add or subtract some, you've only to ask."

"I believe twenty should do nicely," Eliza replied. "It will mean a want of chairs, but I daresay that will be all to the good as it will promote the mingling of the young men amongst the ladies."

An amused little grin played at Huntley's lips.

"The order of the evening shall be conversation, then dancing. I have decided upon twelve dances, which, depending upon the length, should provide enough entertainment to last the whole of the evening. We shall have light refreshments throughout," she ticked off, "lemonade, wine, and punch, with a late supper around eleven or twelve. What do you think?"

"Sounds as if you have planned a good many soirées."

Eliza's dark lashes fluttered against her silken cheek. "Not at all, sir. This will be my first, actually; and I am quite looking forward to it."

"And who is to provide the music for dancing?"

Eliza's expression sobered. "I mean to do that myself, sir. I have been practicing a number of country danses and there will be a quadrille and perhaps, even a waltz."

"Ah. You are very talented, my dear."

Eliza felt herself color. "Not really, sir. I play only adequately, but I mean to step up my practice considerably before the party."

At that moment, Mrs. Allen arrived with the tea tray, and, after Eliza had served her guest, they began again to converse.

"What else must you do in preparation for the party?" General Huntley asked.

"Well, apart from a thorough housecleaning, which I have set the household staff to doing today, I mean to . . ." Eliza paused, realizing that she was speaking quite plainly to the general, as plainly as she did to her father! Of late, however, she'd discovered General Huntley quite easy to converse with. He seemed interested in whatever she had to say, which, of course, prompted her to be open and straightforward with him. Although bringing up vermin in the house was perhaps a bit much. "I . . . I . . . was about to say that I plan to hire a fumigator to deal with the . . . the mouse problem, but, I . . . I expect you did not mean . . ." Her voice trailed off.

Huntley was grinning again. "I rather expected Sailor was detailed to the capturing and disposing of mice. How is the little chap?"

"Sailor is doing very well, thank you, sir. At present, I believe he is fast asleep on Papa's bed."

"Ah, a nap before charge and attack." Huntley chuckled. "Sailor is obviously a well-trained soldier."

Eliza laughed easily, then after taking another sip of her tea, she reached for the pot and refilled both their cups. "I should like you to look over the supper menu I have prepared, if you would, sir. You know better than I what would please the young soldiers. *Oh!*" she exclaimed suddenly.

Huntley leaned forward, a wide-eyed look of concern on his face. "What is the trouble, Miss Eliza? Have you suddenly taken ill?"

"No! I've just been struck with a brilliant idea!"

Huntley laughed aloud. "Another one?"

Eliza's laughter joined his. "I was not aware that I'd already had a brilliant idea, let alone another one!"

"On the contrary"—Huntley's lips were twitching—"you have been struck with several very brilliant ideas, of late, my dear."

A somewhat faraway look appeared on his face. "You must apprise me of your latest inspiration," he said quietly.

Eliza's blue eyes twinkled mischievously. "We shall obtain every last morsel of food that is to be served at the party from Ivy's father's store! And it shall be the very finest he has! It will give Ivy the opportunity to remark upon her father's good taste, and allude to his wealth!"

"Ah." Huntley nodded. "The additional business

should also please Mr. Heathergill. You are quite a good strategist yourself, my dear."

Eliza beamed beneath the great man's praise. "There is one last thing, sir. During the party, you and I, and most especially you, as I will be seated at the pianoforte, must be ever alert to the direction of the young men's gazes. Every last one who casts even the smallest peek at Miss Heathergill must be presented to her."

"Indeed." Huntley nodded, his stern lips still twitching.

"I fear this could very well be my final opportunity to supplant Papa in Miss Heathergill's affections, and I shouldn't want to miss even *one* chance to do so! Now, we must set upon a date for the party, so that I may pen the invitations and have them delivered."

The lively discussion that continued between Eliza and the general was interrupted twice, once by Mrs. Allen, who brought in a plate of fresh lemon cake that Cook had just removed from the oven, and a few minutes later by Sailor, who, with his pink nose sniffing the air, told Eliza that he, too, would like to sample the warm cake.

Eliza put a saucer on the floor for the cat, and, as he was nibbling from it, Huntley knelt to stroke the cat's fuzzy back.

"I suppose Sailor will also be at the party," he mused.

Eliza grinned. "Sailor pretty well goes where he pleases." She, too, knelt to pet the cat, then glanced up at Huntley. "Do you suppose if I issued an invitation to the Duke of Wellington that he might come?"

A considering look appeared on the general's face.

Eliza grinned. "You should have seen Papa's face last evening when I told him that we had met up with the Duke in the park."

"Disappointed, was he?" Huntley chuckled.

"In a word! I told him I thought the Duke remembered me from my come-out ball"—her blue eyes twinkled—"the night you and I purportedly met."

"I daresay *I* clearly recall the night," Huntley teased.

"Do you think he might come? Of course, I do not wish to draw the Duke into our silly charade, but if he should pop in, it would please Papa beyond saying."

Huntley stood, his expression again becoming serious.

"I can see no harm in issuing the invitation, so long as you are not disappointed if it should go unheeded. Despite the commander in chief's great triumph, he remains a man of few words and typically prefers to avoid the limelight."

Eliza nodded as she stood before Huntley, who had reached for his gloves and was now drawing them on.

"The Duchess must be quite happy to have her husband home again," she said. "I understand they have been separated for much of their married life."

"Indeed. The boys have greatly missed having their father about. Only this morning, I overheard Wellington telling General Montrose and Commander Sharpe that he was quite ready for a rest from his responsibilities on the Continent and here at home. The constant round of receptions and balls he and Kitty have been subjected to lately have been quite tiring. So, you see"—he regarded Eliza with a long look before they set out for the foyer—"it is highly unlikely that the Duke will accept your invitation."

Eliza fell into step beside the great general as they headed for the corridor. They walked the length of it together. Near the door, Huntley reached for his cocked hat, which was hanging on a peg there and settled it onto his head. Eliza watched the action, a small contented smile upon her lips.

"The Duke's absence will not make a whit of difference to me, sir," she remarked pleasantly. "I shall have quite enough on my mind without having to worry what Papa might say to the gentleman. Although," she added with a laugh, "of late, I am the one who seems to be having trouble curbing my tongue."

Huntley turned a fond smile upon her. "I should not worry that your little deception, or I expect I should say, *our* little deception, will go a jot farther than it already has.

As I told you yesterday, the Duke has such a great deal to attend to, it is quite likely he has already forgotten all that was said between us when we met in the park.''

"I am certain you are right, sir."

Huntley moved a few steps closer to the door, his gloved hand reaching for the latch as Briggs was nowhere in sight to do the honors for him.

"By the by," he said, "your father issued an invitation to me to accompany him and Miss Heathergill to the theater tomorrow evening. It would please me greatly if you would consent also to join us."

Eliza smiled prettily. "I would be delighted to attend the theater with you, sir. Thank you for asking me."

He stood gazing down upon her for what seemed to Eliza like a very great length. Finally, he said, "The pleasure is all mine, Eliza."

The silent interval between them was broken a few seconds later by an insistent *me-ow!*

Huntley glanced down to find the gray-and-white cat nudging the toe of his boot with his head. "Do you wish also to attend the theater, Sailor-boy?"

Eliza laughed. "I believe he just wishes you'd pet him. He's quite spoiled, you know."

Huntley directed another penetrating look at Eliza. "And you, my dear, are spoiling me," he murmured.

Then he was gone.

CHAPTER 12

"A ROYAL FLUSH"

Despite the fact that she'd be forced to once again endure the sight of Papa with Miss Heathergill, Eliza was quite a-tremor over the prospect of attending the theater in the company of General Huntley.

It being the first time in nearly two years that she'd attended Drury Lane, she dressed carefully, choosing one of her newest and prettiest gowns, a beautiful cream-satin slip with a matching overdress picked out in gold threads and blond lace. Cream-colored kid gloves and dainty gold slippers completed the ensemble. As her abigail Betsy dressed her hair, Eliza endeavored to remind herself that her "pretend romance" with General Huntley was all a sham and that she must give no special meaning to his attentions upon her.

All the same, she could not suppress the charming smile that lit her face that night when the illustrious general arrived to collect them. Looking quite dashing in his smart scarlet coat and white-satin knee breeches, he greeted Eliza most cordially and presented her with a pretty posy of white and red roses nestled in a delicate bed of lacy greenery and tied with white-ribbon streamers.

His solicitations toward her appeared quite genuine. "You look especially lovely tonight, my dear; are you certain you will be warm enough with only the light wrap you are wearing?" he asked, as the party of three headed down the walk toward the shiny black carriage awaiting them at the curb. "This evening's air is a bit chilly," he added.

"I am quite comfortable, thank you, sir." Climbing into the coach, Eliza noted that this large carriage also sported the royal coat of arms. No doubt, it, too, was a castoff of the royal family designated for use now by military notables or visiting dignitaries.

Eliza's father also took note of the coach. "Just wait 'til I show Ivy into this!" he enthused. "Hope her parents have not yet gone; I'd like Heathergill to see it also."

"Ivy's parents are going out tonight?" Eliza asked with interest as she settled herself against the plush velvet squabs. 'Til then it had not occurred to her that persons in the lower reaches of society would also have their little entertainments and whatnot.

"The Heathergills have a box at Drury Lane Theatre," her father replied matter-of-factly.

"A box?" Eliza's eyes grew round as the dimly lit coach rumbled off down the street. Not even they had a box! To be honest, she'd hadn't a clue where they'd be seated tonight. How perfectly dreadful if the Heathergills' aspect proved more advantageous than theirs!

She needn't have worried. Sir Richard led his small party to a sumptuous box that was on the same tier as, and directly opposite from, the royal family's. It afforded an excellent view of the stage, the audience, and the gallery. Just before the curtain lifted on *Industry and Idleness,* the first play of the new season, there was a flurry of activity across the way and HRH himself, the Prince Regent, along with an impressive cortege of elegantly attired persons filed into the spacious crimson-and-gold chamber.

When the orchestra struck up a fanfare, Eliza was certain she saw the Prince Regent stare straight across at their small party. Given General Huntley's fame, she assumed the Prince was taking note of his presence. Feeling an immense wave of pride swell her breast, she elevated her small chin several notches higher. How fortunate she was to have befriended the famous man!

During the short interval between the first and second acts of the lighthearted drama, Eliza and Miss Heathergill struck up a conversation. Ivy looked very pretty in a fashionable ice green satin gown trimmed in row upon row of what Eliza assumed to be lace the girl had made herself. Eliza had earlier remarked upon it and received a pleasant smile of gratitude from her father's lovely companion.

Miss Heathergill now leaned close to Eliza's ear and whispered behind her fan. "A good many ladies and gentlemen appear to be quizzing us. I wonder if it is because you and Huntley have made public your betrothal?"

Eliza shook her head. She, too, had noted the multitude of glasses turned in their direction when they'd arrived, and for quite a length afterward, but expected the quizzers were merely wishing also to catch a glimpse of the decorated general. "I have been invited to accompany a friend of mine to Paris soon," Eliza whispered back. "Huntley and I thought it best to wait 'til my return to England before formally announcing our engagement."

As Ivy's pink lips formed a small O, Eliza bit hers nervously. She had voiced the falsehood so many times, she was beginning to believe it herself!

"By the by"—she leaned again to speak in a hushed tone to the older girl—"March and I are hosting a party for his . . . for the young men who served with him at Waterloo. Papa will be there, of course, and we would very much like you to attend."

Ivy's hazel eyes grew large, and she drew back as if she could scarce believe what she'd just heard. "You wish *me* to attend?"

The girl's obvious delight over being invited to the party sent an immense wave of guilt through Eliza. She suddenly felt positively beastly over deceiving the genuinely sweet Miss Heathergill. "Indeed," she murmured weakly.

Ivy reached to place a gloved hand over Eliza's, which were neatly positioned one atop the other in her lap. Giving a gentle squeeze to Eliza's fingertips, she gushed, "You are every bit as dear a person as your father, Eliza! Thank you so much for thinking of me."

A nervous little smile wavered across Eliza's lips. She was exceedingly grateful when, at that moment, the curtain lifted and everyone turned their attention once more to the stage.

During the lengthier intermission that came at the half-way mark in the performance, however, Ivy again turned toward her. "If you require any help at all with the party, Eliza, I should like to offer my services. Such an undertaking must be doubly difficult without your mother about to help."

As Eliza cast about for something to say, her lashes fluttered downward. Fortunately she was spared making a reply when her father's jovial voice cut in.

"Who'd like champagne and strawberries?" From his chair on Miss Heathergill's other side, he sprang to his feet.

Next to Eliza, Huntley also stood.

"Keep your seat, Huntley. I shall do the honors whilst you entertain the ladies." Sir Richard headed toward the curtained partition at the rear of the box. "I expect there to be a crush in the saloon, but I shall return straightaway." He parted the red-velvet draperies and stepped into the corridor beyond.

As was common during the long lull between acts, the glittering auditorium became alive with activity as patrons on the floor and in the crowded boxes commenced to laugh and talk at once.

A few minutes into the interval, however, a disturbance

of even greater proportions arose, the noise seeming to come from just outside the Foxburn box.

Suddenly, two liveried footmen swished the red-velvet curtain aside and another pair of prim-faced gentlemen stepped into the box, each imperially holding one side of the drapery apart.

Turning quickly in that direction, Eliza, Huntley and Miss Heathergill were suddenly astonished to see the regally attired Prince Regent himself move quite lightly— considering his immense girth—down the few steps toward them.

The three seated there fairly stumbled over one another in their haste to spring to their feet. Huntley's long legs actually managed to topple a chair as the two young ladies beside him melted to the floor in deep curtsies.

"Pray, do get up, Huntley," His Royal Highness commanded, by way of acknowledging the distinguished military man who, once upright, stood a good head and shoulders taller than he.

"Your Majesty," Huntley murmured, respectfully inclining his head, his eyes still downcast.

"Is this the young lady?" the Prince demanded, a royal gaze fixed on Miss Heathergill's suddenly very pale countenance.

"No, Your Grace," Huntley replied. "That young lady is Ivy Heathergill. This is Miss Eliza Foxburn."

Eliza hastily dropped again into a low curtsy. But, feeling Huntley's hand at her elbow, she just as quickly arose . . . and was astonished when His Royal Highness actually reached for her gloved hand, took it, and made as if to bring it to his lips! *Why was the Prince singling her out?*

"The Duke of Wellington has informed me that you plan to host a soirée in honor of the brave young men who defended our country, Miss Foxburn," the Regent stated. "I think it a splendid idea!"

Eliza's blue eyes were so large and round, she feared

they might pop from her head. "I-indeed, sir, er . . . Your Grace; that is, thank you, Your Majesty."

"Where is the event to be held?" the Prince wanted to know. "There are verily thousands of young men home from the wars—will require quite a vast hall, to be sure."

"Well, sir, ummm . . . o-our drawing room is not nearly so large as all that." Eliza flung a helpless look up at General Huntley. "I expect we shall have to . . ." Again, her eyes darted to Huntley's, her troubled blue orbs begging him for help.

"Miss Foxburn's plans have not yet been finalized, Your Majesty," Huntley replied, exhibiting impressive composure, considering the true nature of the subject under discussion.

"Ah," the Prince intoned. "Then the soirée shall be held at Carlton House!"

"Oh, no, sir," Eliza cried, then realizing that she was actually contradicting the Prince, she clamped her mouth shut.

"I insist!" the Regent declared. "The Great Hall and the Gothic Conservatory at Carlton House will serve nicely. You may invite whomever you wish, young lady. I shall send Lady Hertford 'round to assist you with . . . whatever. It shall be a grand affair! I've a number of ideas myself to honor our nation's Royal Army. Splendid plan!" He leveled an intense look at Eliza, then in a grave tone, said, "Until we meet again, Miss Foxburn."

Eliza's heart thundered wildly in her breast as her head dropped again to her chest, and she sank into a low curtsy. Peeking up, she watched the Prince twirl his sumptuous ermine-edged cape about and he and his entourage exit what seemed to her to have suddenly become very cramped quarters.

In a daze, Eliza straightened, then became aware of a deafening hush that engulfed the entire theater. Feeling her knees trembling beneath her silk skirt, she sank weakly onto her chair . . . then caught a glimpse of what appeared to be a sea of faces stretching the entire length and breadth of the gilded house, every last eye trained on her!

A mantle of guilt such as she'd never experienced before settled like a heavy blanket upon her shoulders. *Dear God, she prayed, what folly hath her loose tongue set in motion this time?*

Suddenly, the excited lilt of Ivy's voice mingled with the deep baritone of Huntley's became a disjointed jumble of sentences in her ears. From somewhere, she heard the high-pitched treble of her own voice joining theirs, as they all excitedly pattered on at once.

A split second later, Sir Richard stepped into the box, his authoritative tone directing a footman to set down the tray he carried laden with four long-stemmed goblets of sparkling champagne and two plates piled high with juicy red strawberries.

"Here we are!" he said, striding toward his chair.

"Papa!" Eliza cried, jumping wide-eyed from hers. "You missed him!"

"Missed who?" Sir Richard asked, then looked stricken. "Blast! Wellington here, and I'd gone for strawberries! Can you not get him back, Huntley?"

"Not Wellington, Papa! You missed—" Eliza's voice suddenly broke as she was besieged by a crippling wave of nervous twitters, which dissolved into wave after wave of uncontrollable giggles.

"Who? Whom did I miss, Eliza?" Sir Richard looked a question at Huntley, and then at Miss Heathergill.

"The Prince, Richard," Ivy intoned breathlessly. "You missed meeting His Royal Highness, the Prince of Wales."

Leaving the theater that night, Eliza felt almost like a celebrity herself. To the right and left of her, people she'd never seen before, let alone met, acknowledged her with approving nods and gracious smiles. When she and Huntley, who were leading their small party, began to descend the wide sweep of stairs that led to the rotunda on the ground floor, a smattering of applause actually arose from the smiling crowd assembled there.

"You've become the newest darling of the *ton*," Huntley mused, his lips twitching as he walked close by Eliza's side.

She flung a terrified gaze up at him. She felt positively wretched over the turn of events and longed for an opportunity to unburden her soul upon him.

Reaching the ground floor, the foursome advanced as best they could through the cloying crush of people to the set of double doors that gave onto the street.

"I say," Sir Richard began as they, at last, made their way to the marble steps outdoors, "do you suppose the Prince has already left? Perhaps if he is still abroad, I might . . ." His dark head jerked this way and that in search of the royal party.

Beside him, Ivy tittered. "I expect you will meet His Royal Highness at the soirée, Richard."

"Or, perhaps a jot sooner," General Huntley tossed over one shoulder.

"Do you see him?"

Eliza managed a laugh. "No, Papa. I believe Huntley was referring to the fact that the Regent said he had a number of important ideas to impart to me regarding the Grand Fete."

"Blast."

As the four of them reached the flagway to await the arrival of their carriage, a rush of awestruck theatergoers clustered about them, some being so bold as to actually address Eliza.

"Miss Foxburn, I am Lady Brownlow, and this is my husband, Lord Brownlow. Our son Jeremy was injured in the Battle of Salamanca in Spain. Fortunately he has recovered nicely and is now married to the former Lady Alice Ryder. We attended a rout held at Carlton House in '09," she added imperially.

Eliza had no sooner smiled a reply at the forward Lady Brownlow when she was accosted by a quartet of elegantly attired matrons.

"I am Lady Carlisle, Miss Foxburn. How do you do, Sir Richard?" The woman glanced beyond Eliza's silk-clad shoulder to address her father, then her eyes darted straight back to Eliza. "Your mother and I were very well acquainted with one another, Miss Foxburn, both of us being members of the Society to Benefit Runaway Girls and Orphans. I should like you to take tea with me tomor—"

"Do let the rest of us speak to her!" exclaimed one of Lady Carlisle's companions. "I am Lady Fitzwilliam, Miss Foxburn. Both of my sons served in the Royal Army. One endured a harsh winter in Russia and only just made it home with both limbs intact. Robert is quite acti—"

"And I am—" began another, but before she could get another word said, was interrupted by a shrill voice exclaiming, "Eliza, my dear!"

Eliza turned and found herself engulfed by a crushing embrace from Lady Villiers.

"Confidante to the Prince!" Lady Villiers gushed. "My dear girl!" She turned to address no one in particular. "Miss Foxburn and I are long-standing friends; she and our daughter Jane are bosom bows! Eliza, my dear, I will expect you at teatime tomorrow. We've a great deal to discuss—"

"But, she has promised to take tea with *me!*" exclaimed Lady Carlisle.

Suddenly, even Lady Villiers was roughly shoved aside by another crush of fashionably gowned and turbaned matrons. One of them had actually snatched up Eliza's gloved hand and seemed about to pull her into their midst when Eliza's tall companion, General Huntley, intervened.

"You will excuse us now. Miss Foxburn's carriage has arrived." He placed a protective arm about Eliza's trembling shoulders and guided the frightened young lady toward the large black coach with the royal coat of arms plainly visible on the side-door panel.

"Thank you, sir," she breathed.

"Not at all, my dear."

When the Foxburn party was, at last, safely ensconced inside the impressive equipage, and it had shot off into the night, Eliza turned a troubled gaze on General Huntley.

"How shall I endure it, sir?"

"You will manage," the great man replied confidently.

"You are famous!" Ivy intoned, high admiration evident in her tone.

"Blast," Sir Richard mumbled. "Never once caught sight of the Prince . . . or Wellington."

CHAPTER 13

"THE INCOMPARABLE MISS FOXBURN"

Though she felt positively dreadful over the unexpected turn, Eliza knew she had no choice but to see the dastardly business through to the end. Of course, all hope of the party accomplishing what she'd originally intended was lost forever. Amid the enormous gathering that would be present at Carlton House, Ivy would, no doubt, cling so tenaciously to her escort's arm that presenting her to other young men would prove all but impossible. Considering what had transpired on the flagway outside the theater, Eliza expected, that she, too, would elect to use General Huntley's presence at the fete as a protective shield.

For a week following that fateful night at the theater, Eliza's life became a feverish whirl of activity. She was twice summoned to St. James's Palace to meet with Lady Hertford and the Prince; and once took a turn about Hyde Park with the pair of them in the Prince's yellow chariot with the purple blinds. Eliza found HRH to be a clever man, and, despite Lady Hertford's extreme vanity over being the Regent's current *confidante,* she found she also rather liked the haughty marchioness.

In no time at all the three of them had drawn up exceedingly elaborate plans for the party, which, because it was now to be financed by the Prince, was being heralded amongst the *ton* as the Event of the Year. When word leaked out that the guest list had not yet been finalized, *everyone* clamored to be invited.

The front-door knocker of the Foxburn town house sounded incessantly. Long before teatime every day, the silver salver in the foyer became a veritable mountain of cards, most with the corners turned down. Briggs was in a constant state of turmoil, consuming two and even three bottles of McCutcheon's Tonic before dinner each evening.

"Got so a man don't have a minute to hisself these days," he bitterly complained.

The constant clatter of carriages on the cobblestones in front of the house was enough to chase Sailor completely from the grounds. Eliza hadn't seen her pet in days, and Briggs hadn't the time to go looking for him. Though Eliza was quite distraught over Sailor's disappearance, she saw no way to remedy the matter, nor would there have been time to do anything in the event a solution had sprung to mind.

Because of the increasing demands on Eliza to receive the many visitors who called daily—and every last one of them wanting the selfsame thing, to be assured of receiving a gilt-edged invitation to the Carlton House Fete—she was finally forced to issue an edict to Briggs to the effect that she would be "at home" only between half past two and four of the clock each afternoon, provided, of course, that she was indeed at home.

Lady Villiers was adamant in her demand that Eliza take tea with her and Jane, twice, and then set to boasting to her friends that the Incomparable Miss Foxburn was a frequent visitor in her home.

Because Jane had now completely recovered from her bout of the sniffles, and was as eager as the rest of the *ton* to be invited to the fete, Lady Villiers decided to postpone the Paris trip indefinitely.

"Who knows," she exclaimed gaily, "we may not have to go to Paris at all! With Jane likely to meet every eligible *parti* that exists right here in London, what would be the point?"

Eliza could think of any number of points and all of them in favor of making the trip! In fact, by week's end, had someone offered her a farthing to do so, she'd have foregone the Grand Fete entirely and happily jumped the ditch right then! Yet, every time she felt so inclined, she endeavored to remind herself of General Huntley's quiet admonition delivered that ill-fated night as the coach careened away from the theater, "You will manage," Huntley had said. And Eliza *wanted* to, if for no other reason than not to betray the sterling faith General Huntley had placed in her.

It was now close on a sennight since she'd last seen the dashing military man. Oh, he had called along with most of London . . . but she'd been away every single time, once at St. James's Palace, another time meeting with the principals of the firm Lady Hertford had hired to decorate the Gothic Conservatory at Carlton House, and yet another time at Lady Villiers's. There was so very much still to be done, Eliza wondered if she'd manage to accomplish everything before the Important Day arrived.

She was feeling especially frazzled one afternoon when Briggs rapped at her door to announce yet another caller.

"A young lady to see you, Miss Eliza."

Eliza opened her chamber door the veriest crack and peeked out. "Who is it this time, Briggs?" she whispered. Friend, or foe, she almost added.

Holding the cream-colored card aloft, Briggs squinted at the decorative script. "A Miss Ivy Heathergill."

"Oh!" Eliza flung the door wide, before realizing that in spite of herself, the idea of visiting with Ivy just now quite appealed to her. Unlike so many of her new *ton* acquaintances, the sweet-tempered Ivy had not the least bit of artifice in her.

Ivy was pretty and clever and unassuming. She did not force herself upon others, or push to be included or accepted. Eliza firmly believed that had she not mentioned her party plans to Ivy *before* the Prince Regent burst into their box that night at the theater, that Ivy would have graciously accepted the fact that she was not to receive an invitation and there would be an end to it.

The smile of greeting on Eliza's lips was most sincere when she stepped into the drawing room where Miss Heathergill—looking quite fashionable this afternoon in a pretty walking gown of green-and-brown-checked merino—awaited her.

"How lovely to see you again, Ivy . . . please, do be seated. I've asked Mrs. Allen to prepare a nice tea for us. I do hope you will stay."

Ivy returned Eliza's pleasant smile. "Thank you, Eliza, but I shouldn't wish to impose. Your father has told me how very busy you've become of late."

Emitting a weary sigh, Eliza sank onto a sofa opposite her visitor. "I could never have managed without Lady Hertford's help," she admitted.

"Your father tells me you have seen the Prince above three or four times now, and he has yet to see him even once," Ivy added, a pretty tinkle of a laugh bubbling up from her throat.

"That is true," Eliza said, a grin again lifting the corners of her mouth. "The Prince is very kind. Despite what people say about him, he is quite distressed over the vast numbers of our young men who lost their lives in the war. That is what drew him to my idea of . . ." Suddenly, a sharp pang of guilt assailed Eliza. Unfortunately, since that infamous night at the theater, guilt had become a constant companion, though very often whilst in the company of the Prince Regent and Lady Hertford, or other prominent members of society, she was often able to ignore the nagging feeling, so caught up in the so-called "altruism" of her idea to honor Britain's young soldiers did she become. But in her own drawing room, gazing into the trusting countenance of Miss Ivy Heathergill, who was so very unaware of the part *she* played in the drama, Eliza could not thrust aside the wretched emotion.

"Oh, Ivy . . ." As hot, stinging tears swam before her eyes, Eliza's voice dissolved into a wrenching sob.

Ivy sprang from her chair and was beside the younger girl in an instant. "Do tell me what is troubling you, Eliza, dear." She slipped an arm about Eliza's small shoulders in an attempt to console her. "I fear you must have been working far too hard. This is too great an undertaking for one small girl to manage alone. Despite Lady Hertford's help." She pulled a distraught Eliza into her arms and murmured, "There, there."

Eliza sniffed back her scalding tears and tried to collect herself. "I-I am being silly," she murmured.

"You are not being silly!" Ivy drew a scrap of linen from her pocket and pressed it into Eliza's trembling fingers. "The Prince is expecting far too much of you! Your plan to host a simple party in your own drawing room has gotten quite out of hand. It was not what you intended at the outset at all!"

Eliza gulped back a sudden fierce urge to tell Ivy everything! All of it. Even the part about hoping to lure her away from Papa. But, no! She couldn't do that. Ivy must never know what really lay behind this taradiddle.

"You are right," she said instead. "I am overtired. I did not sleep well last night." That was not a lie. She hadn't slept well in weeks, and very little of the blame for that could be laid at the Prince's doorstep. Every last whit of this bumblebroth was Eliza's own doing, and well she knew it! She worked to collect herself, but was only moderately successful.

"I have brought you something that might cheer you up," Ivy announced suddenly. She sprang to her feet and darted to the chair where she'd dropped her cloak and snatched up a small parcel from beneath the folds of it.

Smiling sweetly, she handed the package to Eliza, who, completely dry-eyed now, turned back the tissue paper and found a pretty new pair of limerick gloves edged with a flounce of delicate lace that Ivy had made herself. "Oh!"

"I have been making these up to sell at the bazaar when it opens next week," Ivy said. "I wanted you to be the first young lady in your set to own a pair."

"They are exquisite, Ivy!" Eliza blinked away the final droplet of moisture clinging to her lashes. "Thank you so very much. I am certain every one who sees them will want a pair. I promise to direct them all to the bazaar."

A troubled look flitted across Ivy's pretty face. "Oh, I didn't mean—"

"It is all right," Eliza said hastily. "You offered to do up a pair for me long before *I* became fashionable." She was unaware of the note of derision that colored her tone.

"Has it been so very dreadful for you?" Ivy asked, a look of genuine sympathy on her face. She slipped again onto the sofa beside Eliza.

Eliza's lips thinned as she looked away. It was a long moment before she could voice the thought uppermost in her mind. "The worst of it is"—she felt a fresh sob rise in her throat—"I-I've not seen Huntley even once since that night. And I . . . I miss him *dreadfully!*"

"I am so very sorry, Eliza. I don't know what I should do if I were unable to see your father," Ivy intoned.

But Eliza didn't hear her. She was too caught up in the

mix and stir of painful emotions that weighed like granite upon her own shoulders.

During the following week, Eliza accepted invitations to two routs and a musical evening, not because she particularly wished to attend the social gatherings, but because she hoped General Huntley might be there. She had begun to feel as if she might burst if she did not see the gentleman soon. She longed to speak with him . . . and if not speak with him, then just to *look* at him.

At first, it had alarmed her that she missed the older man so very greatly, missed their little talks and the safe feeling she experienced when she was with him. But it did not alarm her now. Why would she *not* miss him? He was a wonderful man, and she enjoyed his company immensely. She'd met several young men in the past weeks who'd taken to calling on her, but not a one of them could compare in any way to the dashing military man. Next to him, they appeared insipid and dull. They'd accomplished nothing of import in their young lives and consequently had nothing of import to converse about. Eliza found their talk of gaming and horses and the routs they'd attended quite boring. And, of course, they, too, badgered her about receiving one of the coveted invitations to the Carlton House Fete.

By the end of the following week, her longing to see General Huntley had escalated to such a degree that when she was not being put upon by demanding members of the *ton,* or seeing to minute details of the party, she seemed unable to think of anything save Huntley. Thoughts of him kept her awake at night, and when she did drift off, his handsome face invaded her dreams.

Over and over again in her mind, she relived the few delightful moments she'd spent in his company, beginning with the night they'd acted out the charade in Lady Hamilton's drawing room, when he'd drawn her into his arms,

and the delicious tingling sensation that had assailed her
then. Only now . . . now that she felt she truly *knew* the
gentleman, had talked with him, had shared a laugh with
him; now that she *knew* what a kind and caring and
thoughtful man he was, and how very, very wise he was . . .
the tingly sensation seemed to intensify. She'd never felt
such a *yearning* to see anyone before in her life!

She was especially eager to see him now . . . now that
the little plan *they'd* hatched together for a simple party
in the Foxburn drawing room had become a full-scale
extravaganza that involved the Prince Regent and nearly
everyone of consequence amongst London's upper ten
thousand. She needed *his* strength, *his* guidance, *his* wise
counsel. She needed him to tell her how to go on and to
hear again his pronouncement of faith in her that she
could.

Papa was certainly no help in that quarter. All he could
think of these days was how very much *he* wished to meet
the Regent, that and his silly electrifying machine. Papa'd
got it into his head that once word got out that he'd
invented the clever device, the Prince Regent *and* Wellington and all manner of Important Personages would seek
him out!

"The ramifications of such a device are endless, Eliza,"
he told his daughter one day over luncheon. "Electrical
charges to the body have been known to have extraordinary
healing effects . . . why, it's said electrical impulses can
even make hair grow."

His lively blue eyes darted to Briggs's bald pate as the
stodgy retainer reached for a remove at the far end of
the table. Catching his employer's gaze on him, Briggs
"harrumphed" and shuffled from the room in haste, as
hastily, that is, as one who shuffles can.

"What do you say, Eliza?" Sir Richard turned again to
his daughter, who thus far, hadn't said a word. "Did you
hear me, sweetheart? I was saying that—"

"I heard you, Papa." She hadn't responded because she

already had far too much on her mind. She only hoped that before he was through experimenting with his electrifying machine, he didn't accidentally kill someone!

"It occurred to me the Prince might find a demonstration fascinating," Sir Richard remarked. He put a heaping fork full of new potatoes and green peas into his mouth, then reached for the large glass of ale before his plate to wash down the vegetables.

When no answer seemed forthcoming from Eliza, he added, "If you were to tell him about my invention, sweetheart, perhaps he'd request to see it. I've given Huntley leave to tell Wellington."

Eliza's ears perked up. "You have seen General Huntley?"

"Indeed. At Tattersall's yesterday." Sir Richard cut off a bite from the thick slice of roast beef on his plate. "And again last night at Boodles."

"Did he . . . ask about me?"

Her father chewed up his food. "Said he hadn't seen you in a spell." His brow furrowed. "Haven't had a spat, have you?"

Eliza shook her head. "No. I've just been . . . busy." Her lashes fluttered downward, and she again fell into a moody silence.

A moment later, her father said, "Well, will you tell him?"

Eliza didn't even glance up. "Tell who what, Papa?"

"The Prince! Blast, Eliza. I've yet to meet His Royal Highness, or Wellington! Dammit, I insist you tell the Prince about my electrifying machine. I am certain he will find it as amusing as Heathergill and I do!"

Eliza's lips thinned. Since that fatal night at the theater, it seemed every last person she came in contact with wanted her to tell the Prince something. Either about a son or a brother, or a cousin who'd served valiantly in the war, or . . . or any number of things. One Lady Somebody-or-other had actually insisted that Eliza tell the Prince her son deserved to be *knighted* for his deeds of valor!

Of late, the only person who *hadn't* wanted something from Eliza was Ivy Heathergill! Eliza's visit with Ivy had been quite refreshing. Although she still did not believe Ivy and her father were suited for one another as man and wife, she quite admired Ivy's lack of pretense and her, well, her . . . her *normalcy*.

"We could make a party of it," her father began again. "The Prince, Wellington, Huntley, and myself. Would be quite entertaining. You'll tell him, won't you, Eliza?"

Eliza exhaled a frustrated breath. "Yes, Papa. I'll tell him."

Because Eliza'd not yet made the obligatory calls that society dictated she make after attending functions hosted by members of the nobility, she added two more calls to her long list of stops to be made that afternoon. After leaving a card at Lady Brownlow's and one at Lady Wyndham's, thanking her for the lovely musical evening, she proceeded on to Lord and Lady Maitland's lovely home located just beyond Mayfair.

Despite the fact that good breeding demanded it of her, she was quite weary of traipsing about the city day after day, and smiling 'til her cheeks actually ached! At Lady Maitland's, however, while sipping listlessly from the fourth or fifth cup of tea she'd already been offered that day, it struck her that her father's idea to demonstrate his electrifying machine was not entirely without merit.

Not that she had any intention of mentioning the device to the Prince Regent—or that HRH would accept an invitation to their home to behold the wonder if he did know of it—but a simple dinner party that included certain others of their friends would not be amiss. Lord and Lady

Hamilton, who were always on the lookout for new and amusing ways to entertain their guests would surely come, and she could invite Lord and Lady Villiers, and Jane. And, the Heathergills.

And General Huntley.

It was a splendid idea!

Eliza had not felt so uplifted in days.

Not only was her father delighted when she told him of her plan to host a small dinner party where he might demonstrate his new toy for their guests—and yes, she again promised she *would* mention the wonder to the Prince the very next time she saw him—Eliza was thrilled when her invitation to General Huntley netted a prompt reply, in the affirmative!

Because she just plain enjoyed Ivy Heathergill's company, and because Ivy was the only one of her friends who truly *understood* how she felt about the elderly general, Eliza decided to send a note to Ivy soliciting her help with the preparations for the small "do." Ivy was especially pleased to be asked, and the two girls spent a long afternoon thusly occupied.

When the designated evening rolled around, Lord and Lady Villiers, and Jane, were the first to arrive, followed almost at once by Lord and Lady Hamilton. And then the Heathergills, whose consequence, Eliza had duly noted, had been substantially elevated by the fact that Ivy had had the good fortune to be presented to the Prince.

Ivy had confided to Eliza the afternoon they spent together that since that infamous night at the theater, she'd received upward of half a dozen invitations to one society event or other, and that she and her mother had been kept quite busy with a steady stream of callers.

"I confess, the bulk of them merely wish to quiz me about you," Ivy told Eliza, with a grin. "I expect they believe I might be influential in persuading you to issue them an invitation to the Grand Fete."

Eliza told Ivy that quite a number of people she'd met had remarked upon Ivy's beauty. And, it was true. They had. Both girls marveled over how one single event in one's life could so quickly alter it.

As Briggs exited the drawing room that night to answer one last summons at the front door of the Foxburn town house, Eliza, who was seated on a small settee beside Jane, anxiously glanced up. The only guest who had not yet appeared was General Huntley.

Even as she heard the familiar deep rumble of the gentleman's voice coming from the foyer, she was obliged to turn her attention to Lady Villiers, as that woman had only just addressed her.

"I daresay you have become quite the social butterfly, Eliza! Jane quite envies your success."

"I do nothing of the sort, Mama," Jane protested.

"Has the final number to be invited to the Grand Fete been tallied yet, Eliza, dear?" Lady Hamilton asked, with high interest.

"At last count, the number was near two thousand."

"My stars!" Lady Villiers cried.

"The most are young men," Eliza added. "The Prince sent 'round several lists for Lady Hertford and me to review. I confess, settling on whom to invite and whom to . . . leave out has been quite a daunting task."

"Well," said Lady Hamilton, with a laugh, "so long as our names are not overlooked!"

"Indeed!" added Lady Villiers, also laughing gaily.

"Your names were at the top of my list," Eliza assured them each again.

She cast another anxious glance toward the drawing-room door. *What was keeping Huntley,* she wondered?

Just then, Briggs's stooped form appeared, and, catching Eliza's eye, he headed toward her. She rose to her feet and met the elderly man midway across the carpeted expanse. "Is something amiss, Briggs?"

"Your gentleman caller is asking for ye, Miss. In the foyer."

"Thank you, Briggs."

Her heart thundering in her breast, Eliza hurried past the butler on her way to the foyer. *What on earth can be the trouble now, she wondered?*

CHAPTER 14

"A SHOCKING EVENING"

General March Huntley had been exceedingly pleased to receive the hand-lettered card from Miss Eliza Foxburn inviting him to dine at the Foxburn town house and to view a new gadget or other that Sir Richard Foxburn had lately been tinkering with. March didn't care a flip about Richard's latest invention, but he was delighted for the opportunity to visit once more with his old friend's lovely daughter.

Since he'd last seen Miss Foxburn, he knew she had been excessively busy with the myriad details dictated by the Regent in regard to the Carlton House Fete. He felt a bit guilty that he hadn't been able to forewarn the young lady that the Prince had got wind of her party idea before the Regent himself burst into their box that night at the theater. When Wellington questioned Huntley about the soirée the day after he and Eliza met up with him in the park, Huntley hadn't the least notion then that the Duke meant to bring the matter to the attention of the Prince. If he'd had any inkling what was to transpire, he'd have called a halt to the proceedings straightaway.

Miss Foxburn's impromptu idea had since grown to gargantuan proportions, with every noncom officer and foot soldier in London a-twitter over the Palace's plan to recognize them. And such elaborate plans they were, too!

During the past fortnight, Huntley had heard any number of accounts of what the Prince meant to do, from bestowing honors and medals in a special ceremony to personally conducting interviews with every last soldier present. Though considering the vast number that would be there, Huntley could not imagine how the Prince, or anyone, could accomplish that!

As a result of the wild rumors that were circulating, Huntley had purposely put a wide berth between himself and Miss Eliza Foxburn. Firstly, because it alarmed him to realize how very attached he was becoming to the spirited little minx. Secondly, because he thought it high time the imaginative young lady realized what serious consequences could result when one failed to consider one's words before one spoke!

He knew that, in truth, Richard's sweet daughter was all that was good and proper. He greatly admired her fierce loyalty to her father and did not fault her genuine desire to protect him from himself. But he still felt the young lady needed to learn that certain matters—especially ones that involved persons a good deal older and wiser than herself—were essentially none of her affair. For instance, the fact that her father loved Miss Ivy Heathergill and wished to marry the girl was, in truth, none of Eliza's concern. Another name for trying to force the outcome of events to one's own liking was . . . meddling.

And March Huntley had no desire to marry a meddlesome woman. Harmony in marriage was difficult enough to maintain without stacking the deck against oneself by marrying a managing female.

Standing now in the foyer of the Foxburn town house, waiting for the charming young lady to come and greet him, Huntley silenced his ruminations and shifted the somewhat squirmy item he carried tucked under one arm but shielded from view by his cape.

Catching sight of the warm smile on Eliza's pretty face, he felt his pulse quicken. "Good evening, Miss Foxburn." His lips curved upward in response. "A pleasure to see you again."

"Thank you, sir. Briggs tells me you wished to—"

Suddenly, as if announcing *its* presence, the item concealed by Huntley's cape poked one fuzzy paw through a convenient opening.

Me-ow . . . Me-ow!

"Oh!" Eliza's sapphire blue orbs widened with surprise. "You've found Sailor!"

Tossing aside the folds of his wrap, Huntley gently deposited the soft bundle of fur into Eliza's outstretched arms. "I believe it more apt to say that Sailor found me," he replied.

Hugging her beloved pet to her cheek, Eliza cried, "Where have you been, you naughty boy?"

Because Briggs had not yet returned to his post, Huntley himself took care of the business of draping his cape over a chair and hanging his hat upon a peg beside the door.

"I recently acquired lodgings near here," he told Eliza, who was now lovingly stroking Sailor's backside and being rewarded with quite audible purring noises. "One day I arrived home and found this little chap, looking quite pleased with himself, awaiting me on my doorstep."

Eliza laughed. "I imagine he was quite proud of having found you all on his own.'

"Perhaps." His lips twitching, Huntley reached to also scratch Sailor's ears.

"It has been quite frantic here, of late," Eliza remarked. "I expect poor Sailor grew weary of the constant interruptions to his cozy naps on our doorstep." She addressed the cat in her arms. "Promise me you shan't run away from home again, Sailor-boy!' "

She glanced up at Huntley. "He doesn't look too awfully ill treated, or hungry."

"I daresay he is quite adept at fending for himself," Huntley replied with a grin. "Although he did not refuse the daily scraps of fish and chicken I set out for him."

"Thank you for looking after him." Eliza gingerly set the cat down on all fours, and Sailor, with his tail at a jaunty tilt, promptly trotted off toward the kitchen, where the delicious smells of the dinner soon to be served to the humans apparently smelled quite tempting to him, as well.

Eliza turned a charming smile on Huntley. "I am glad to have him home again. Now I shall know where to look for him the next time he disappears."

They moved down the corridor together and into the drawing room, whereupon everyone looked up and cordially greeted the general. Moments later, Mrs. Allen announced that dinner was on the table.

Eliza had dearly wished to place General Huntley's name card next to hers for the meal, but because she wished also to keep Ivy and her father apart, she'd thought it best to mix up all the couples present.

Consequently, for her—seated between Lord Villiers and Jane, with Huntley quite a distance away next to her father at the head of the table—the dinner hour seemed to drag on interminably.

As was common in mixed company at such gatherings, the gentlemen at the table turned to discussing what was of primary interest to them instead of deferring to, or joining in, conversations initiated by their feminine counterparts.

This evening, the *only* subject being addressed by the ladies was the Grand Fete. Both Lady Villiers and Lady Hamilton fired a barrage of questions at Eliza regarding it, wanting to know everything from the size of the orchestra, to what would be served at supper, to what theme the decorations were to depict. Despite the fact that Eliza wished to discuss anything *but* the party, and that she would much prefer to be conversing exclusively with General Huntley, she tried her best to answer all of the questions put to her, knowing full well that by tomorrow every word she'd said tonight would be bruited about in drawing rooms all over London.

At length, the gentlemen were also drawn into the conversation, but it was General Huntley who eventually summed it up best.

"I believe Miss Foxburn's idea to honor England's brave soldiers is long overdue. It has been my experience that the muster-roll of fame following an important battle always closes *before* the rank of captain. If a lieutenant, ensign, sergeant, or private has distinguished himself for bravery or valor, the young man's deeds seem never to be brought to the attention of the nation. The sovereign and the country ought to know who it is who really fights the great battles of the war."

A moment of near-stunned silence followed Huntley's frank remark. For a military officer to deflect *any* honor or glory to a soldier of lesser rank than himself was quite rare, indeed.

"Very well put, Huntley!" Sir Richard finally enthused. "Well put, indeed." He lifted his glass in a toast.

After it had been drunk, Huntley turned an intent gaze upon Eliza. "And to Miss Foxburn, whose indomitable spirit in forwarding this oh! so noble cause is to be applauded."

Though Eliza beamed with pleasure beneath Huntley's admiration, his kind words were still not enough to dislodge the familiar burden of guilt that had served for weeks to keep her spirits low. *How she yearned to consult privately with him now about her feelings!* She determined to look for a moment this very evening in which to draw him aside for a private coze.

Following the meal, the small companionable group retreated once more to the drawing room. Eliza instructed Briggs to bring in fresh pots of tea and coffee for the ladies and glasses of her father's best aged port for the gentlemen. During dinner, a pair of footmen had set up Sir Richard's electrifying machine in readiness for the demonstration.

After he and Mr. Heathergill made a few final adjustments to the fair-sized apparatus, comprised of a large metal cylinder with a crank-type handle and a complicated series of coils and wires fastened to a flat wooden stand, the men, looking quite pleased with themselves, were ready to proceed.

Sir Richard clapped his hands together in order to arrest everyone's attention, then invited the ladies to seat themselves upon the straight-backed chairs one of the footmen had thoughtfully drawn up for that purpose. The men, eyeing the strange gadget with varying degrees of interest, had already drawn close and stood hovering over it.

Ivy Heathergill slipped onto a chair beside Eliza. "Richard is quite ingenious," she announced proudly.

Eliza cast a wary glance at her new friend. "I do hope he does not catch the house afire."

Ivy laughed. "It is quite safe, really. The sparks are very pretty."

"Sparks?" Eliza's worried gaze flew from her smiling companion to her father. "Papa, you assured me the thing would not catch fire, and now Ivy tells me it gives off sparks!"

"Sparks!" exclaimed Lady Hamilton with rising interest. She moved to stand beside her husband, who, with quizzing glass in hand, was quite intently inspecting the curiosity.

"Apart from 'sparking,'" Lord Hamilton inquired, "what else does it do, old man?"

Ignoring his daughter's beleaguered plea, Sir Richard launched into an explanation. "It emits electrical impulses of quite low power, harmless really, though it's said they can be beneficial to the human body."

"Electrical impulses?" mused Lady Villiers.

"Indeed," replied Mr. Heathergill, nodding. He was a short, rather paunchy-looking man in his early fifties, whose carriage and bearing was not the least unlike that of the titled gentlemen present. "The shock can be compared to the sort of 'jolt' one receives after walking across a woolen carpet and upon reaching to touch another, feels a bit of a start. The friction generated by the movement across the carpet creates a power known as 'electricity.' "

Sir Richard took it up again. "One person is the conductor of the charge, and the other person—"

Lady Villiers began to titter. "My stars, Richard, do be still! Not a one of us is clever enough to understand the inner workings of the thing! Scientific mumbo jumbo is far too complicated for the likes of me!"

"I quite agree, Isobel," Lady Hamilton chimed in. "I, for one, simply wish to see the sparks. Are the colors quite brilliant?" she asked Ivy.

Ivy had no chance to reply, as Sir Richard began again to speak. "Very well, we shall get right to it. I should like everyone to join hands and form a semicircle . . . just so," he directed, as they all stood and arranged themselves into a crescent shape.

"Now, then. I shall turn the crank thusly, and when sufficient power is generated—"

"Wait!" cried Jane, who was positioned first in line. "I've no desire to receive the bulk of the jolt. Father, do change places with me!"

Several others decided to switch places, which quite pleased Eliza, for when all was said and done, she ended up holding hands with Huntley, who now stood last in line.

Once again, Sir Richard grasped the crank and began to turn it, slowly at first, then faster and faster.

Suddenly, Lord Villiers exclaimed, "By Jove!"

As the charge of electricity skittered up and down the arms of each participant in the half-moon, each person in turn registered awareness of it.

No one had noticed that Eliza's gray-and-white cat had ambled nonchalantly into the room or that a split second before the jolt reached Huntley, Sailor had commenced to rub his head and ears against the gentleman's trouser leg. But, not a single person missed the earsplitting caterwaul that Sailor let out when the electrical charge shot straight through his small body!

With lightening speed, the cat, whose fur was standing on end, bolted across the room just as Briggs was shuffling into it, balancing a heavy tray laden with the pots of steaming hot coffee and tea, and five glasses brimful of Sir Richard's finest blood red port.

"Briggs! Look out!" cried Eliza.

But the warning came too late.

Sailor had already hurled himself clean into the butler's legs. On impact, Briggs simultaneously pitched forward and appeared to toss the contents of the tray up, up, up into the air. Boiling hot coffee and black Irish tea intermingled with splashes of bright red wine, bone china cups and sparkling crystal came raining down upon the hapless butler's head.

The whole mish-mash soiled not only his crisp white shirt front but pooled and stained the freshly cleaned Aubusson carpet on the floor.

Both Huntley and Eliza made a mad dash in that direction, Huntley lending the dazed butler a hand, Eliza skirting past the men on her way after the cat.

Before she'd caught up to the still-mewling Sailor, she encountered a wide-eyed Mrs. Allen, two housemaids, and a near brace of footmen, who'd all heard the crash and come running to see what was amiss.

"Fetch a mop and some damp rags, Mrs. Allen, and put another pot of coffee on to boil!" Eliza cried, as she streaked past them.

She captured the frightened cat just as he was escaping through a door at the far end of the corridor that very often stood ajar, allowing a cool breeze to waft into the kitchen and stale cooking odors to escape.

"Sailor!" Eliza fell to her knees and scooped up her pet. "Did Papa's old electrifying machine scare you to

pieces?" She set to smoothing the cat's still-crackling fur.
"There, there, sweet kitty," she purred. "I shan't let anyone hurt you ever again."

She continued to stroke Sailor's disheveled backside, 'til
she'd once again coaxed contented purrs from his throat.

Some moments later, she heard footfalls behind her.
"How is the little chap?" inquired General Huntley, genuine concern evident in his rich baritone.

Eliza glanced up, the fretful look still furrowing her
brow. "He's never been so ill treated before! I am certain
he meant to leave home this time and never come back!"

Huntley knelt beside Eliza and began affectionately to
scratch Sailor's ears and head. "He appears to have recovered nicely. Perhaps he has changed his mind about
leaving."

"I do hope so." She glanced up. "How is Briggs?"

"Took quite a spill. Your father offered him a glass of
port."

Eliza grinned. "He'd best offer him the whole bottle.
Briggs has taken to his bed over less than this."

Huntley laughed. "I daresay a lively sense of humor is
an essential requirement for anyone living in this house."

Eliza turned a quizzical look on the older man. It pleased
her to note that his full lips were twitching. "I fear it is
very often akin to bedlam around here," she added with
a laugh.

In the dimly lit hallway, Huntley turned to meet and
hold Eliza's gaze. "I find the Foxburn household . . .
delightful," he replied sincerely.

Throughout the long pause that ensued, Huntley and
Eliza's gazes remained locked. Not until Sailor squirmed
from Eliza's loosened grasp did the significant moment
end.

"Oh, no! He's gone again!" Eliza darted into the garden
after the cat.

Huntley followed her.

But, in the small square of moonlit-splashed garden

behind the tall house, they could both see that the cat did not intend running away this time. Casting a backward glance at his mistress, Sailor merely scampered to a grassy spot, where he promptly lay down and rolled lazily onto his back.

Eliza drew in a relieved breath . . . and wondered if she and General Huntley ought not to return to the drawing room?

As if reading her thoughts, Huntley murmured, "Considering the commotion indoors, I expect we've time for a short stroll before we are missed."

Eliza's heart began to thump wildly in her breast. She'd wished for a few moments alone with the general, but . . . to be *this* alone with him was not quite what she'd envisioned. She'd never before taken a stroll with a gentleman in the garden on a moonlit night, or on any other night, for that matter.

As they silently stepped onto the cool flagway that encircled the pretty yard, she wondered if the dashing military man would take her arm.

He did.

As each step drew them farther and farther from the house and deeper and deeper into the shadowy thicket of shrubs and trees and close-clipped hedges that lined their little plot of land, she wondered if he were feeling the selfsame breathless anxiety she was?

He was.

Huntley wasn't quite sure why he'd suggested they steal away from the others just then. Miss Eliza Foxburn wasn't the sort of woman a man lured into dark corners and stole kisses from. She was . . . he turned a sidelong look on the innocent beauty walking so quietly and trustingly by his side . . . she was the sweetest, the most adorable young lady he'd ever met.

And, he heartily suspected he was falling hopelessly in love with her.

These last weeks with her, he'd discovered a quality to

his life he'd never known before. He'd grown up believing that order and adherence to principle were essential to success. It was, after all, the military way. But order precluded spontaneity and bursts of sunshine and pure joy, all of which Miss Eliza Foxburn's youth and innocence had unwittingly brought into his life.

Her fresh outlook made the most ordinary of events fun, the simplest of pleasures special. *She* was special. She was sweet and adorable and precious, and since she'd come into his life, he'd thought of little else but her.

Before Eliza, his life had been discipline and rules and schedules. He'd known exactly what to expect each and every minute of each and every day. Even during wartime, in the midst of a raging battle, there were few surprises. But not with Eliza. With her, none of the rules applied. Her spontaneous laughter and antics were making mice-feet of his hard-and-fast rules and regulations. She was a woodland sprite whose sparkling sapphire blue eyes kept him awake at night and led his thoughts on a merry chase during the day.

Though he did not know quite how to accomplish it, he knew now he wished to make her his bride. He wished to love her, to cherish her, to spoil her shamelessly, and, above all else, to keep her smiling and happy for the rest of her days.

After he'd succeeded in his quest to win her, he would not let the rigors of everyday living, of bearing his children, of raising them and looking after him, destroy her. Eliza's bright light would not be snuffed out before her time, as his beautiful mother's had been. Eliza would stay young and lovely and vibrant forever. He would see to it.

But, first he had to see to winning her, to thinking up a scheme that would show her, once and forever, that *he* was the man of her dreams. Persistence and patience had won him innumerable battles in the war; perhaps the same qualities would lead him to victory now.

The sound of her soft voice penetrated his deep

thoughts. "I have been hoping for the opportunity to speak with you, sir," she said.

They were nearing the far corner of the moon-splashed garden that lay directly behind the tall, narrow house. Huntley spotted a stone bench beneath an elderberry tree and guided his charming companion toward it. There, the swash of moonlight was near as bright as day. Long shadows from a stand of evening primrose fell across the path and bench.

"Is something troubling you, my dear?" he asked gently.

Seated beside Huntley on the bench, Eliza fiddled with the folds of her long mulberry silk skirt that lay bunched in her lap. *"Everything* is wrong, sir. I confess I have felt quite wretched since the night the Prince burst into our box and . . . Oh!" She turned an appealing look upward. "I haven't the least clue what to do, Huntley! I can't tell Papa, or Ivy, the truth, although I feel I ought!"

Huntley nodded compassionately. "I daresay, for sheer topsy-turvydom, this taradiddle is unsurpassed."

Eliza sighed dejectedly. "It is not at all what I wished to happen."

Huntley could not suppress a small grin. "I recall you once pined for adventure and excitement, my dear. Appears you now have it in full measure."

Another frustrated sigh escaped Eliza. "But, what am I to *do?* I feel so . . . guilty about it. If the truth were known . . . if Ivy knew . . . or Papa . . ."

"I do not believe you can be faulted for what has come about, my dear. Even though you initially spoke without thinking, the Prince merely leapt upon what was, indeed, *your* idea at the outset. And it was a good one, with a great deal of merit to it. You cannot be faulted for that," he said again.

"But, I never meant to embroil anyone, least of all the *Prince,* in my silly little scheme," she moaned.

Huntley turned a gaze upon her. He reached to cup her chin and tilted it upward. "Are you admitting that your

plan to come between your father and Miss Heathergill
was ill conceived?''

She dropped her gaze. ''I admit I have come to care a
great deal for Ivy myself. She is a dear girl, not the least
bit set up in her own conceit, as . . . as so many others
are.'' She chewed fretfully on her lower lip. ''I quite enjoy
her company. She is clever and thoughtful, and . . . and I
believe she sincerely believes she loves Papa, but . . . oh,
I've such a tremendous lot to tell you!''

''It will have to wait.'' Huntley glanced toward the house.
''It is time I took you back.'' He stood and reached a hand
toward her.

When he felt her small fingers curl neatly 'round his,
something irresistible took hold of him, and, before he
knew what he was about, he'd slipped both arms around
her tiny waist and drawn her petite body close to his. As
one arm held her tight against him, his free hand stole
upward to cup the silky dark curls at the back of her head.

''Eliza . . .'' he breathed hoarsely.

''Oh, Huntley,'' she gasped. Standing on tiptoe, she
twined both arms up around his sturdy neck. ''I need
you . . .'' she began, but got no further.

His mouth came down hard on hers, and without meaning to, his tongue parted her soft lips and drove hungrily
into her mouth. In seconds, flames of white-hot passion
pulsed through his parched veins, and he felt his body
spring to life beneath her caresses. He'd never wanted a
woman so much in his life. He must have her!

But . . . no!

Of course, he could not take her. She was a child. She
had no idea what turmoil, or need, she was inspiring within
him. Struggling to regain himself, he grasped her by the
shoulders and pried her sweet form from his.

With ragged breath, he murmured, ''Forgive me. I
shouldn't have . . .'' His chest heaved as painful sparks of
pleasure continued to pulse through his body.

"But, March, I wished you to kiss me," she softly protested.

As smoldering passion darkened his gray eyes, he gazed into the innocent blue pools of hers and willed discipline and control once again to the forefront of his mind. "Nonetheless . . ." he said, "I shall not let it happen again."

Setting his jaw, he determinedly wrapped her fingers over the crook of his arm and forced his long legs into motion. "It is time we joined the others."

They walked a few steps in silence, then Eliza said, "You've not yet told me what to do, sir."

"About what, my dear?"

"About . . . the muddle I'm in!" she cried.

His chin held aloft, Huntley replied gravely, "For the nonce, I see nothing for it but to carry on as you have been." He paused, then added, "On a positive note, your little falsehood has already been turned to good account. Apart from drawing attention to those brave young soldiers whom no one has noticed, you are causing a great many people to be at ins with a great many others. Take Lady Villiers and the Heathergills, for instance. A fortnight ago, Lady Villiers would have refused to sit at the same table with a mere tradesman and his wife. And now the families are becoming fast friends."

Eliza turned a perplexed gaze upon her distinguished escort. "But, I did not think you condoned the idea of . . . mixing the classes, sir. Have you now changed face on that head?"

Huntley kept his eyes forward as he spoke. "An astute military man is willing to look at all sides of an issue if circumstances warrant it."

A moment later, Eliza said, "I am not at all certain I understand what you mean, sir."

"I mean, my dear, that in view of all that has happened, *you* have become quite a powerful young lady. Being presented to the Prince elevated Miss Heathergill's stature immeasurably, but the very fact that *you* are befriending her is ensuring that she will never be given the cut direct by anyone. Your friendship is in itself enough to render her acceptable in the eyes of the *ton*. You, my dear, have all the consequence necessary to bring Miss Ivy Heathergill, the young lady your father loves deeply, up to the mark.''

Eliza's lips thinned.

So . . . that's how it was now. During the past fortnight, whilst she'd been engaged with the myriad details for the upcoming Fete, her father had managed to twist General Huntley's opinion askew.

Huntley had allayed a bit of her guilt over the disastrous turn, but the knowledge that he'd suddenly decided her father *ought* to marry Ivy Heathergill was an outcome she hadn't counted on. And was an additional worry she scarcely needed. In fact, it was almost enough to make her wish she'd not allowed the handsome gentleman to kiss her.

Almost.

CHAPTER 15

"A NIGHT TO REMEMBER . . . BUT NOT BY ALL"

By eight of the clock on the designated evening, a solid bank of carriages extended from Carlton House all the way to the top of St. James's Street. By nine of the clock, carriages were packed in to the top of Bond Street, with the empty coaches being ranged in on St. James's Square.

Before the elegantly attired guests had even made their way to the balustrated portico of Carlton House, they were entertained with lively tunes from the full band of the Home Guards playing in the courtyard, regal in their state uniforms of red, blue, and gold.

At the entrance to the Great Hall, guests were required to present their official gilt-edged invitations before being admitted. They were then greeted by members of the royal family, the Dukes of Clarence and York, Sussex and Cambridge, and Ernest, the Duke of Cumberland, looking quite menacing with his eye patch, worn over the eye he'd lost in battle. Also in the receiving line were several sisters of the Prince, the Princesses Augusta and Elizabeth, and even the invalidish Princess Sophia, who'd become an especial favorite of Eliza's. Last in the receiving line were Lord and Lady Hertford and Miss Eliza Foxburn.

Her heart aflutter, Eliza had dressed with special care, donning her gorgeous new gown of white lace over a white-satin slip, the bottom of the skirt trimmed with a drapery of white lace entwined with pearls and full-blown roses above a *rouleau* of white satin. The Empire bodice and short puffed sleeves were of rose-colored satin, the sleeves slashed with white lace and both the scooped neckline and sleeves finished off with a scalloped edge of delicate white lace encrusted with pearls.

At her throat and ears, she wore a necklace and earrings of fine white pearls that had belonged to her mother, and just that evening, her father had presented her with a beautiful pearl bracelet to match, which she fastened over the wrist of her long white-kid gloves.

Eliza's shiny dark curls were artfully arranged in an upswept style with wispy tendrils fringing her brow and dangling over each ear. Nestled in amongst the curls bunched atop her head was an exquisite amethyst-and-diamond tiara, lent her by the Princess Sophia. Though Eliza was not a member of the royal family, dressed as she was tonight, she felt just as if she were.

She could hardly wait for General Huntley to see her. Since the night he'd kissed her in the garden, she'd thought of little else but him. She'd never been kissed before, and as she lay in bed at night, reliving the wondrous experience, she'd marveled that her reaction to Huntley's lips pressed to hers felt amazingly akin to the charge produced by Papa's electrifying machine. The kiss had actually sent tiny pinpricks of exquisite pleasure sparking all over her body! It was a most extraordinary sensation . . . and one Eliza fervently hoped would be repeated tonight.

From time to time, she'd wondered if she might be falling in love with the elderly gentleman, but always she pushed that thought from mind. It was not possible, she'd tell herself firmly. Her friendship with the general was . . . well, much like Ivy Heathergill's fanciful infatuation with Eliza's father. When she met the gentleman she was meant to marry, she'd forget all about General March Huntley. Until then, however, she had no objection to enjoying to the hilt her association with the famous man. For tonight, she was simply too caught up in the thrill, the excitement, the *importance* of this marvelous occasion to refine too seriously upon anything else.

Nearly every person who appeared before her on their way into the Great Hall of Carlton House had something wonderfully admiring to say to her: "My dear, Miss Fox-burn, you are a paragon! You have single-handedly set London on its ear!"

"What a marvelous career you have before you, my dear!"

"I would that my daughter could be more like you!"

"You simply must meet my son!"

Long before the full two thousand guests had passed before her, Eliza's ears fairly rang with the words of high praise being heaped upon her head.

"You are a stunning success, my dear," said the aristo-cratic Lady Hertford, a somewhat proprietary smile upon her lips. "I predict you will receive a dozen offers before the night is over."

Eliza smiled shyly. There was only one man she wished to impress tonight . . . and thus far, she hadn't even seen him. It already seemed like hours since Mr. and Mrs. Heath-ergill and Papa and Ivy had arrived. Where was Huntley?

When the line of arriving guests dwindled to a mere trickle, with still no sign of the great man, Eliza grew alarmed. When the receiving line broke up, she worked her way through the huge swarm of people still crowded onto the sweep of steps that led to the ground floor and hurried through the large hall that gave on to the Prince's library. Both the hall and library, with its massive oak book-cases in the Gothic style, were thronged with people, most curiously inspecting the Prince's priceless furnishings, complete with the Regent's badge—a plume of feathers; or his renowned collection of Dutch paintings, or the min-iature sculptures of triumphal arches displayed in buhl cabinets.

Hurriedly scanning the sea of faces as she made her way through the Golden Drawing Room, a curious combina-tion of Corinthian pillars and modern lacquered furniture, Eliza took little note of her surroundings, so intent was she upon locating the great general. When he was nowhere to be seen here, she raced into the heavily gilded Blue Velvet Room with its profusion of gold-leaf furnishings, and an immense blue-and-gold crystal chandelier.

Still in search of him, she entered the spacious dining chamber, the entire room a riot of crimson and gold, the plush Sheraton chairs and sofas lining the wall upholstered in blazing scarlet. The ceiling of this room was painted to resemble a summer sky, complete with puffy white clouds and a bird or two soaring amongst them. The Prince, always in the vanguard of fashion, had insisted that Holland paper the dining-room walls with patent yellow, the controversial new color made popular by Sir John Soan. Rush matting on the floor provided a stark contrast to the luxurious carpeting that graced the remainder of the royal home.

From the dining room, Eliza burst into the main archi-tectural glory of Carlton House, the Gothic Conservatory. The long, glassed-in rectangular hall was designed on the order of a cathedral, with a nave and two aisles on either side. An intricate tracery of delicate stained glass added dimension to the high, arched ceiling. The gold-filigreed Gothic lanterns hanging from the points of every arch cast a kaleidoscope of brilliant colors in all directions. In keeping with the military theme of tonight's occasion, the Union Jack and hundreds of other flags, displaying the insignia of various companies and batteries, fluttered everywhere.

Because supper would be served in the Conservatory to those guests specially invited to partake of the meal indoors, a two-hundred-foot-long table ran straight down the center of the room, set with the finest bone china and gleaming crystal the Royal Household had to offer. The table was decorated with festoons of flowers and even a silver fountain with a stream of water trickling from it, overlaid with golden brides and featuring live gold and silver fish.

Through the illuminated stained-glass windows of the Conservatory, Eliza could see onto the long, covered walkway that extended into the garden. Also decorated with flags, mirrors, and flowers, it, too, was thronged with people, many inspecting the tables set up in three additional walkways where the majority of tonight's guests would partake of the elaborate supper. An additional six thousand soldiers and their families had been invited to come to Carlton House the next day to view the decorations and to meet the Prince. Light refreshments would also be served to them.

Unable to catch even a glimpse of General Huntley, or of her father and Ivy, Eliza's anxiety grew as she rushed from room to room. The Golden Drawing Room was packed with people, but, unfortunately, there was no sign of the tall, distinguished military man.

Upon hearing the lilt of music rising above the deafening roar of hundreds of people laughing and talking at once, Eliza rushed to yet another chamber beyond the Conservatory and the Golden Drawing Room. Stepping into the noisy room, she surmised from the large clearing in the center of the highly polished parquet floor and the group of musicians seated on the dais, all producing lovely sounds from their wind instruments, which Eliza knew comprised the Prince's private band, that this was the dancing room, although it appeared the dancing had not yet begun.

Suddenly, a voice proclaimed, *"There she is!"*

Every head in the room turned toward Eliza, and every eye fixed upon her. Spontaneous applause broke out as the crowd of cheering persons surged forward and swept a somewhat startled Eliza to the empty expanse in the center of the room.

The band struck up a fanfare and from somewhere not seen by Eliza, another procession of people appeared and as the cheering accompanying *this* presence reached a crescendo, Eliza suddenly found herself standing face to face with the rotund Prince Regent himself, splendidly turned out tonight in an elaborate field marshal's uniform, said to be of his own design. Heavily decorated with bands of gold braid and gilt embroidery, and with a host of heavy medals and multicolored ribbons upon his broad chest, Eliza thought the scarlet coat alone must weigh at least a hundred pounds!

As the band launched into a French quadrille, the smiling Prince took one of Eliza's gloved hands and lifted it aloft. Led out for the first dance of the evening on the arm of HRH, the Prince of Wales, Eliza lost herself once again in the thrilling adventure of this magnificent evening.

When the dance concluded, the Prince thanked her most cordially for it, and for her part in making the soirée the huge success that it was. He then led her to the sidelines, where he was instantly swallowed up by a veritable crush of people who seemed intent upon pressing attendance upon the royal personage wherever he might be going.

Left once again alone and having not yet spotted General Huntley, or her father and Ivy, Eliza felt somewhat at loose ends. But, the feeling was short-lived. Almost at once, she was besieged with offers from scores and scores of young gentlemen, and some not-so-young ones, to dance, to partake of a glass of champagne, to take a stroll about the grounds, to take *them* on a stroll through the house, which it was erroneously assumed that Eliza was as well acquainted with as she was her own home.

Eliza danced and talked and smiled 'til her feet and head ached from sheer exhaustion. And still, she'd not laid eyes upon General Huntley.

Not until moments before supper, as she was returning from a necessary trip to the withdrawing room set aside especially for use by ladies, and crossed again through the Blue Velvet Room, did she spot Ivy Heathergill seated alone on a small gilded sofa.

A smile lit up Eliza's face as she hurried over. "Ivy have you seen Huntley?" she blurted out.

Ivy's expression brightened visibly as Eliza approached. "Eliza! How lovely you look! I fear I failed to remark upon your beautiful new gown and the lovely tiara when first we arrived. I confess I was breathless with excitement even to be here! Mama and Papa, too. They are the envy of all their friends!" she gushed. "Your father and I saw you dancing with the Prince. You looked positively splendid!"

"Have you seen General Huntley?" Eliza asked again.

"Huntley? Why, yes. He and Richard are . . ." She leant to see around the crush of people standing elbow to elbow in the gilded room. "There." She lifted a gloved finger. *"Where?"*

"In that far corner, next to the ebony statues and the porcelain vase."

Eliza craned her neck to see, and indeed, over the tops of heads and around silk-clad shoulders, she caught a glimpse of Huntley's dark head and the white wings of his hair feathering from his temples. She continued to stare in that direction and eventually spotted her father and the group of people—most of whom, she noted with an odd pang were *women*—clustered about the men.

She turned back to Ivy. And noted the somewhat morose look clouding her sea-green eyes.

"Appears your father is acquainted with a . . . great many ladies," Ivy said, a sad little smile twisting her lips.

"But surely you danced with Papa."

"Indeed." Ivy nodded. "Once. I also stood up with General Huntley."

A raging stab of envy shot through Eliza. "Huntley has been dancing?"

Ivy nodded again. "Near every dance. I only just . . . followed the men in here," she confessed sheepishly. "I . . . hardly know anyone. But, I have been enjoying myself immensely," she hastened to add, the lovely smile returning again to her pretty face. "I have never seen so many stunning gowns and exquisite jewels. And the gentlemen look positively divine in their court dress and military colors. Huntley looks especially handsome tonight. He is a very handsome man," she added firmly.

Anger pulsed through Eliza's veins. Huntley had been here *all* evening, and he had not *once* sought her out? Why? *Why?* She fought the urge to fight her way across the room and storm the crowd of women clustered about him and demand an explanation! He had *kissed* her, for pity's sake! Did that not count for something?

She fought for control as she murmured, "I do not recall greeting the general in the receiving line."

"Huntley told me as we danced that he and the Duke of Wellington and a number of other high-ranking officers were ushered in a side door and taken to the Prince's private quarters on the first floor."

"Oh." Eliza stood still gazing toward Huntley and her father. "Did Papa meet . . ."

"The Duke?" Ivy laughed, her honey brown curls shaking. "Not yet. I suspect that is why he is dogging Huntley's footsteps. Richard is quite determined to be presented to at least *one* of them tonight."

Eliza's lips thinned. "Well, I think it quite rude of them to abandon you!" *And, of Huntley to ignore me,* she added to herself. How dare he kiss her in the garden and pretend that she wasn't even here tonight! *How dare he?*

Suddenly her thoughts were interrupted by a resounding

gong that signaled the guests that it was time to assemble for supper. There was a mad dash for the Conservatory, and, caught up in the flow of people headed in that direction, Eliza again lost sight of her father and Huntley, and even of Ivy.

Eliza had seen to it that both her father and Ivy received the special invitations to dine with the Prince indoors. She, of course, along with Lord and Lady Hertford, and the royal dukes and princesses, would be seated quite near HRH. Because she expected that Huntley and the Duke of Wellington and others of the commanding officers would also be near the Prince, her hopes rose once more that she might be accorded the opportunity to exchange a few words with the great general.

A few words was all it was to be.

Her blue eyes peeled for the least glimpse of him, Eliza'd been seated for quite a spell when she felt a hand touch her shoulder and glanced up. Her pulse quickened when she saw that it was he.

"You look *breathtakingly* beautiful tonight," Huntley said.

Although he was smiling down at her, Eliza's hopes for anything more were dashed when the handsome man said nothing further and, instead, continued to move past her, his long gray eyes scanning the name cards in search of his place at the overlong table.

Throughout the lengthy meal, which lasted above two hours, Eliza caught only snatches of the general's head or, at times, his shoulder. Seated on the same side of the table as she, it was only when she leaned quite far over her plate and directed a long stare in that direction that she caught even the merest glimpse of him. As it was quite an uncomfortable, and unseemly, position to maintain, etiquette demanded she not employ the tactic too terribly often.

As her own dinner companions, two *quite* elderly army officers, seemed not to take much note of her, but kept up a running conversation above her head, Eliza spent the bulk of the dull meal wishing it were over and done with.

She'd had no more than a dram or two of wine all evening, and now she was far too anxiety-ridden over Huntley's strange behavior to consume more than a few bites of the hot and cold soups, venison in currant sauce, partridge pie, roast beef and fowl, asparagus in cream sauce, and the assortment of sauteed and buttered vegetables, poached lobster, and pickled oysters that was set before her.

Served by the Prince's own servants, wearing dark blue livery trimmed in gold lace, more often than not, Eliza's plate was taken away in the exact same state it was when it was placed before her. She even waved away all manner of delicious-looking desserts, the chocolate mousse, tansy pudding, puffed pastries and assorted biscuits and tarts smothered in pieces of fruit, rich sauces, and icings.

All she could think of was Huntley, and why he was treating her with such cool indifference? Had she done something to drive him away? Should she have *not* let him kiss her in their garden? Because he'd sent her a beautiful bouquet of roses the following day and a lovely box of chocolate confections the day after, she'd assumed she'd done nothing wrong . . . and that he still held her in high regard, or at least, in *regard*.

Now, she wasn't certain of anything . . . except that he hated her! That he despised her! That he wished to have nothing whatever to do with her! And, she hadn't the least notion why.

She tried for another peek at him, but was interrupted by the sound of yet another gong, signaling the end of the meal and the start of the Special Ceremony to honor those young soldiers who'd exhibited especial bravery during the war or performed an outstanding act of valor on the battlefield.

Since the whole concept for tonight's gala was being attributed to Miss Eliza Foxburn, she was scheduled to play a vital part in the award presentation. As a sort of prelude to the festivities, the Prince had requested that she deliver a short address.

Her heart in her throat the entire time, Eliza managed to get through her little speech and then, taking up a position to the left of HRH, she held the crimson-satin pillow, upon which the Regent himself placed each and every medal that the commander in chief, the esteemed Duke of Wellington, then pinned upon the proud chest of each recipient.

It was a glorious presentation, punctuated by round after round of spirited applause from all the onlookers, including those who'd taken their meal outdoors, but who attempted now to squeeze into the Conservatory to witness the award presentation. When Lieutenant Charles Langston's name was called, his beaming young bride, the former Lady Constance Torbett, the young lady Eliza'd assisted to escape at Lady Hamilton's dinner party, actually broke ranks and surged forward to embrace Eliza, tearfully expressing her gratitude for all Eliza had done to help her and her young man.

Eliza couldn't help feeling proud that this ... *this* extraordinary event, unprecedented in her country's glorious and colorful history, had all come about because of ... her.

With immense pride swelling her breast, she managed to *not* remind herself what selfish motive of hers actually lay behind it. Instead, she chose to hark back to General Huntley's words, spoken that night in the Foxburn garden, that despite everything, a great deal of good had sprung from her little falsehood.

She only prayed she could be equally successful in thrusting from mind the *other* thing that had happened that same night in the Foxburn garden. It was quite obvious Huntley had forgotten it ... and that he wished her to do the same.

At the conclusion of the ceremony, the guests again scattered about the mansion to take part in the various amusements—dancing, card playing, billiards, or simply to roam freely about the grounds.

Because Eliza was certain she'd spotted General Huntley, and consequently her father and Ivy, head for the dancing room, she also hurried in that direction. But she was held up on the way there by a beaming Lady Villiers, who could hardly contain her excitement over the fact that Jane had met a young man who seemed quite enamored with her.

"I intend doing all in my power to further the match!" she cried. "Lord Tremayne's credentials are excellent! Heir to an earldom, no less!" she concluded with high satisfaction.

The overjoyed mama gave Eliza a delighted squeeze. "To think, my dear, Jane will virtually owe her future to you!"

Linking an arm through Eliza's and still nattering on excitedly, Lady Villiers strolled alongside Eliza into the dancing room.

"Now, we must find you a beau!" the delighted woman concluded magnanimously. A wide smile splitting her face, she gazed anxiously about the room.

"I take it you and General Huntley have abandoned that silly charade you were forwarding some weeks back," Lady Villiers said absently. "Huntley is a dear, but he is not a'tall in your style." She was still gazing calculatedly about. "Although, he and the widow Jamison suit quite nicely."

"E-excuse me?" Eliza stammered.

"I said I believed General Huntley and the lovely widow Jamison suit. He has danced with her a number of times this evening. They are even now in the garden."

"I-In the garden?" Eliza gasped. Her breath suddenly grew quite short, even fitful. *Huntley had taken another woman into the garden?* Thoughts of her father's electrifying machine flitted through her mind. But the unsettling thought was suddenly shattered by the shrill sound of Lady Villiers's voice calling to someone.

"*Hallo!* Come dear, I shall introduce you to several nice young men!"

For Eliza, the remainder of that glorious evening passed in a painful blur.

CHAPTER 16

"A CAT NAP"

"I fear we have attached ourselves to a couple of rake-hells," Ivy Heathergill lamented to Eliza a few days later.

The two young ladies were commiserating with one another over a second, or third, cup of tea one afternoon in the Foxburn drawing room. It was a gray day, both indoors and out, with sheets of cold, hard rain relentlessly pounding the cobblestones all over London.

"That does appear to be the case," Eliza replied glumly.

Since the Carlton House Fete, neither she nor Ivy had laid eyes on their gentlemen friends. Which meant that, in a backhanded sort of way, the party had accomplished exactly what Eliza intended. It had separated her father and Ivy. But, not in precisely the *way* she'd intended. Papa was now squiring about several *tonnish* women, each closer in age to him than Ivy, whilst, to Eliza's immense dismay, Huntley seemed—to borrow a word from Lady Villiers—*enamored* with the flame-haired widow, Lady Jamison.

Feeling another surge of rage swell within her, Eliza huffed her displeasure at the direction her life had taken and absently ceased stroking Sailor's backside. The cat, curled into a tight ball on her lap, was presumably sound asleep.

When the pleasurable caresses Sailor was enjoying halted so abruptly, he twitched an ear and commenced insistently to bump his mistress's hand 'til she again resumed her soft stroking of him.

Exhaling another noisy sigh, Eliza further realized that the mere idea of General Huntley with another woman was more unsettling than anything she could imagine. Not only was it hurtful, it made her see red! And green! Why, a veritable rainbow of brilliant colors sparked angrily through her mind. *How dare that . . . that rakehell kiss her in the garden and then turn to igniting the same sort of electrifying passion within another woman as if she didn't even exist? How dare he?*

She shifted beneath the weight of the cat snoozing on her lap.

It wasn't just the "sparks" that had her back up. No, there was more to it than that. The bald truth was, despite the vast difference in their ages, she just plain liked Huntley. And she missed him. She'd come to think of him as a friend. He was as easy to talk to as . . . well, as Ivy was. And, now, he'd *abandoned* her, with no logical or reasonable explanation that she could see.

And, the same was true where Papa was concerned for Ivy.

"I feel so . . . lost, and empty without Richard about," Ivy complained, as if reading Eliza's thoughts. "I'd never been so happy as I was with him." She paused, a faraway look clouding her sea-green eyes. "Father misses him, too."

Eliza heaved another sigh. "I'm so very sorry, Ivy. I wish I knew what caused men to behave in such a beastly fashion."

Suddenly, she flounced to her feet, the action quite upsetting Sailor, who, when awakened in so rude a manner, had to scramble to right himself, and then sat staring sleepily at his mistress, who was now absently pacing back and forth upon the carpet.

Presently Sailor hopped to the floor and began to follow along behind Eliza, a few steps one direction, a few steps another. Back and forth, back and forth.

"Do you suppose they think us too *young* for them?" Eliza asked. She came to a sudden standstill and leveled an expectant gaze at Ivy. Of course, Eliza already knew the answer to that question. They were too young for both elderly men. Obviously, her ruse to get that fact across to Papa had worked equally well on Huntley. It was quite plain now that he agreed with her on that head. So, why didn't getting what she'd wanted all along not make her happy?

As Ivy considered the question, Eliza set to pacing once more. Sailor, however, apparently deciding he'd had quite enough exercise for one day, instead ambled over and jumped onto an overstuffed chair that sat invitingly near the fire blazing in the hearth. Apparently feeling secure in the knowledge that he'd not be ousted from this bed anytime soon, he curled up and soon fell fast asleep again.

"I suppose that could very well be the case," Ivy offered. "I admit that the vast difference in our ages worried me at the outset. But, when your father repeatedly assured me that my youth did not matter to him, I ceased to think of it." She sighed with frustration. "Unfortunately, we've no way of knowing what the gentlemen truly think."

Eliza flung herself onto the sofa again. "I suppose I could ask Papa what his feelings are now on that head, although I rarely see him anymore. He seems to be staying excessively busy, or . . . he is avoiding me altogether."

"I expect he fears an interrogation from you . . . on my behalf," Ivy replied morosely.

Eliza shrugged. "Perhaps. He is aware that we have become fast friends."

Ivy managed a small smile. "That is the only outcome

in this wretched business that pleases me. I did so wish to become your friend, Eliza.''

Eliza returned Ivy's sincere smile. In all candidness, she had to agree with Huntley's assessment that a great deal of good had come from this taradiddle. Eliza couldn't imagine her life now *without* Ivy Heathergill. Ivy was a true bosom bow. Still . . . she was not yet ready to concede her position on all points. She truly liked Ivy, but she was not eager for the young lady to become her stepmama! "I . . . expect you knew that I was quite . . . set against you when we first met,'' she replied somewhat haltingly.

Ivy nodded. "I confess I might have felt the very same about you if the situation had been reversed. As it was''— she grinned—"I was determined to win you over.''

Since the girls were exchanging intimate confidences, Eliza toyed with the idea of telling Ivy the entire truth behind her party idea and how she'd deliberately hoped to separate her and Papa. But she quickly rejected the notion. She and Ivy both felt low enough without adding another adjunct to their pain. In any event, the party was over and done with, and Papa and Ivy were no longer a twosome, and Eliza hadn't had a hand in the doing of it after all. Still, in all honesty, a part of her deeply regretted anything she might have done that led to this pass.

"I should have left well enough alone,'' she murmured, more to herself than to her new friend.

"Richard straying from my side was none of your doing,'' Ivy rushed to say, her sweet tone consoling. "I just wish I'd never introduced Huntley to the widow Jamison.''

Eliza's ears perked up. 'Til now, she hadn't known how Huntley'd come to be acquainted with the older woman. It was on the tip of her tongue to question Ivy further about that happenstance, when both girls—and Sailor, who jerked his sleepy head up when, he, too—heard the sound of a raised voice coming from the foyer.

"For pity's sake, do step aside, Briggs! Can you not see I am in a rush? I shall show myself in!'' declared Lady

Villiers impatiently. A scant second later, that lady sailed grandly into the drawing room, enveloped by a crisp gust of cool, damp air.

"Eliza, dear! I simply had to deliver the news—hello, Ivy—in person!" She headed for the hearth and began to shake the wet raindrops from her fur-lined pelisse.

Not particularly liking the shower-bath he was receiving, Sailor let out a disgruntled mewl, hopped to the floor, and, indignantly holding his head aloft, stalked from the room, all hope for a cozy nap by the fire driven from his mind.

"Do join us for a cup of tea, Lady Villiers." Eliza forced a pleasant tone to her voice. "The pot is still warm," she added. She reached to lift it from the cozy and proceeded to pour a cup for her guest.

Lady Villiers moved to join the young ladies, seated in the center of the room, a few yards from the fire. Her glowing countenance was in stark contrast to Eliza and Ivy's glum demeanors.

After taking a quick sip from her cup, Lady Villiers nestled it into the saucer and brightly announced, "My Jane is betrothed! The Viscount Tremayne only just presented his suit. He and Lord Villiers are this minute drawing up the agreement." Without pausing for breath, she popped to her feet, and added, "So, I really must be off!"

With a loud clatter, which, had he still been in the room would have given Sailor a start, Lady Villers clapped her teacup and saucer onto the tea tray.

"I am off to spread the news ... far and wide!" She laughed gaily as she headed back toward the door, a gloved hand waving farewell over one shoulder. "You've my permission to tell everyone you know!"

Upon reaching the threshold, she turned to address Eliza once again. "By the by, dear, I fear we shall have to abandon our little trip to Paris. No need now, is there? Ta!"

* * *

That night, as she lay in bed, Eliza decided her life had never looked so dismal. During the past weeks when she'd been busy with the party plans, and it had begun to look as if she'd be *un*successful in turning Papa from his pursuit of Ivy, she had half begun to relent. She truly cared for Ivy, and as her affection for General Huntley grew, it seemed quite hypocritical of her to scold Papa for doing the exact same thing she was doing.

But . . . now that things had worked out . . . satisfactorily on their own, why did she feel so . . . perfectly *dreadful?*

Perhaps it was because she no longer had the lovely trip to Paris to look forward to.

Or, perhaps it was . . . because she no longer had *Huntley* to look forward to.

All of the young men Lady Villiers had introduced her to at the Carlton House Fete only furthered the conclusion Eliza had earlier drawn. Not a one held a candle to General Huntley. They were all pups, whereas he was a *man.* A strong, kind, thoughtful, wise, and wonderful man. A man Eliza was coming to realize she cared a *very* great deal for.

Perhaps . . . she even loved him.

Only, he did not love her.

And, Papa no longer loved Ivy.

And, Jane was set to marry Lord Tremayne, and *no one* was going to Paris!

Suddenly, her life felt more wretched and dull than it ever had before! And she hadn't a clue how to remedy it this time.

CHAPTER 17

"THE DELECTABLE LADY JAMISON"

Eliza was surprised the following morning to find her father seated at the breakfast table in the little nook where, until lately, the two of them had been accustomed to break-fasting together every day.

"Papa!" A small, but genuine smile of pleasure lifted the corners of Eliza's mouth. "You have been so busy these days, I feel I never see you."

Sir Richard looked up from the copy of the *Times* he was holding open before him. "I have missed you, as well, sweetheart." He laid the newspaper aside and fixed his full attention upon his only daughter. "Now that the Carlton House soirée is over, I trust your life has returned to normal?" He gazed expectantly at her.

Eliza smiled ruefully. "It is true, I have fewer obligations to discharge, and I think it pleases Briggs that we've far fewer callers now. Although we are still receiving a goodly number of invitations," she added. Then in a somewhat calculating tone, as if to to see what her father might have to say on the subject, she said, "I have received a few gentlemen callers."

There was a pause, and then, in an unusually *grave* tone, unusual in that her father's voice generally always reflected his carefree attitude toward life, he said, "I have been giving a great deal of thought to the idea of you marrying General Huntley, sweetheart, and, I find I must now advise against it."

The unexpected pronouncement caused Eliza's heart to thunder wildly in her breast. Had Huntley taken it upon himself to speak to her father? Was he "crying off" in order that he might freely pursue the widow Jamison? Why did it hurt her so that he'd said nothing to her about it? Suddenly, she wished to flee from the room and fling herself across her bed and sob her eyes out. But, of course, she could not do that. Papa would demand an explanation and . . . what would she say? She didn't know herself why she felt so . . . so awfully wretched!

". . . was pleased to see you standing up the other night with a number of eligible young men," her father was saying. "You must not let the circumstances of your . . . previous entanglement overset you. Since the betrothal announcement did not appear in the newspapers, no one, save Lady Villiers and the Heathergills, are the wiser. There should not be a breath of scandal attached to your name." He paused to take a sip of coffee. "I am proud of you, Eliza, and your mother would have been very proud of all that you have accomplished these last weeks. You looked like a princess standing next to the Regent at the Special Ceremony."

Eliza fought for control. She had ceased to listen to her father when he ceased to speak of Huntley. She knew that her betrothal to the general was a sham. So . . . why did it overset her so that he had "cried off" in such a heartless fashion?

With great difficulty, she tried to force down a bite of creamed eggs. Presently, in as bright a tone as she could muster, she said, "You are quite right, Papa. I, too, had reached the conclusion that Huntley and I do not suit. It was fortunate, indeed, that the announcement was never published in the papers. It is as if . . . as if we never knew one another. I—I have every intention now of . . . of making a new life. In fact, I am planning to attend a dinner party at Lady Hertford's at week's end. And there are a score of other invitations on the sideboard in the foyer."

"There's a good girl." Sir Richard nodded with approval. "You are very wise, Eliza." He took another sip from his coffee cup. "Huntley has been seen at various functions this past week." His sharp gaze did not leave Eliza's face for a second.

At the mention of Huntley's name, her lips pressed tightly together. But since she could think of nothing further to say on the subject, she made no reply.

Sir Richard, however, went on. "I expect you are also aware that I am no longer squiring Miss Heathergill about. I decided to heed your excellent advice, sweetheart, and cast about for a . . . more mature woman."

Still fighting to remain calm, Eliza murmured, "Ivy has mentioned to me that she has not seen you of late. She and I have become quite good friends."

Her father nodded. "I am pleased to hear that. Ivy is a dear girl, and I continue to think fondly of her. But, I am convinced that both you girls belong with gentlemen *much* younger than either Huntley or myself."

A long pause ensued, during which it took every ounce of Eliza's courage to keep a civil tongue in her head and *not* lash out against both her father and Huntley's callous treatment of herself and Ivy.

Presently, by way of changing the subject, somewhat, she said, "Jane is to be married."

"Ah." Her father smiled agreeably. "Met a young man at the Grand Fete, did she?" He turned back to his breakfast, scooping up a forkful of buttered kidney and eggs, then swallowing the mouthful. "You seemed rarely to lack for dancing partners at the soirée. Huntley and I were both astonished by the vast number of young men who sought you out. You were quite the belle.''

Eliza said nothing for a moment, then because she couldn't help herself, she murmured, "Do you think it possible that General Huntley perceived my standing up with other gentlemen as a . . . a lack of interest in him?''

Despite the faint gleam of satisfaction in her father's bright blue eyes, he shrugged noncommittally. "You would do well to forget Huntley, sweetheart.''

It was not the answer EIiza hoped for. Nothing made sense anymore. Not Huntley's odd behavior, or her feelings in regard to it. She had known all along that their "betrothal" was false and that as soon as Papa broke off with Ivy, their charade would also come to an end, but . . . she just hadn't expected to feel so . . . so . . . As she tried to sort out her feelings, she was unaware that instead of eating her breakfast, she was merely pushing the food around on her plate.

"You are not taking ill are you, Eliza?''

When her father's voice penetrated her thoughts, she blinked herself to awareness. "No, Papa. I . . . I am just not hungry this morning.'' She purposefully set her fork down and pushed her plate aside. Forcing a small smile to her lips, she said brightly, "I had wished to stand up with you at the Carlton House Fete. Did you ever come face-to-face with the Prince? Or Wellington?''

Her father chuckled. "I was never presented to the Duke. Seems he does quite avoid the limelight. Left immediately following the Awards Ceremony. Though I did meet the Prince. Likable chap. Not the least bit pompous.''

"I found the Regent quite agreeable. Despite what people think of him, he is very genuine . . . and he has exquisite taste.''

"Indeed.'' Her father nodded. "Never saw such a fine collection of Dutch paintings.'' He paused and leveled an intent look at Eliza. "Huntley quite admired them.''

A pang shot through Eliza. As if again struck dumb, she clamped her lips shut and said nothing further.

An uncomfortable silence ensued. Eliza had no intention of eating another bite. Yet, despite the fact that she did not really wish to hear another word about General Huntley, she was loath to leave the table lest her father mention something else of import about him.

Presently, Sir Richard lifted his napkin to his lips, then tossed the crumpled piece of linen across his plate. "I will be out all day and much of the evening. I have met a beautiful woman who I find quite suits me. She is a widow by the name of Lady Jamison."

"Lady Jamison!" Eliza sputtered. "But I was given to understand that Huntley had been dancing attendance upon Lady Jamison."

Her father smiled, though once again, Eliza was far too overset to notice the devilish twinkle in the sky-blue orbs that were closely regarding her.

"So far as I am concerned," Sir Richard said with a shrug, "until a woman is wed, she is fair game. Lady Jamison quite appeals to me, and I intend to do all in my power to win her." He pushed up from the table. "Let that be fair warning to Huntley," he added in a challenging tone.

Stunned, Eliza rose as well and followed a few steps behind her father into the drawing room, where she stood wordlessly beside the double doors that led to the mews. After he'd dropped a fatherly kiss upon her flushed cheek, and exited the house, she absently latched the door firmly behind him.

If her father had set his cap at the lovely widow Jamison, then perhaps *she* still had a chance to win General Huntley's affections.

Before making her way to the upstairs sitting room to tend to her household duties for the day, Eliza walked to the foyer and scooped up the handful of unopened invitations that lay next to the salver on the sideboard. Tearing open the seals on several, she paused when she found one that looked interesting—a rout to be held that very evening at Lord and Lady Carlisle's. General Huntley, she recalled, was very well acquainted with Lord Carlisle.

To cheer herself, Eliza chose to wear the favorite of her pretty new gowns that evening, an elegant lilac sarcenet trimmed in silver lace. With its tiny cap sleeves and slim skirt, she thought the gown made her appear quite mature.

In the company of Lord and Lady Villiers and Jane, who was every bit as taken with the Viscount Tremayne as he was with her, she arrived that night at the lovely home of Lord and Lady Carlisle.

All day long, she'd been distracted by pleasant memories of her intimate talks with General Huntley. He was so very dashing and handsome, and she adored listening to him talk of his war experiences. Again and again she relived the feel of his lips on hers and the delicious tingling sensation she'd experienced when he held her close. She also recalled how in the past weeks, he'd often gazed at her with a look of genuine concern, as if he truly cared for her. And, the remark he'd made that afternoon about Sailor coming to live with them after they were wed warmed her anew. Surely, when taken altogether, it meant that he cared for her a little, didn't it?

Buoyed by her newfound knowledge that her father had set his cap at Lady Jamison, Eliza determined tonight to uncover Huntley's true feelings for her.

With a determined tilt to her chin, she pasted a bright smile on her lips as she and Jane—who was in quite good looks tonight, with a rosy glow replacing the wan look on her cheeks—entered the Carlisle drawing room and gazed expectantly about.

At almost the same instant Jane espied her intended, Lord Tremayne, Eliza spotted General Huntley. Engaged in conversation with two other gentlemen, he was standing quite near Lord Tremayne and his companion. "Come!"

Jane took Eliza's arm. "I shall present you to William. He is the dearest man in the world, and has no intention of *ever* entering the military."

Despite Jane's betrothal signaling the end of their Paris trip, Eliza was quite happy for her longtime friend.

After the introductions had been made and Eliza had expressed her sincere well-wishes to the groom-to-be, the talk turned to other things. Lord Tremayne was possessed of a lively sense of humor, and in no time, he and his companion, a Mr. Wilcott, whom Eliza had met at the Carlton House Fete, had both young ladies laughing aloud.

From the corner of her eye, Eliza was pleased to see that their gaiety very soon attracted the notice of the three gentlemen standing nearby. She was even happier when one of the gentlemen, the one with the distinguished white wings of hair feathering from either side of his temples, strolled over.

"Good evening, ladies, Lord Tremayne, Mr. Wilcott," General Huntley said. Dressed in his highly decorated scarlet military coat, white knee breeches, and gleaming top boots, he stood a good head taller and prouder than any other man in the room. Eliza also thought him easily the most handsome.

"A pleasure to see you again, sir," she said brightly. Standing so very near him again after so long a time apart made her feel quite breathless, but she managed quite admirably to stay calm. "Lord Tremayne was just remarking upon a particularly amusing cartoon that he'd seen a day or so ago in the *Times.*"

"Ah. Believe I saw the very one. Napoléon launching an elaborate campaign to defeat his opponent at deck bowling?"

Everyone laughed and Tremayne nodded. "Old Boney has plenty of spare time on his hands now, don't he?"

"Indeed." Huntley replied. He turned to Jane and congratulated her and William on their recent betrothal.

Jane laughed gaily. "I daresay Mother has told everyone!

The announcement will not appear in the newspapers until Wednesday next.''

"Rather a waste of ink now, wouldn't you agree?" her intended remarked dryly. "Perhaps we should insist on a cartoon instead.''

Everyone tittered again.

With a grin on her lips, Eliza protested. "A cartoon would not look nearly so pretty pasted in Jane's memory book.''

General Huntley addressed her. "I rather expect your memory book is filling-up rapidly. The *Times* account of the Carlton House Fete was quite glowing, indeed.'' He smiled into her shining blue eyes. "The praise credited to you was very well deserved.''

Eliza beamed with pleasure beneath the great man's praise. He was being as agreeable and cordial as ever. But she reminded herself not to attach too much significance to the remark. Huntley was a gentleman quite adept at charming the ladies. All of them. Still, she decided to take advantage of the opening he'd given her. "I had hoped for the opportunity to stand up with you, sir, at the Grand Fete," she remarked pleasantly.

His gloved hands clasped behind his back, Huntley inclined his dark head a notch. "You will allow me to make up for the oversight tonight. I understand there is to be dancing later.''

Eliza was about to reply to his kind offer when the muffled sounds of new arrivals in the foyer reached their ears. Huntley turned an anxious gaze in that direction, as if he were expecting someone.

Eliza, as well, looked toward the doorway of the already-crowded drawing room, and was a bit taken aback to see her father and the stunning Lady Jamison walk in together. Her father had said nothing earlier about attending Lady Carlisle's rout.

Almost at once, Huntley murmured a near-imperceptible, "Excuse me," and hurried that way.

Squaring her small shoulders, Eliza also hurried over and was gratified to reach her father's side a scant second before Huntley did.

"Papa! Do introduce me to your lovely companion."

He did, and Eliza smiled agreeably into the warm brown eyes of the beautiful Lady Jamison. In her mid-to-late thirties, the young widow was wearing a champagne-colored gown that, although Eliza thought it displayed far too much of her ample bosom to be considered entirely proper, was, nonetheless, quite attractive on her.

"I am very pleased to meet you, Eliza," the pretty woman said. "Your father speaks of you often." She reached to take one of Eliza's small gloved hands and bent to affectionately kiss the younger girl's flushed cheek.

During this exchange, General Huntley stood quietly to one side, watching. Presently, he stepped forward. " 'Evening, Foxburn. How lovely you look, my dear."

Lady Jamison favored the tall military man with a flirtatious smile. "You look lovely yourself tonight, Huntley."

Both Eliza and her father stiffened at that remark, the saucy tilt of the widow's auburn head causing Eliza to alter her assessment of the woman's character somewhat. She might be beautiful, but she was far too brazen to be called a lady in every sense of the word!

When Huntley'd managed to drag his eyes from her shapely form, he again addressed Sir Richard. "With your leave, Foxburn, I desire a private word with Lady Jamison."

Noting the scowl that flitted across her father's face, Eliza held her breath for fear that he'd take umbrage at Huntley's forwardness. Instead, he handed his companion's arm over without a word and the smiling twosome strolled contentedly away.

Sir Richard, however, did utter an oath beneath his breath. "I'll not give the reprobate more than five minutes with her."

"Papa!" Eliza cried hotly. "Huntley is not a reprobate! Though, I daresay, Lady Jamison is little better than a

Covent Garden trollop!" She flung a contemptible look after the pair. "There are plenty of other lovely ladies here tonight." She linked her arm through her father's. "Besides, the dancing is about to begin, and I should like you to lead me out."

Though Eliza tried her best all evening to refrain from gazing longingly at the dashing military man, it seemed everywhere she turned, she came face-to-face with him . . . and his ever-present companion, the voluptuous Lady Jamison. As the evening progressed, and her father remained perpetually alone, he grew increasingly more sullen and withdrawn. It was plainly evident to Eliza that both men were smitten by the auburn-haired beauty.

The one time Sir Richard stood up with Lady Jamison, Huntley stood on the sidelines wearing an angry scowl on his face. When Huntley escorted the widow into supper, Eliza's father stormed up to their table and demanded that the gentleman to Lady Jamison's other side relinquish his place to him. It got so Eliza feared the gentlemen's little skirmishes to gain ground with the delectable woman would erupt into all-out war.

Though Eliza was not yet ready to admit defeat in her own efforts to win Huntley's notice, by two of the clock in the morning, which was far later than she generally lingered at parties, she was ready to give up the battle for that night. She'd been all too aware of Huntley's whereabouts all evening long and was quite weary of jockeying to stand near him on the sidelines of the dance floor, or when they filled their plates at the buffet table for supper. Once, while forming a set for dancing, she'd made certain that she and her partner, with whom she'd purposely kept up a running conversation, stood opposite General Huntley and Lady Jamison—who was the only woman Huntley stood up with all evening—so that, when the pattern of the dance brought the two lines together, Huntley would be forced to take Eliza's hand for the brief span of a turn or a single step.

As the evening wore on and Huntley had barely spoken to her, Eliza worked to conceal her growing irritation with him behind a mask of indifference. By the close of the evening, she was so tired that, if left unchecked, she feared her expression would be near thunderous, and yet, despite her failure to attract his notice all night, she was determined to approach him one last time.

As usual, he was engaged in conversation with Lady Jamison; still, she marched boldly up to the pair of them now.

"The Villierses and I are leaving," she announced.

Huntley turned a cool look upon her. "Ah. And you have come to remind me that you and I have not yet danced?"

The sudden wave of white-hot anger that swept over Eliza made her want to smack the arrogant so-and-so's handsome face! Her nostrils flared with indignation, still she managed to school her features into placidity. "I am far too weary to dance with anyone now," she replied sweetly. "I merely wished to invite you to take tea with me . . . that is, with us, with Father and me . . . tomorrow," she stammered. "I fear I have not yet thanked you properly for all of your excellent help with the—"

"I beg your forgiveness, Miss Foxburn, but as it happens, I have a previous engagement tomorrow," he cut her off briskly.

That the always-polite general might refuse her had never occurred to Eliza. She stood stock-still, staring into his hard gray gaze as if she hadn't heard correctly.

She was so very stunned by his curt reply that she failed to detect the flicker of regret that momentarily softened his rugged features. "You have thanked me sufficiently, my dear," he remarked crisply, then, with a dismissive nod, he turned back to his lovely companion.

Eliza's heart lodged painfully in her throat as she darted away. She'd never felt so spurned and rejected in all her life!

Scrambling into the Villiers coach, she thanked God for the concealing darkness that enveloped her. Leaning her throbbing head back against the cool leather squabs, she squeezed her eyes shut against the gathering tears that swam to her eyes. Despite her valiant efforts to check them, in seconds she felt the scalding moisture trickle in rivulets down her cheeks.

She'd been a fool to think that she, a green girl of eighteen, could stand a chance against an experienced older woman whose delectable charms no man in his right mind could resist. She had no choice now but to accept the harsh reality that, no matter how much she desired it, General March Huntley would never be hers.

CHAPTER 18

"AN UNEXPECTED TURN"

For upward of a week following Lady Carlisle's rout, Eliza's efforts to do as her father insisted she must—forget she'd ever known March Huntley—all came to naught. Eliza could no more explain the attraction she felt toward the older man than she could fly. All she knew was that each time she saw General Huntley, each time she spoke with him, the longing she felt to be with him grew stronger and stronger. Despite both her father's admonition to forget the man and Huntley's seeming rejection of her, she yearned still to be with him.

It hardly helped matters any when night after night, at one soirée or another, she was forced to watch, not only Huntley making a veritable cake of himself over the beauteous Lady Jamison, but her father, as well.

That her father was also in desperate need of wise counsel in matters of the heart was quite plain to Eliza, but she had learned her lesson well in that quarter. She was not about to offer unsolicited words of wisdom now on a subject where she could boast of even less success than he.

Near a fortnight following Lady Carlisle's rout, Eliza's

spirits had sunk so low she finally decided to forgo all society functions altogether. Winter was fast upon them, and although the Christmas season would soon be there, she knew no desire whatsoever to take part in any of the holiday festivities.

"I simply cannot smile my way through another party, or dinner, or rout," she told her father morosely. The two were ensconced in the drawing room one especially cold afternoon, their hands wrapped 'round warm cups of steaming hot tea.

"I worry about you, Eliza," Sir Richard said. "You've not been yourself of late."

Eliza stared moodily into the fire. Even the brilliant red flames reminded her of Huntley. The scarlet plumes were the exact same crimson as his military jacket, the gold tongues licking the flames the same gleaming brilliance as the coat's shiny brass buttons and dazzling braid. A sigh of longing escaped her.

Blustery days such as this only made her yearn for him more. She missed the warmth of his friendship, the tender look in his eyes when he gazed upon her, and the unique way he had of making her feel that he thought her special.

But she dared not confess her true feelings to her father. How could she explain to him that, against his better judgment, and her own, she had fallen top over tail in love with March Huntley, a man far too old for her? Especially after she'd so fiercely championed against his match with Ivy Heathergill? And won. How would that look? Still, she wondered how long she could keep the ironic truth to herself.

Her ruminations were interrupted by the rich timbre of her father's voice. "Jane Anders's wedding and marriage celebration is but a few days away." His tone was kindly.

Eliza emitted another sigh. A mere handful of weeks ago, she'd been excessively worried over Jane because she'd persisted in spending each and every day in the exact same manner Eliza was doing now. But . . . she couldn't help how she felt, could she? She drew her feet up beneath her body on the sofa and pulled the invisible blanket of gloom and despair she wore like a shield a deal tighter about her body.

"I don't feel like attending a wedding, Papa," she muttered glumly.

"Jane and her mother will be most disappointed if you are not on hand."

Gazing trancelike into the fire, Eliza made no reply.

As the stillness stretched between them, Sir Richard regarded his daughter with a worried frown. Noting that she'd hardly touched her tea, or taken a single bite from the sandwich or the sugar-coated biscuit on her plate, he urged, "Try to eat something, Eliza. You will waste away."

"I am not hungry, Papa."

Her father set his own nearly empty teacup aside and continued to study his daughter. Finally, he ventured, "Would you like me to send for Ivy, sweetheart? She was most disappointed when you failed to receive her a few days back."

A spark of interest appeared in Eliza's red-rimmed eyes. "You have spoken with Ivy?"

"No." Her father shook his head tightly. "Briggs informed me that Miss Heathergill had called . . . and that you had turned her away."

Eliza choked back a sudden sob of anguish that bubbled up from her throat and threatened to strangle her. It was true. She'd felt so forlorn she feared sharing her sorrow with Ivy . . . feared blurting out the shameless scheme she'd engineered to destroy the genuine love that existed between Ivy and her father.

"Oh, Papa . . ." The wrenching plea was barely audible.

"What is it, sweetheart?"

Hot scalding tears began to trickle down Eliza's cheeks.

Her father was beside her in an instant, his strong arms drawing her to his chest.

"I have ruined everything, Papa," she sobbed into his shoulder.

"Hush, now." His hand cupping her shoulder, Sir Richard patted his daughter's arm soothingly. "I daresay I can remedy whatever is amiss if you'll just tell me what it is."

Now that her pent-up tears had begun to fall, Eliza felt helpless to halt them. "I—It's too late!" she sobbed.

"It is never too late," her father protested. Holding her from him, he gazed with concern into her troubled face. "Tell me what has happened, sweetheart. Did that scoundrel Huntley trifle with yo—"

"No!" Eliza quickly shook her head. "Huntley has been the perfect gentleman." She tried valiantly to blink back her tears and still her trembling chin. "It is me. I have ruined everything, and I am so very sorry, Papa."

Sir Richard fixed his daughter with a curious gaze. "Whatever do you mean, sweetheart? You have ruined nothing that I can see." The solicitous gaze on his face was replaced by one of fatherly amusement.

Eliza bit down hard on her lower lip to keep from confessing everything. But it was no use. She had to tell her father the truth. She had wronged both him and Ivy. And, it was plain as day that what she had done to them had now come back to haunt her. She needed their forgiveness as much as she needed Huntley's love. A fresh sob rose in her breast. "I am so very sorry for what I did to keep you and Ivy apart, Papa. Ivy loves you and I . . . I believe you truly cared for her at one time. I did not understand then, but . . . I do now."

"Do you, Eliza?"

"Yes." She nodded sadly. "Oh, Papa, I tried not to give way to my feelings. But, the truth is, I am terribly in love with General Huntley. I have tried to forget him. And I tried to make myself care for some other young man, but next to him they are all . . . dull and . . . unremarkable. And now . . ." The tears began to flow again. ". . . now, I shall become an ape leader and spend the rest of my life on the shelf!''

Her father could not halt the burst of merry laughter that bubbled up inside him. ''I hardly think you've anything to fear on that head, my dear!''

''Oh-h-h, Papa.'' She flung herself into his arms again. The smile still on his face, her father hugged her to him. ''Your broken heart will mend, sweetheart. In no time, you will forget all about General Huntley.''

''No!'' Eliza wrenched from him, her blue eyes snapping with fury. ''I will never forget Huntley! I love him!''

Her father stared into her troubled blue orbs. ''Well, I . . . don't know what to say, sweetheart.''

Sniffing back her sobs, Eliza looked away. ''There is nothing to say. He does not love me. I doubt he . . . ever did. I only wish I had not ruined things for you and Ivy. I should not have interfered. One cannot make another person love or not love someone, Papa.''

Her father studied her. ''Are you certain of that?'' he asked gravely.

''Very certain.'' She nodded eagerly. ''I cannot help how I feel about General Huntley.'' She gazed intently at her father. ''And although I truly understand why you do not wish me to settle on him, I . . . still love him.'' She gave a helpless little shrug. ''I cannot help how I feel about him, Papa. I think him the most brilliant man in the world.''

Her father's lips twitched with affection. ''More brilliant than I?''

Eliza managed a watery grin. ''Perhaps not quite so brilliant as you, Papa. But, he is kind and thoughtful, and I rarely cease to think of him. I shall . . . always love him. Are you terribly angry with me?'' She gazed raptly into her father's eyes.

''No, my dear. I am not angry with you. But, I am pleased that you have learned your lesson. One cannot make another person love, or not love, another. Love . . . just happens,'' he concluded, if a bit sadly. ''I would that I could remedy the situation for you, but I fear that no matter how clever I am, this is one matter I cannot fix.''

Eliza felt fresh tears welling up in her eyes. ''I have lost him forever,'' she murmured. ''Just as you have lost Ivy.''

Sir Richard studied her a moment longer, then he squared his shoulders and rose to his feet. ''Perhaps I have,'' he said. ''But I shall not lose Lady Jamison.'' An angry scowl stole over his face. ''Huntley be dammed!'' he spat out as he stormed from the room.

Eliza didn't know what to do. In the past, when she'd been confused or needed advice, she'd felt free to seek Huntley's counsel. But asking his advice now was no longer an option; nor was commiserating with Ivy. How could she confide to Ivy that her father harbored ill will against General Huntley because he'd stolen away the woman Papa now loved?

How things had come to such a pass, Eliza could not think. It was all a muddle, and she had no one to turn to. Neither Jane nor Lady Villiers would be any help. They were far too caught up in their joyous plans for Jane's wedding.

Eliza'd never felt so lost and alone in all her life. Her thoughts strayed to her mother, although she knew precisely what her mother would say to it. In her prim, firm voice, Mama would echo Papa's advice to put away all notions of becoming General Huntley's bride and set her sights on a more appropriate, *younger* man.

Eliza fretted over her horrid life the rest of that day and long into the night. She did not see her father for supper. In fact, she hadn't seen him since he stormed from the house, his face a thundercloud, that afternoon. Not seeing her father for long stretches was, in itself, not unusual. Of late, she rarely knew where her father was for much of the day, or evening, or when, or even if, he'd return home. She had learned not to let his long absences cause her alarm. It was just that . . . today seemed somehow different.

He knew now what was troubling his daughter, and for some reason, Eliza feared there'd be grave consequences.

It was not until the wee hours of the morning that she finally fell into a fitful sleep, only to be startled awake just before daybreak by a persistent rap-rap-rapping on her bedchamber door.

"Eliza!" a feminine voice called insistently. "Let me in, please!"

Blinking the cobwebs from her mind, Eliza flung the warm coverlet back and sleepily padded across the carpeted floor in her bare feet.

"Eliza, do wake up, please!"

Eliza sprang the latch and opened the door. "Ivy!" She blinked to clear her vision and assure herself that she was not, indeed, dreaming.

Her green eyes wide, Ivy Heathergill burst excitedly into the room, the long, flowing, green woolen cape she wore swirling about her slim body. "I had to come, Eliza!" she cried, her generally placid tone reflecting a state of high anguish. "Your father and General Huntley came to blows over Lady Jamison at a rout tonight. Richard has challenged Huntley to a duel and asked my father to stand as his second."

"Oh!" Eliza cried.

"They are even now on their way to Land's End."

"Oh, dear! I knew something dreadful would happen, and now it has!"

With Ivy's assistance, Eliza hurriedly dressed, and the two girls flew down the stairs and into the stately Heathergill coach that awaited them at the curb. As the well-sprung carriage careened 'round the square and onto Oxford street, heading toward the outskirts of London, Eliza turned a fearful look on Ivy. "I do hope we are not too late!"

"So do I." Ivy wrung her gloved hands together with despair. "I prayed Father would dissuade him, but Richard was exceedingly angry. He called Huntley a bast''—she paused—''he said very unkind things about him.''

Eliza could well imagine what ungentlemanly things her father might say. His tongue often grew loose when he was overset. ''But your father did try to stop him?'' she asked anxiously.

''I . . . cannot say for certain. I was awakened by Richard pounding at our door, but I did not wish anyone to know I was awake. I fear your father may have had a bit too much to drink,'' she confessed in a small voice to Eliza.

''I do not doubt it,'' Eliza murmured, then, in a distraught tone, she urged Ivy to go on.

''I thought it odd that Mother did not try to get Richard to take some tea or coffee, but . . . after only a bit of talk, he and Father set out.''

''Did Papa speak with you?'' Eliza probed, her tone anxious.

Ivy's brown head shook beneath the hood of her cape. ''They neither one saw me. I slipped out the back door just as Father and Richard left in Richard's coach. I came straight for you.''

Eliza smiled thinly. ''I am glad you did, Ivy.''

She reached for her friend's hand and wrapped her gloved fingers 'round it in the semidarkness. The glow of the lamps flickering on the outside corners of the coach illuminated the tear stains on Ivy's pale cheeks. Clearly, she was as distraught as Eliza over the disastrous turn.

''Can you ever forgive me for not receiving you when you called, Ivy?''

Ivy squeezed back fresh tears that had begun to gather in her eyes. ''Of course, I forgive you. I shouldn't have come tonight,'' she said. ''Richard loves another. He is fighting over . . . Lady Jamison. He no longer cares for me.''

Eliza blinked back her own tears of sorrow over her friend's helpless plight. She turned to stare from the coach window at the slumbering city, the dark silhouettes sweeping past them in a mist-shrouded blur. "The same is true for me," she confessed. "Huntley no longer cares for me."

"I could not bear it if Richard were killed and . . . I was not there."

"Oh, Ivy, don't say such a thing!" Eliza cried in terror. She attempted to gulp back her own fear. "Surely your father will be able to make the men see reason."

She and Ivy fell silent for a spell, each of them consumed by her own private grief.

Eliza, torn by her love and loyalty for both of the gentlemen fighting to the death on a damp stretch of greensward still some miles beyond their reach, tried to remind herself that March Huntley was a principled man. Despite the steel gray hardness she, herself, had lately observed in those long gray eyes, surely he would not, could not, take her father's life! Though how the lovesick men would decide which of them would win the war over Lady Jamison's hand, she did not know. That both men must love her dearly was a realization almost too painful to bear.

As light began to peek over the horizon and glance off the ice crystals formed along the edges of the coach windows, they at last wheeled into the secluded clearing where for centuries Englishmen had met to settle their differences. A scant second after the high-sprung carriage had jerked to a standstill behind the pair of other vehicles already parked in the lane, a lone gunshot reverberated through the stillness. Both Eliza and Ivy screamed with alarm.

"Papa!" Eliza called out. But before she could tumble to the ground and race to his side, she was forced to wait patiently while the Heathergill footman let down the steps.

"Papa!" she screamed afresh as she ran toward the tight knot of shadowy figures assembled in the center of the dew-kissed meadow, the thick morning fog swirling ominously about them. Behind her, a worried look on her pale face, Ivy Heathergill hung back.

The four men standing in the clearing had heard the

heavy coach lumber up the tree-shrouded lane. The second it drew to a halt, Sir Richard Foxburn had purposefully raised his dueling pistol into the air and fired one shot at random. Now, wearing a mixture of satisfaction and mischievousness on his handsome face, he stood gazing down upon his "handiwork."

"Lie still, Huntley," he told the man stretched out on the ground. "You are dying."

Mr. Heathergill stood to one side of the gentleman lying in a pool of what appeared to be his own blood on the ground. Having just smeared another bright red splotch upon the gentleman's crisp white shirtfront, he tossed a furtive glance over one shoulder before hastily recapping the vial of thick red liquid and slipping the bottle into an inside pocket of his multicaped overcoat. "Looks convincing to me," he muttered to no one in particular.

Racing toward the men, Eliza spotted a fourth gentleman, whom she presumed to be a doctor—it being her understanding that a physician was always on hand when gentlemen dueled—on his knees administering to the poor slain man on the ground.

"Papa!" she screamed as she drew nearer, still unsure which of the men she loved had fallen.

When her father turned toward her, her eyes widened, and she screamed afresh. "Huntley! Papa, you've killed him! How could you?"

As she darted past, her father caught her about the shoulders and held fast. "You should not be here, Eliza," he said gruffly.

"Ivy and I had to come," she protested. She struggled with all her might to free herself from his grasp.

"Ivy is here?" Sir Richard flung a questioning look over one shoulder, but from this distance, the fog was far too thick to make out much beyond the bulky shapes of the carriages ranged along the lane.

Eliza was still gazing with fright at the silent figure lying prone on the ground. "Is he—?"

The fourth man looked up. "The general is not yet . . . gone," he replied solemnly.

"Oh, Papa!" Eliza commenced to wriggle again. "Let me go!"

"This is no place for ladies, Eliza. You and Ivy must—"

"Oh, Papa, you have killed him!" Eliza cried. She buried her dark head in the crook of her father's arm as tears of grief began to course down her cheeks.

"It was a fair fight," Mr. Heathergill intoned.

"Come along, sweetheart." Sir Richard attempted to propel his daughter back toward the coach.

"No!" She managed to at last wrench free from his grasp. "I cannot leave! I will not!"

"E . . . liza," came a weak voice from the ground.

When the gentleman lying there stirred slightly, Eliza hurled herself to her knees, her blue eyes wild with fright. "I am here, Huntley." She clasped the "dying" man's cold hand to her soft breast, but upon catching sight of her beloved general's very lifeblood oozing from what could only be a gaping hole in his chest . . . everything went black.

For a tense second, the four men in the clearing said nothing. Then, Huntley tentatively lifted his head a few inches from the ground and, peering, furtively from one opened eye at the clump of damp skirts and fur-lined pelisse bunched near his chest, he murmured, "She appears to have swooned."

"Sh-h-h," Sir Richard hissed. "Ivy might hear you." He tossed another wary glance over his shoulder. "Heathergill, you and Dr. Walker cart Huntley to my coach. I'll see Eliza and Ivy home."

As the Heathergill coach pulled up in front of the Foxburn town house, Eliza's father said, "You mustn't fret, sweetheart. Huntley will recover." His tone was soothing as he cradled Eliza's limp head in his lap.

Eliza's eyes fluttered open. "What happened? Where is Huntley?"

"The surgeon is seeing to him now—"

"Oh-h, Papa," Eliza moaned, as the horrid details came flooding back to her.

"Dr. Walker assured me that Huntley will recover. Come." He helped her to a sitting position. "We must get you inside before you catch a chill."

"Where is Ivy?"

"She is home . . . where she belongs." Sir Richard gathered his daughter into his arms and carried her up the steps to the house.

"Miss Eliza taken ill, has she?" Briggs asked, when he flung open the door and his employer skirted past him into the foyer.

"Have Mrs. Allen bring up a pot of hot coffee, Briggs."

"Miss Eliza don't like coffee."

"Very well, then, Briggs, tea! But, make haste!" Sir Richard Foxburn ordered irritably.

"Yes, sir. Right away, sir."

After assuring her father that she did, indeed, feel quite herself again, Eliza insisted that he go and see to General Huntley. "It's the very least you can do, Papa! You might have killed him." Eliza was propped up in her bed, a fluff of pillows at her back. Her father had coaxed her to take two cups of steaming hot tea and eat as many hot, buttered scones.

"I am certain Huntley is . . . healing nicely, sweetheart," her father replied. "It was little more than a . . ." he shrugged, "a flesh wound. The bullet merely glanced off—"

"But you cannot be certain of that, Papa!" Eliza cried. "I shan't rest easy 'til I *know* he is safe!"

"Very well, sweetheart." Sir Richard rose uneasily to his feet. "Though this is hardly the way things are . . . done.

Huntley and I are still at daggers drawn, you know. The contest at dawn settled nothing between us.''

Eliza huffed her displeasure. That the illegal duel this morning had been fought for naught made it all the more damming. But she wisely refrained from ringing a peal over her father's head. He was a grown man, and the manner in which he conducted himself was none of her affair.

Before leaving the room, Sir Richard turned to address his daughter once more from the door. In quite a firm voice, he said, "Just so you know, sweetheart. Even if Huntley should change face in regard to his feelings for you, after what he revealed to me of his character today, I could never countenance having that bounder for a son-in-law.''

Eliza folded her arms across her chest and glared stubbornly at her father. "You have made your feelings in regard to Huntley perfectly clear, Papa. Regardless what happens, if *I* must endure having that trollop Lady Jamison for a stepmama, then the very least you can do is put aside your grievances against General Huntley and respect *my* choice in a life mate.''

The veriest hint of a smile played at her father's full lips. "Well said, Eliza.''

By afternoon, feminine tongues in drawing rooms all over London were telling and retelling accounts of the duel fought at dawn over the delectable Lady Jamison. Though Eliza'd been there herself and knew *parts* of the story firsthand, she was loath to repeat what sketchy details she did know lest she contribute to the on-dit's long life. So far as she was concerned, the sooner the deed was relegated to oblivion, the better. That her father, and Huntley, had sunk to such a low was both off-putting and embarrassing.

Long before teatime, she was subjected to highly embroidered accounts of the tale from three different sources.

Lady Villiers was the first to burst in, repeating her version even before she'd demanded to hear all that Eliza knew of it. Lady Hamilton and Lady Brownlow soon followed, each recounting her take on the story, although no one seemed to have an accurate fix on why, or how, the contest had come about.

When the last of her callers left, Eliza, who was now convalescing in the drawing room, began to grow anxious once more over her father's unaccounted-for whereabouts. What was keeping him, and why had he not returned with an updated report on Huntley's injuries?

She had just requested that Briggs bring her a fresh pot of tea when, instead of doing her bidding, the elderly retainer shuffled back into the drawing room and handed her a card.

"General March Huntley," it said.

CHAPTER 19

"THE DANCE OF LOVE"

Eliza started. "Show the gentleman in, please, Briggs; and bring the tea and *two* cups, if you will."

"Which, Miss?"

"Which, what, Briggs?" Eliza asked irritably.

"Which shall I bring first, miss? The tea and cups, or the gentleman?"

Meow-meow!

Eliza glanced 'round Briggs's rotund shape and spotted Sailor, his head and tail held aloft as he trotted toward her, General March Huntley on his heels, er, his paws.

"Master Sailor showed me in," Huntley remarked, a grin twitching at his lips.

Eliza sprang to her feet, her blue eyes wide with alarm. "Sir, are you quite well enough to be out and about so soon?" she cried. "Briggs, do see to the tea!" she added, her tone rising.

Briggs bent to scoop up the cat. "Come on, Sailor-boy. We's been dismissed."

Sailor wriggled free from the butler's grasp and darted

instead to where General Huntley stood, gingerly warming his hands and backside before the blazing hearth.

Still stunned by the gentleman's unexpected arrival, Eliza asked again, "Are you certain you feel well enough to be out, sir?"

"I am quite well, thank you, Miss Foxburn. Is your father at home?"

Realizing that the general had called to see her father, and not her, Eliza's heart sank. "No. He . . . I was concerned for your . . ." she began hesitantly. "I asked him to please go and check on you, sir. He has been gone quite a length now. I expect he will be home soon," she concluded in a fairly even tone, considering her acute agitation. "Please, do sit down." She indicated the comfortable-looking overstuffed chair near the fire that both he and Sailor seemed to favor.

"Thank you." Huntley moved to take the proffered seat, whereupon Sailor promptly hopped up and curled himself into a tight ball on his lap. "Perhaps the three of us"—Huntley commenced to stroke the cat—"might have a coze while we wait. If you've no objection, that is?" He cast an inquiring look at Eliza.

"No." she shook her head. "Not at all." What did his sudden appearance mean, she wondered. Had something *else* untoward happened? Had he come to concede defeat in this morning's battle and to mend the riff that had sprung up between him and her father? Did that mean her father was, indeed, to marry Lady Jamison?

"Your father informed me that you were not . . . feeling well," Huntley began politely, his long gray eyes closely regarding her.

Feeling a wave of anxiety overtake her, Eliza glanced down. "I . . . Papa feared I had caught a chill this morning, but I . . . am much recovered now, thank you." Did he not remember that she was *also* at Land's End this morning? Did he not recall speaking her name when he seemed . . . near death? She longed to inquire further after the general's injuries, but if he did *not* recall her being there, she would prefer not to remind him.

A long pause ensued, during which both Eliza and General Huntley cast guarded glances at one another, each of them appearing uneasy as they cast about for a safe topic to broach.

Eliza's mind reeled with questions to put to him . . . but for each of the questions burning in her mind, she feared hearing the answers, especially those that concerned his feelings for the alluring Lady Jamison.

Huntley had a number of questions to ask of Eliza, also. But, before posing the All-Important One, there were a few related matters regarding which he desired assurance. He knew very well that the lovely Miss Foxburn cared deeply for him. Since he had, in fact, *not* been injured in the meadow that morning, he had, indeed, heard her cries of alarm when she thought he'd been about to expire.

In truth, none of the participants in the *faux* dueling party had expected the young ladies to turn up, nor had the gentlemen intended that their sham scare the girls. That they had gotten wind of the contest and been on hand, however, was simply hastening the outcome of Huntley's carefully orchestrated scheme.

Sir Richard was even now with Miss Heathergill. Huntley expected the pair of them to announce their betrothal before the day was out. He hoped the same would be true for himself and the delightful Miss Foxburn. But, first, he had to ease his mind on a number of Important Issues that, if not resolved now, might later prove the ruination of their union. Huntley did not want the same circumstances that had spoiled his father's marriage to destroy his own.

He chose his words carefully before beginning. "I daresay I owe you an apology, my dear. I realize that my demeanor of late may have seemed somewhat aloof and distant. I wish you to know that I never meant to be cruel, or to hurt you. I value your friendship deeply, Eliza." He paused and noted with pleasure the look of relief that spread across her face.

"I appreciate you saying as much, sir," she murmured. "I, too, value our friendship, and I . . ." She looked down. ". . . have greatly missed your company," she concluded softly.

When she glanced back up, the sad look in her corn-flower blue eyes tore at Huntley's heart. He hastened to speak again. "It appeared to me that you had become quite caught up in your plans for the Grand Fete, your visits at the Palace, and whatnot. The entire happenstance seemed to . . . considerably elevate not only your conse-quence, but your confidence. I did not wish to interfere." He studied her. "You did enjoy a good bit of the attention, did you not?"

Eliza smiled thinly and with some reluctance, finally nodded assent. "It is true, I did enjoy . . . parts of it. But, on the other hand, I felt such immense guilt over deceiving Papa and Ivy, that, in the end, a good bit of my enjoyment was marred." She wished to say more on the charged subject, but . . . she refrained. "I confess your behavior . . . did confuse me," she added, "especially when you failed to . . . approach me at the soirée. I did so wish to stand up with you," she added sadly.

"Forgive me. But there were other reasons why . . . suf-fice to say, the omission could not be helped," he replied obliquely.

They again fell silent, Eliza darting uneasy looks and half smiles at the handsome man seated so very near, and yet, so very far away from her. Sailor, purring contentedly on the general's lap, seemed the only one not afraid to express his true feelings.

At length, Eliza ventured to address the general again. "I wish to thank you for all of your excellent advice . . . and for coming to my aid when I asked it of you." She paused. "I confess I grew accustomed to seeking your coun-sel," she added. "It meant a great deal to me when I believed that you . . . cared." The final word was spoken so softly, it was barely audible.

But Huntley heard it, and smiled. "I wished you the opportunity to learn to rely on your own judgment, Eliza," he said gently. "You are far stronger and wiser than you think."

She digested that. Perhaps she was. It was beginning to dawn on her that both her father and Huntley's actions, though often mystifying to her, had been well-intentioned all along. In their own way, they were both trying to show her how to get on in the world. Something that if her mother had been alive, she'd have undertaken in a far less painful, and considerably easier to understand, manner.

The answering smile on Eliza's lips was serene. "I daresay, you are correct again, sir. Though I do admit, delivering my little speech at the Grand Fete quite terrified me."

"You were splendid."

Huntley held her gaze a spell before adding, "Your father tells me you have received a goodly number of gentlemen callers these last weeks. I believe you told me once that you'd given no thought to marrying. Is that still the case?"

Eliza shifted nervously. There was only *one* man she wished to marry, but she could not tell *him* that. "I . . . have considered it," she replied softly.

"Ah. And, have you settled on a . . . particular gentleman?"

For some reason, that particular question caused Eliza's heart to thunder wildly in her breast. She bit down so hard on her lower lip she feared it might bleed. She dared not speak, or meet his eyes, lest the adoring look in hers betray her.

It was not necessary that she speak. Apart from her flushed cheeks and shy glances, Huntley already had the knowledge he sought. "How would you react if the gentleman you married wished you to leave London?" he persisted. "If he wished you to take up permanent residence in the country . . . apart from the social whirl and the glittering parties and the London Season? Would you find such an arrangement acceptable . . . or would you feel . . . deprived?"

Eliza finally glanced up, her alert blue eyes searching his probing gray ones. For the first time since he'd entered the room, she noted that he was not wearing his military uniform today, but was instead attired as any other fashionable London gentleman—in dark trousers and coat over a forest green waistcoat and tucked white-linen shirt. The snow-white cravat at his throat was tied in a simple Mathematical.

"I would be happy living wherever my husband wished to live," she replied firmly. "To be with him is all that would matter to me."

"And what of your father?" he pushed. "Would you not miss him terribly?"

Holding the gentleman's steady gaze, Eliza spoke in a strong tone. "My father has his own life to lead. I expect him to marry soon and get on with it. It is not my place to look after him forever, you know."

"And you've no objection to his . . . choice in a marriage partner?"

"Whomever my father chooses to wed is none of my affair."

Huntley drew in a long breath. In an effort to further collect his thoughts, he made a slight move to rise to his feet. Remembering, however, that Sailor lay snoozing upon his lap, he shifted the curled-up cat to one side before he fully arose and walked to stand again before the fire. The scarlet-and-gold flames blazed brightly behind him. Presently, he fixed his full attention again upon Eliza.

"I do regret that we never shared a dance."

Eliza smiled coyly. Then, on impulse, she sprang to her feet. "We shall dance now!"

"Now?" Huntley looked puzzled. "Here?"

Eliza's chin shot up. "Indeed, right here!"

Huntley took a tentative step or two forward as Eliza approached him. A determined look shining from her bright blue eyes, she announced, "I should like to dance the waltz with you, sir."

"But . . . we've . . . no music," Huntley protested weakly.

Her dark head cocked to one side, Eliza's determined gaze pinned his. "You and I have no need for music, General Huntley."

Caught completely off guard by the opposition's unexpected maneuver, the highly acclaimed general could only manage a tight nod. "Very well, Miss Foxburn."

Eliza smiled sagely. Suddenly it struck her that she knew exactly how to outwit Wellington's Master Strategist. All that was required of her was to be herself—her unpredictable, impulsive, spontaneous self. The very traits her mother had tried to school out of her, the ones she, herself, had chided her father for—but that she'd been lucky enough to inherit from him—were the very things missing from the general's rigid, well-ordered life. He needed her uniqueness as much as she needed the qualitites that he possessed: his strength, his wisdom, and his stability. With him, she felt peaceful because she never had to worry what he might do next. His actions were predictable. He would never set the house afire, or embarrass her. He would be her rock in time of crisis. And she, she would bring love and laughter and delight over the simple things in life to his well-ordered one. He needed her, and she strongly suspected that . . . he loved her. Although she was not entirely certain that he yet *knew* he did.

Standing directly before him, her pert nose in the air, she positioned both arms expectantly for the dance, one hand resting in the air near his shoulder, the other hand palm down, her fingers extended as she awaited his grasp.

Poised thusly, Huntley was very nearly overcome by a compelling urge to gather the little minx into his arms and kiss her 'til she begged for mercy! But, the commanding officer in him checked the impulse and disciplined his errant body into submission. There would be plenty of time for passion later. First he must assure himself that marriage, and marriage to *him*, would satisfy the impish little minx.

He slipped an arm about her slim waist, and, when he felt her melt into his strength, he realized the magnetism between them was undeniable. She meant everything to him. He'd never wanted a woman so much in his life, and he strongly suspected she felt the same about him. He'd already taken the first step toward making his dream to wed her a realilty. He was no longer active in the military. He'd elected to go on half pay. He was now but one step away from settling down in the country . . . with Miss Eliza Foxburn by his side, as his bride. There remained one last vital thing he must do . . . fetch the ring and . . . ask her.

With pent-up love darkening his eyes, Huntley suddenly drew apart from her. "I regret to say that I must be off now, Eliza. Thank you for the dance."

He was halfway to the door before Eliza's closed eyelids fluttered open. The abruptness of his departure stunned her, almost as much as his unexpected arrival had. What had she done now to cause him to flee so quickly from her?

She was not accorded the time to reflect upon the matter, however, for Huntley had no sooner exited the house than her father returned to it.

Striding into the room, he bent to drop a fatherly kiss upon her flushed cheek. "I am glad to see that your color has returned, sweetheart." He glanced about the empty room. "No callers?"

"H-Huntley was recently here," she stammered. So recently, in fact, she wondered that they had not tripped over one another on the doorstep!

"Ah. Anyone else?"

Eliza returned to the sofa where she'd been seated and absently sat down. "Lady Villiers and Lady Hamilton were here a bit ago. It seems all of London is agog to learn the details of the . . . duel.''

Sir Richard grinned with satisfaction as he shrugged out of his topcoat and stripped off his driving gloves. "And what are the gossipmongers saying?"

Eliza grimaced. "That you and Lady Jamis—"

"Ahem," came an interrupting cough from the doorway.

Eliza and her father glanced toward Briggs, who, quite unlike himself, stood as primly as any butler could on the threshold. "A Lady Jamison to see you, sir."

"Ah! Show her in, Briggs!" Sir Richard enthused.

Noting the pleased grin on her father's face, a rush of white-hot anger rose in Eliza's breast. But, recalling her recent remark to Huntley that her father's choice in a marriage partner was none of her affair, she forced her anger down and schooled her features to remain impassive.

A polite smile was in place upon Eliza's lips when her nemesis, Lady Jamison, glided into the room, looking the very picture of loveliness in an ermine-trimmed, green-velvet pelisse, with a green plume atop the bonnet that perfectly set off her rich auburn hair.

"How nice to see you again, Lady Jamison," Eliza murmured, rising politely to her feet as the older woman glanced her way. Eliza fully expected her father to happily announce that he and the lovely widow were soon to be wed.

The attractive woman merely tossed a quick "hello" over one shoulder at Eliza and made a bee-line for Sir Richard's outstretched arms.

"How lovely you look, my dear," he enthused. The pair quickly embraced. "Appears Huntley has already come and gone," Sir Richard told her.

The comment baffled Eliza somewhat, but she was far too overset at the moment to dwell upon the oddity.

"No matter," Lady Jamison shrugged. "Our little ploy

worked famously! News of the duel has spread all over town!'' She laughed gaily. ''Huntley is a genius!''

''I take it details of the challenge have reached the *right* ears?'' Sir Richard queried.

''Indeed, they have!'' The beautiful woman drew off one white-kid glove and waved a slim hand beneath Sir Richard's nose. ''I have just come from a meeting with Major Sheldon at the Home Office. We are to be married in a fortnight! I am deliriously happy!''

Married? Eliza's mouth gaped open. Lady Jamison was not to wed her father . . . *or* General Huntley? Then who was Papa to wed?

''Ahem!'' came another throat-clearing noise from the doorway.

All three persons in the drawing room looked a question at Briggs.

''A Miss Ivy Heathergill to see you, sir.''

''Splendid! Show her in, Briggs!''

Eliza's eyes widened once more. Ivy, *here?*

Looking equally radiant as Lady Jamison, Ivy fairly flew into the room. She directed a warm smile at Sir Richard before her smiling green eyes darted from his to the bewildered countenance of his daughter.

''Is it not wonderful, Eliza, dear?'' Ivy moved to embrace her friend, who merely stood staring blankly at her.

''I confess I haven't a clue as to what is going on, Iv—''

''A-hem!''

''What is it now, Briggs?'' Sir Richard asked, a slight edge of irritation creeping into his tone.

''Miss Eliza's gentleman caller is here, sir.''

''Well, devil take it, Briggs! Show the fellow in!''

Eliza's head jerked up. *Who could possibly be calling on her now?*

When she caught sight of General March Huntley striding purposefully into the room—for the second time that day—she very nearly swooned. If Ivy hadn't had a firm grip upon both her hands, which had suddenly gone clammy, Eliza was certain her knees would have buckled beneath her.

"Afternoon, Huntley!" her father said, *quite* cordially, considering that at their last meeting he'd very nearly put a bullet through the man's heart!

"Afternoon, Foxburn, Lady Jamison. How do you do, Miss Heathergill? Eliza," Huntley concluded, quite warmly.

Lady Jamison had already rushed to link her arm through his. "Our little ploy worked famously!" she exclaimed, her face aglow. "Major Sheldon and I are to be married in a fortnight!"

"Is it not delicious?" Ivy asked Eliza. "It is very like a romance novel."

Eliza was too confused to utter a single word.

"You are such a clever man!" Lady Jamison exclaimed, still smiling up into Huntley's alert gray eyes. "Both you gentlemen pretending to be in love with me was the perfect plan! When Sheldon heard that not one, but *two* men wished to marry me, he proposed in an instant!"

Admist her gay laughter and the gentlemen's hearty congratulations on her betrothal, Ivy turned again to Eliza.

"You recall, I met Lady Jamison some weeks back at a musicale that Mother and I attended. At the time, she was quite distraught over the disappearance of her beloved Major Sheldon. As he had not yet returned to England from the war, she feared he'd lost his life at Waterloo. Considering General Huntley's vast connections, I was certain he could help locate the major." Ivy smiled warmly. "And, indeed, he did. Although, unbeknownst to me, when Major Sheldon returned to London, he was reluctant to take up where he'd left off with Lady Jamison."

Though Eliza was still vastly perplexed, she was beginning to get a clearer picture of the rather convoluted scenario. "Are you saying, Ivy, that you were unaware that Papa and Hunt—?"

Ivy laughed gaily. "Indeed! I was as convinced as anyone that *both* Richard and Huntley had fallen top over tail in love with her." She glanced at the stunningly beautiful widow. "You must agree she is lovely enough for that to be the case."

At that moment, Sir Richard, wearing a self-satisfied grin on his face, stepped up. He planted an affectionate kiss on Ivy's upturned cheek. "I had the devil of a time explaining the taradiddle to Ivy," he told Eliza. He slipped an arm about the younger girl's slim shoulders. "But, I daresay, I convinced her."

"C-Convinced her of what?" Eliza queried. Despite Ivy's explanation, she was still a good bit mystified over this latest turn.

Her father directed a solemn gaze at his only daughter. "That I love her dearly and that I wish her to become my bride."

Eliza stared openmouthed at the smiling twosome before her. "Then, you are to be—?"

"Yes!" Ivy cried joyously. "We are to be married!"

The two girls embraced. When, at last, they drew apart, both girls had happy tears glistening in their eyes.

"I am *so* very happy for you, Ivy!" Eliza exclaimed. "Oh, Papa . . ." She sniffed as she hugged her father. "I love you dearly!"

From the doorway, Lady Jamison's voice interrupted the tender moment. "I must be off, Richard!" she called. "I shall never forget what you and March have done for me!" In a flurry of rich ermine and lush green velvet, the lovely widow was gone.

Sir Richard turned to address Eliza. "Ivy and I will be in the library, sweetheart." Leading a beaming Ivy from the room, he flung a significant look at Huntley.

As yet, Eliza had not yet gazed directly upon the handsome man *she* so dearly loved.

She ventured to do so now.

And found his long, gray eyes regarding her quite intently. Huntley advanced a few steps closer to her. "I hope you can forgive my little deception," he said gravely.

Still a bit dazed from all that she had just witnessed, Eliza managed a wavery smile. "I forgive you, sir. Although I confess I do not fully understand the secrecy behind your and Papa's perfidy. You might have taken Ivy and me into your confidence," she chided gently.

"For a campaign to be entirely sucessful," the Master Strategist replied solemnly, "complete secrecy is a must. I also felt that secrecy in this case was necessary, for other reasons."

He moved a few steps closer to Eliza. When he was standing mere inches from her, he announced, "You see, I, too, am planning to be married."

Again, Eliza felt near faint as a sickening wave of anguish washed over her. But, she tamped the feeling down and gazed steadily into the ruggedly handsome face of the most brillant man she'd ever met. "Am I . . . acquainted with the young lady?" she asked evenly.

Huntley's full lips softened as he gazed lovingly into her guileless face. "Indeed, you are. She is the most adorable imp I have ever had the good fortune to meet. The young lady quite stole my heart the minute I laid eyes upon her."

So painful were his words to her, Eliza could barely draw breath. She wished both to flee from the room *and* to fling herself into his strong arms and beg him to reconsider. As the conflicting emotions warred within her, she watched in a daze as Huntley reached into his waistcoat pocket and withdrew a small glittering object, which he held up for her inspection.

"Do you think this an appropriate token to bespeak my love, Eliza?"

A mix and stir of emotions flickered over Eliza's face as she gazed upon the most beautiful diamond-and-sapphire ring she'd ever seen. Then, suddenly, General Huntley reached for her left hand, and, before she knew what he was about, he'd slipped the ring onto the third finger of her left hand!

In a voice husky with emotion, he asked, "Will you do me the very great honor of becoming my wife, Eliza?"

She darted a wild look from the ring sparkling on her finger to General Huntley's suddenly, quite blurry face and then, for the second time that day . . . everything went black.

It was certainly not the reaction Huntley had expected. On the other hand, perhaps it was. That his future bride-to-be was so very *un*predictable, was becoming . . . well, predictable.

Mere seconds before she crumpled into a heap on the floor, he scooped up the unconscious Eliza into his arms. As he was casting about for a sofa or settee upon which to deposit her, there came an insistent mew at his feet.

Huntley glanced down. "Perhaps you can help me awaken her, Sailor-boy. I admit I am a bit anxious to know if she'll have me."

He laid Eliza's limp body upon an Egyptian sofa in the center of the room, being careful to tuck her long woolen skirt properly about her ankles.

Sailor, apparently curious over what ailed his mistress, hopped up beside her and began to nudge her shoulder with his nose. Eliza's eyelids fluttered open, but upon realizing what had happened and where she was, and how she must have gotten there, she sprang upright at once.

Scrambling to her feet, she glared at Huntley. "You and Papa hoodwinked me!" she cried.

Huntley shrugged. "Guiltly as charged."

Her pretty nostrils flared with anger as she flounced back and forth before him, pausing every second step or so to glare at a very subdued commanding officer. "I think the entire scheme was . . . well, I think it was outrageous!"

Huntley turned palms upward.

Eliza continued to pace. "And now, you suddenly wish to up and marry me." It was more a statement than a question.

"Highly arrogant of me, I agree." A grin began to twitch at Huntley's lips.

Her blue eyes narrowing, Eliza studied him. At length, she said, "Well, I expect it was also rather . . . brillant of you to carry off such an involved charade. The duel was . . . quite convincing."

She continued to study the maddeningly clever military man whom she found so *very* attractive and so *very* intriguing. Perhaps he was not nearly so predicatable as she thought. Perhaps she'd hadn't yet learned how to outwit Wellington's Master Strategist, after all.

Perhaps to do that would take a bit longer.

A good bit longer.

A slow grin spread over her face.

Thrusting her pert nose in the air, she said, "Yes."

"Yes, what?"

"Yes, I will be your bride."

Breathing a huge sigh of relief, Huntley closed the distance between them and gathered the saucy minx into his arms. Moments before he kissed her soundly, he murmured, "I'm glad that's over."

Over? Eliza thought as she joyfully welcomed her beloved's lips on hers. On the contrary, the fun was just beginning.

Dear Reader,

If you are like me, you also feel an overwhelming longing to experience life as it was in the romantic time period known as the Regency. Then, a real man was a gentleman, right down to his polished Hessians, and a proper young lady still blushed when caught staring overlong at milord's broad shoulders—not to mention his thigh-hugging inexpressibles!

For me, the pull was so great I simply had to delve deeper, to learn more about the past I found so intriguing. Not even traveling to London, or visiting Brighton and Bath, was enough to satisfy me. I had to know more! From this longing grew *The Regency Plume,* a bimonthly newsletter dedicated to accurately depicting life as it was in Regency England.

Each issue of *The Regency Plume* is full of fascinating articles penned by your favorite Regency romance authors. If you'd like to join me and the hundreds of other Regency romance fans who experience Prinny's England via *The Regency Plume,* send a stamped, self-addressed envelope to:

> Marilyn Clay
> c/o *The Regency Plume*
> Dept. 711-D-NW
> Ardmore, OK 73401

I'll be happy to send you more information and a subscription form. I look forward to hearing from each and every one of you!

In the meantime, I hope you enjoyed reading *Miss Eliza's Gentleman Caller* and will want to read my next Regency romance, *Miss Darby's Debut,* coming out in October, 1999. Thank you!

Sincerely,
Marilyn Clay

ROMANCE FROM JO BEVERLY

ROMANCE FROM FERN MICHAELS

DEAR EMILY   (0-8217-4952-8, $5.99)

WISH LIST   (0-8217-5228-6, $6.99)

AND IN HARDCOVER:

VEGAS RICH   (1-57566-057-1, $25.00)

LOOK FOR THESE REGENCY ROMANCES